CW01654427

Pennywise

Stormy Souls MC Book 4

by

Payton Hunter

This is a work of fiction. Names, characters, places, and incidents either are the product of the author's imagination or are used fictitiously. Any resemblance to actual persons, living or dead, events, or locales is coincidental.

Copyright © 2024 by Payton Hunter

All rights reserved. No part of this book may be reproduced or used in any manner, including generative AI, without the written permission of the copyright owner except for the use of quotations in a book review.
For more information, address:
paytonhunter.author@gmail.com.

First e-book edition February 2025
Book cover design by: Joetherasakdhi
Editor: Nicola Thorpe
ISBN print 978-1-0685340-1-0
ISBN ebook 978-1-0685340-0-3
www.paytonhunterauthor.com

ABOUT THE BOOK

This is the book I always wanted to write but never dared to. It is a pure work of fiction, featuring what I love most—badass bikes and the hot men to go with them!

It contains no cheating and has a HEA, though there may be backstory elements stretching over several volumes.

TRIGGER WARNING

This book includes scenes of physical violence and deals with the subject of pregnancy loss. There are explicit sexual acts and strong explicit language. It is not suitable for people under the age of 18 or people with triggers relating to any of the above.

ACKNOWLEDGMENTS

Thank you to my editor, Nicola Thorpe. I would not have been able to do this without you.

Thank you to my family and friends for continuously supporting me. Gretchen Calder, thank you for your hard work, and my Beta and ARC teams. All of you are important to me.

DEDICATION

To all those mothers who never got to see their children grow up. To those who went through the worst experience any parent can go through.

Dad's Poem

We never had the chance to play, to laugh, to rock, to wiggle
We long to hold you, touch you now, and listen to you giggle
She'll always be your mother, and I'll always be your dad.
You'll always be our child, the child we never had.
But now you're gone … but yet you're here, we sense you everywhere.
You're our sorrow and our joy. There's love in every tear.
Just know our love goes deep and strong, that we'll forget you never.
The child we had, but never had, and yet will have forever.
Author Unknown

STORMY SOULS MC CHARACTER LIST

Road Name	Rank
Raven	President
Vegas	Vice President
Slender	Sergeant at Arms
Pennywise	Enforcer
Dawg	Secretary
Clusseaud	Road Captain
Ferret	IT Guy
Moggy	Member
Sparks	Member
Ratchet	Member
Zippy	Member
Dougal	Member
Halfpint	Member
Striker	Member
Spen	Nomad
Greg	Prospect
Caleb	Prospect
Mom	Club mother, mother to Pennywise

Others

Neil	Bar Manager
Chris	Bar Man, Security Staff
Darcie	Therapist
Ellie	Slender / Founder Debs' Haven
Jade	Foster child Sarah & Dougal
Amy Owens	Resident of Debs' Haven
Mel	Resident of Debs' Haven
Eve	Tattooist Apprentice

Old Ladies

Chloe	Raven
Ashley	Vegas
Ellie	Slender
Caroline	Dawg

Restless Slayers MC

Fury	President
Ghoul	Vice President
Masher	Sergeant at Arms
Ghost	IT

Wild Pixies MC

Rainbow/Ally	President
Jules	Vice President
Hazel	Sergeant at Arms
Tanya	Enforcer
Caroline	Secretary
Gypsie	Member

Table of Contents

1 — PENNYWISE

Is my head thumping me awake, or is it Ally's rude banging of pots and pans for the rally breakfast? Man alive. The smell of bacon, sausage, and egg is making me want to hurl right now. Never again will I touch tequila. My eyes and brain are fuzzy as I crawl out of the tent on my hands and knees, not daring to lift my head or make any quick movement, as I know I'll barf before I can get out of my way.

"Bad night, huh?" Slender smirks at me.

"You kill a cat in there last night?" Dawg scoffs.

"What the fuck are you talking about?" I rack my brain, but for the life of me I can't think what they are talking about. Damn idiots.

"Leave off, you limp dicks," I throw over my shoulder while walking to the gazebo kitchen, grab not one but two cups of Java, make a plate, and plonk my ass on the nearest seat.

"Jesus, Pennywise, you look like you're getting ready to scare kids at Halloween early." Raven, my Prez, shakes his head at me, his eyes alternating between me and Chloe, the chick helping us with the donor drive. I realize he's gone for her; unfortunately, he doesn't, so he keeps making moony eyes from afar. Sucker!

I hate it when he calls me by my full road name. I earned it as a prospect. They sent me shopping at the last minute, so I left my scary clown costume on and rode into town.

At the checkout, I scared some little kids shitless, and an old lady beat me with her purse, screaming, "You sick pervert! Scaring me to death. Go to hell, stupid boy!"

Slender kindly took a video and showed it to the brothers. Hence, I became known as Pennywise. Though I prefer Pen, or even Penny. I hate Pennywise. I pleaded with the club to choose another road name. The response was howling laughter and being called Pennywise at least once per sentence. I gave up after that.

I grew up in the club. My dad, an officer, died in a shootout when I was still a kid. My mom looked after me, and the club looked after my mom. She's well loved by everyone and loves all of us with everything she has. Over the years, she's turned into everyone's Mom. We are a big, loyal, if a little dysfunctional family, tied by brotherhood and love rather than blood. They say blood is thicker than water; I say brotherhood is thicker than blood.

It appears the club is in constant flux now. Slowly, more old ladies are beginning to creep in. First, just Ally and Debs; now it's Caroline as well, and Ashley, Raven's sister, has recently become Vegas' old lady. Vegas frequently hangs with me and Slender, our SAA, who's also my closest friend.

I tune out the noise, sip my coffee, which is as black as my soul, and push my food about on my plate, not convinced it'll stay put if I eat it. Gratefully, I nod at Ally as she places a bottle of water and two pain relievers in front of me. I take the pills and chug the water without ceremony, despite it making me feel like a bloated water buffalo.

Though I try to chill out, my worries still nip at my heels, regardless.

I've been the Enforcer for a few years now, and I've seen more shit than I care to remember. Sometimes, I'm tired of doing the dirty work. It's made me jaded and regularly fucks with my head. I try to keep my temper leashed, but recently I've found it exceedingly hard.

Things are brewing. The fact I have no idea what or who is coming for us doesn't displace that dark gnawing feeling deep in my bones. Now, Rusty is our first concern. Our VP is a menace and will be dealt with in due course, but that's not what's scratching the inside of my brain like a whore's fingernails on a chalkboard.

Before I can get too deep into my head, a giggle whisper almost has me shooting straight off my seat.

"Naughty boy, Pen, watch what you're doing. Last night has to be a one and done."

Caroline. Of course. I wish she'd keep her nose out. And what is she talking about? As I shake my head, memories flood my brain, making me desperately wish they wouldn't.

I watch Caroline, who now sits opposite me, winking, with a knowing grin.

Shit. Fuck. Hell's bells. What did I do?

Sitting back with a groan, I rub my forearm over my eyes, wishing I could erase the picture of the naked beauty above me, riding me like a barrel racer.

Her hazel eyes dark with need, squealing as she came hard, then licking and sucking me clean, before getting dressed and crawling out of the tent, giggling. We were both fully loaded; however, that does not excuse our actions, and I guarantee that fire and brimstone will rain down on both of us if we're found out.

One thing is certain. I'll never drink tequila again! Not only did it make her clothes fall off, but mine too.

Caroline studies me intently while the images from last night parade through my consciousness.

"Is it coming back to you?" she teases me mercilessly, smirking at me the whole time.

"Yes, woman, and I wish it hadn't," I groan at her.

"Don't worry, Pen, your secret is safe with me," Caroline says, her smile belying the sincerity of her tone.

"Thanks, Caroline. Let me assure you, it was definitely one and done. No repeats, no backsies. Ever."

"Pen, I don't judge. Just concerned for you. I'm there for you if you need an ear to bend." Caroline squeezes my shoulder as she gets up and walks away. She is one of the good ones. Dawg's old lady is an amazing person, and Dawg's fiercest supporter. She'd take a bullet for him before any of us could react.

Glancing down at my plate of eggs and bacon, which are now cold, my stomach rumbles. It takes me all of thirty seconds to shovel the contents of my plate into my mouth, chew, swallow, and wash everything down with my second cup of coffee.

My back cracks as I stand, groaning and feeling a hundred years old. Thank fuck we're leaving today. I busy myself taking down my tent and throwing it in the club support vehicle, then I help everyone else with their jobs, until our site's picked clean. The Restless Slayers MC, our dominant MC, will see to the gazebo and donor stall.

Following Raven, we throw our legs over our bikes, start the engines, and pull out of the rally site in formation. Thank fuck this shower of shite is over.

◊◊◊

The four hours it takes to ride home are the longest of my life. My head's still crushing from the hangover, not helped by the noise and fumes of the formation of bikes all around me. Man, I can't remember the last time I was so glad to see the clubhouse gates. As we park up and dismount, I spot Mom standing in the open clubhouse door.

"Come on, boys, food is ready for you to chow down. You look as though you need it." She smirks, then catches sight of me and shakes her head. "Son, you look like death warmed over, and you get no sympathy from me."

I wish I could roll my eyes as hard as I would like right now, but it hurts too much to move them. Last thing I need is Mom on my case. There's enough shit flying without a dose of her sarcasm added into the mix.

Look, I love my mom fiercely, but she can be a royal pain in my butt.

Giving Raven, Slender, and the rest of the gang a chin lift, I grunt, grab my stuff out of the support vehicle, and trudge up to my cabin. After throwing my shit up in the loft space, I jump in the shower, trying to soothe my sore muscles under the hot water. When I'm done, I sling a towel round my hips, take two more pain relievers, down a bottle of water, and fall into bed, exhausted.

Despite my soul-deep tiredness, my mind won't stop turning. An uncomfortable feeling creeps over me like ice through my veins. Bile rushes up my throat, making me sit up straighter in bed. Dark times are speeding towards us.

I can tell, and I have an ugly premonition that there's little we can do to stop it. We worked so hard to clean up the club, yet it feels as though we're standing at the abyss, looking down, with Rusty behind us, ready to give us a massive shove over the edge.

I'm not looking forward to Church tomorrow. Closing my eyes, I lay back and take deep breaths, trying to cleanse the impeding blackness on my soul. Yet not quite succeeding. I try hard not to think of the blonde, hazel-eyed beauty who made me forget my troubles for a while this weekend. She's trouble personified, and I'm trying to banish her from my overworked and underpaid brain.

Should never have gone there; we both knew that, but the fizzing chemistry between us was overwhelming. One and done. We agreed on that beforehand, so no one gets hurt. No harm, no foul.

But, man, that woman is so damn hot, strong, with an undeniable vulnerability. Not to mention those legs, and, Jesus, those eyes. Spitting fire at me one second, cold as ice the next, and all the while turning my insides into lava with their heat.

She's a spitfire, and I pity whoever ends up with her. That girl sure is trouble.

2 — TANYA

Damn, what a weekend. I wish I could say it was a great party, but I can't. Too much tension and too many mishaps. Dad running around like a headless chicken half the time. Ghoul showing too much interest in that Stormy Souls' chick. Meghan disappearing, and then, to top it off, the Stormy Souls bringing their drama to our rally… What can I say?

The Restless Slayers MC were none too pleased. And when the Prez ain't happy, no one is. I'm lucky. My dad, Masher, the SAA of the Restless Slayers, is a little more laid back. In fact, he's almost horizontal. In stark contrast to Fury, Ghoul, Ghost, and the rest of the officers. There's been tensions within the club for a long time now, but the Stormy Souls pissing Fury off sure as shit isn't helping matters.

Neither did Meghan's disappearance last night. One moment she was there, the next she was gone, vanished. She can say all she wants, continue to assure us all that she's fine, but I can see it in her eyes. She's a terrible liar, and the pain behind her eyes speaks so much louder than words. Watching her trying to carry on as normal makes my guilt even worse. I should have looked after her, but I didn't. I trusted she'd be okay at our own damn rally. Yeah, my stupidity is biting me in the ass now.

Damn the Stormy Souls MC for the tension they're bringing and damn me for not being able to keep an eye on Meghan like I was supposed to.

"You alright, kid?"

Darn, how did Dad manage to sneak up on me?

"Yes, Dad, I'm fine, just tired from the long night last night. Megs is okay too, just tired and quiet; I think getting lost scared her a little." I force a smile on my face as I turn to look at my father.

"Okay, darlin, we're done here now. Prospects are tidying up. Time to get home." He nods at me, then tips his head towards the van, where I spot Meghan already waiting.

"Sure, Dad, see you at home." I nod back at him and stalk over to the van and Meghan.

Giving her a gentle shove inside, I follow her, before slamming the door shut and fastening my seat belt. I can't wait to get home.

◊◊◊

The journey back, as short as it is, passes in deafening silence, Meghan stares out of her window, not even making eye contact with me. I breathe a sigh of relief when the door opens in the compound.

We jump out of the van, and I immediately feel the prospect's leering eyes on my ass.

"I swear, I'll kick you in the nuts if you don't remove your eyes from my ass!" I hiss at him.

He's the gall to snicker! I turn within a millisecond and watch his eyes go huge as my steel-cap toes connect with his balls. He sinks to the floor, yowling like a kicked dog, which in effect he is.

Meghan walks straight up the path to her and Fury's house. As I watch her disappear through the front door, a sense of foreboding rolls over me like a dark wave.

Grabbing my bag, I head towards our house. It's a small two bed, one bath, but it's home. Most of the time, I'm here on my own anyway, as Dad mainly stays at his room in the clubhouse. He partakes not only in the sluts but also in doobies.

The smell of those makes me gag. Both the sluts and the weed. So, he keeps that shit away from me. I've often wondered what the hell he is doing at the Restless Slayers MC, a down-and-out one percenter club, with their sticky fingers in many illegal pies. Drug running, prostitution, gun running, extortion, you name it, and it's on their list.

Dad is careful not to let me hear any of the '*Club Business.*' Others… not so much. I keep my mouth shut and pretend I know nothing. It's the safest thing to do.

I grew up in the club. My mother died soon after I was born, and those rough men and a couple of old ladies brought me up. Old ladies are few and far between here. There aren't many women who can put up with this life and the trouble that inevitably follows these men.

My dad, though, is my hero. He bandaged every scraped knee, read me bedtime stories, loves me unconditionally, and encourages me in everything I do, especially if it's away from the club. He doesn't want this life for me, but this is home. I don't know how to live differently; this has been my only existence.

Dad pushed me to take my bike test and encourages me riding. When everyone said I can't ride cause I'm a woman, he went and bought me a blood red Fatboy 114, just to prove a point and to show his love and belief in me. I love that machine, almost as much as I love my dad, and ride it every chance I get.

He won't be back for hours, so I head to the bathroom, run the taps to fill a nice hot bath, and luxuriate in the hot, sweet-smelling bubbles, trying to chill myself out from the weekend.

◊◊◊

Wow, waking with my hand between my legs isn't something that happens often. Not that I'm not averse to giving into my urges. Hey, I'm only human after all, but to wake up horny as hell, pleasuring myself to a dream? Nah, not my usual routine.

Damn that man! His hard, steel-gray eyes still have me captivated. Not to mention his skillful tongue and hands. He's my guilty secret, and I like it like that. His long, dark hair in a ponytail, the strength oozing out of his every pore, the way he made me feel completely feminine, vulnerable, strong, yet safe.

One and done. That's what we agreed. I wish it could be different, but it can't. He's miles away from the type of man I normally go for. With his slim physique, I normally wouldn't have given him a second glance, but somehow, his body belies his strength. You can tell he's a boxer, a scrapper with an iron will. Maybe that was the attraction. Not that it matters now, it's done with, over before it even began.

A quick rally passion. Everyone knows what happens at a rally stays at the rally. So why, oh why, can't I get his eyes and hands out of my head? Why does the memory of the two of us plague me like a cat in heat?

Groaning, I stretch, roll over, grab my vibrator out of my bedside drawer, and set about relieving my feverish need, concentrating only on the vibration on my clit, nothing else. No eyes, no hands, no tongue. After about five minutes, I groan in frustration. B.O.B is not getting me there today. Looks like I need to take a cold shower to wake myself up and cool off.

Getting dressed, I decide to grab Meghan and take her out for breakfast. Might help to shift her mood and keep my mind off other things. Meaning, my rally lay.

On my short walk to Meghan's, I suck in the fresh air of Grand Forks, which is a nice place to live. Nature surrounds us, and our small town can give a picturesque appearance if you're not aware of its seedy underbelly. I try not to look too closely at that side of town. I prefer to ignore the bad and just see the positive. Otherwise, it'd drive me nuts.

I step up to Meghan's front door and knock. It takes a few minutes before the door opens. A tousled, red-eyed Meghan stares at me.

"Come on, girl, get dressed. We're going for breakfast."

My chirpiness clearly false, as I'm shocked at what I see in Meghan. This is a girl with a ton of weight on her shoulders. I cajole her along, and thirty minutes later, we're in the car and out the clubhouse gates, heading for the town center. Meghan has always been the silent type, but today she seems to be not even present. She stares out of the passenger side window, almost completely ignoring me.

Her pain emanates out of her every pore, and I hate that she believes she can't open up to me. Meghan is like my little sister. We've always been there for each other, despite our age difference. She's just turned eighteen, and I'm twenty-three.

We find a place in our favorite cafe, take a seat, and put in our orders.

"Meghan, what's going on?" I ask her, unable to keep the worry out of my voice.

"Nothing, Tan. I'm fine. Just tired from the weekend."

I call bullshit.

"Meg, I wasn't born yesterday. I can see you're not right. I'm here for you. You can talk to me, you know?"

"I know, Tan. There's just nothing to talk about. So, drop it, please? I promise, if there ever is anything, you'll be the first person I'll turn to."

I see the lie in her eyes, but there's nothing I can do.

"What do you fancy doing today?" I decide to change the subject instead. With that, she perks up a little.

"Can we go to Andy's?" she asks.

I laugh at her enthusiasm, remembering well how eager I was to turn eighteen so I could buy my first motorcycle. I can't blame her. So, the Harley dealership it is. That's killing two birds with one stone, as Fury tasked me to find out what she wants for her birthday present. Well, he'll have a shock, but I can't see him denying Meghan her coming-of-age present.

3 — PENNYWISE

THREE MONTHS LATER

Holy fucking shit. My heart stops as I race up to the gruesome scene. The station wagon we've been looking for is parked on the verge, and there are bodies littering the road. Caleb is kneeling next to one of them, trying to stem the blood welling out of it. He's got a lot to learn. We don't rescue our enemies. At best, we keep them alive to face their fate in the bunker.

"Where the fuck are the girls?" My teeth are grating so hard I may have to see an orthodontist. After I slapped some sense into the prospect.

Slender runs past me, bawling, "Ellie, Ellie!" like a madman. He's losing his ever-loving mind over his old lady. Everyone with half an ounce of sense can see that they're made for each other. Out of the corner of my eye, I clock Ellie coming out from behind the station wagon. *Clever girl.* Gave herself just enough cover to stay out of the spray of bullets.

"Caleb!" I bellow at the prospect, still waiting for an answer.

As he turns towards me, all the blood drains from my head. *Fuck!*

In front of me, Caleb's face is tear-stained, and on the ground in front of him lies Tanya, slowly bleeding out from several gunshot wounds. I guess she tried to kill the bastards who took them. And took fire herself.

"FUCK!" My voice sounds almost otherworldly even to my own ears as I dial 911.

"Get this shit cleaned up. EMTs are on their way," Raven growls.

Slender grabs Ellie, and after a terse exchange with Raven, they climb on his bike and leave.

Masher roaring, "No, Tanya, hang on, baby!" reaches me as though through a fog.

Time seems to have slowed. Sirens in the distance punch through my muffled brain, and I jump into action. Grabbing Greg, I haul one of the dead guys, Benito Lacasa, to the van, shut the door, and watch Greg jump in, driving off in the opposite direction from where the sirens are coming. Blue and red lights are now flashing closer.

Shit, the last thing we need is the cops on our asses, but with Tanya on the ground, we can't avoid it.

◊◊◊

Bikers and old ladies pack out the hospital waiting room, not to mention the cops hanging around, questioning all of us. We all tell the same story. Flesh traders took Tanya. The prospect followed them. She freed herself but must have gotten shot in the exchange. Caleb fired to protect Tanya.

The cops hate the fact they can't pin this on us, but since all our stories match, there's little they can do, other than glare at us. Masher has gone to wait outside the operating rooms, where Tanya is undergoing surgery. Only family is allowed through there, which leaves the rest of us pacing.

Masher and Tanya have been hanging around for weeks. Raven is keeping zipped over the reasons. I'm getting frustrated with it. I'm the Enforcer. Slender is the SAA. It's our job to keep the club safe. We can't do that if we're kept out of the loop.

Something cold begins to crawl up my back, sending involuntary shivers down my spine.

My intuition screams at me that the worst is yet to come. It's like a premonition, without an actual vision. Yes, I believe in listening to my gut, even if it sounds wussy. And my gut is screaming at me right now.

Watching the EMTs work on Tanya, then load her into the waiting ambulance, had every muscle, every sinew in my body pulled so tight, I thought they were gonna snap. My mind refused to work, and everything around me seemed muffled.

It took Masher ramming me out of the way to get into the ambulance with Tanya, to shake me out of my funk.

Our one and done has quickly morphed into a casual as long as we both fancy and done. Somehow, we can't seem to resist one another.

She's a spitfire, and to my amazement, she warms my ice-cold, jaded insides a little every time we get together. Sex with her is off-the-charts hot.

She has a magic pussy for sure, since I can't seem to get enough of it. I'm aware I'm playing with fire. Not just because I can't help myself when it comes to fucking her, but if Masher finds out, we're both toast. There's no way the Restless Slayers will accept me fucking one of theirs, whether our two clubs happen to be on friendly terms or not.

The door to the waiting room slams open, pulling me from my thoughts, and Masher strides in.

"She'll be okay," he announces, relief lacing his tone. "Doc says she took a bullet to her thigh that nicked a vein, and one to her abdomen, which only barely missed the liver. Plus, two of her ribs are cracked. I'll kill the motherfucker who laid hands on her." By the time he finishes, Masher is a breathless, hot, furious mess.

"Can we see her?" Ally asks.

"They're taking her to a room now. They'll call me as soon as she's settled." He waves his cell around, visibly shaking as his anger slowly evaporates. No longer Masher the SAA of the Restless Slayers MC, but Masher the father, who nearly lost his little girl today.

When his cell finally rings, Ally and Chloe are the first to go in and see Tanya, followed by the rest of the club, two at a time. When I enter with Slender, his hand is on my shoulder. Since he caught me and Tanya, he looks at me with a perpetual smirk on his face, and he's really starting to get on my nerves.

Nevertheless, I'm glad I don't have to be on my own when I walk into the room. Tanya is flat on her back, eyes closed, skin deathly pale, with the surrounding monitors beeping. So many wires and IV lines going into her, it makes her almost unrecognizable.

We sit on the chairs placed either side of her. Slender grabs her hand and cradles it. I'm glad he has because if I touch her now, I'll go to pieces, and I can't afford that. There's work to be done still.

Silently, I vow to catch those bastards and make them suffer. Their pain will be ten times worse than Tanya's. I'll make sure she gets her revenge!

Slender watches me like a hawk.

"You still hitting that?"

His question makes me want to throttle him. He doesn't mean any harm, but his glib attitude grates on me.

"None of your fucking business," I snap at him, and his eyebrows rise to his hairline.

"What the fuck, Pen, get your head out of your ass, will you? I'm the one who caught you in your room. I take it no one else knows?" He skewers me with a glare, then shakes his head. "Nah, of course they don't, because if this was out in the open, you'd be in shit so deep not even an excavator could pull you up.

"Masher is gonna shoot your ass when he finds out. We have enough shit going on without this extra load you and her are dumping on us. So, excuse me if I want to know whether I have to put eyes on you to prevent you getting clubbed in a dark alley!"

Wow, Slender is pissed. In fact, it's been a long time since I've seen my best friend *this* infuriated. He's not wrong, either.

Feeling suitably chastised, I wind my neck in. "Sorry, man. I've not been with her since you found us, and that's the truth. Don't get me wrong, she's hot. Mega hot, but, man, that woman is high maintenance. Not to mention the Restless Slayers' connection. If she was anyone else, I'd probably make her my regular, but she isn't, so I'm not going there again." I put as much conviction into my words as I can muster.

If it's the truth, why do I feel like shit?

"Change of subject, man." I glance at Slender, hoping he understands my back-to-front apology. "What the hell is going on with the Restless Slayers, Slender? Something doesn't sit right."

"I understand, man, my gut is screaming too. Whatever it is, it ain't good. I think we need to investigate, just as soon as the cops are off our backs," Slender answers, his brows scrunched, staring right at me. It's obvious how seriously he takes his and my gut feelings.

A groan rips us out of our conversation, and our heads shoot round, giving Tanya our full attention. Her eyes are fluttering, and she shifts around her hospital bed.

"I'll grab someone," I offer as I stand, open the door, and walk up the corridor to fetch a nurse, who quickly follows me back to Tanya's room.

"Gentlemen, can I please ask you to leave? I need to see to this young lady. I'll speak to her dad after that. He can tell you what's happening."

That put us in our place. I want to close my hands around her throat and slowly cut off her air supply. Slender's hand stops me dead, though.

“Come on, man, let’s find Masher. Let him know she’s waking. Time to get out of here.”

I nod at him in complete agreement. My monster is too close to the surface. I’ll snap if I don’t leave.

Back in the waiting room, we put Masher in the picture. I watch as Slender draws Ellie to him, kissing her like his life depends on it. They are so right together. Always have been. It’s a shame my soul is as black as Satan’s asshole. I don’t qualify for a good woman. I’d only drag her down the pits with me, and I don’t want that for anyone.

So instead, I keep my feelings locked up tight. It started when my father died. I couldn’t stand the looks of pity from the brothers. Mom tried to make life as normal as possible, but at the end of the day, my father was still dead. He was my hero. A great man. I was old enough to watch him being consumed by darkness and ultimately, into his untimely death. Mom has never dated again, not as far as I’m aware, anyway.

Some days, I wish things were different. That life was different. But it ain’t, so I deal and carry on. Some brothers think I hate my job as an enforcer. To be honest, I need it; it gives me a sense of belonging and helps me manage my inner demons.

To everyone I'm a brother, friend, enforcer, someone who is devoted to the club and my mom. She's the only person who's caught glimpses beyond what I let everyone else see.

Well, apart from Tanya. She seems to enjoy being around my darkness. That's why my door is locked from now on. She has her own darkness and doesn't need to be drowned in mine.

4 — TANYA

Light blinds me as someone pulls my eyelids back and shines a flashlight into them.

A soothing female voice creeps through my muddled brain. “Hello, Miss Frost, I’m Nurse Heather. You are in hospital and recovering from an operation. Please stay calm and still for me so I can check your dressings, okay, honey?”

I try to answer, but all that leaves my throat is a painful croak. Right now, I wish that asshole had shot me properly and put me out of my misery.

My mind is racing at a hundred miles an hour, but my body’s struggling to keep up. The last thing I remember is that bastard shooting at me, the searing pain that followed, then me hitting the deck. Everything after that is vague.

A muted conversation between what sounded like Pennywise and one of his brothers. I doubt I heard everything, but what I did hear was enough. Enough to make me want to scream at myself and kick my own ass for letting him anywhere near me. The ignorant pig.

“I’ll give you something for the pain,” Nurse Heather says to me, and that’s the last thing I hear as my vision retreats once again into darkness.

The next time my consciousness rises to the surface, overwhelming agony is all I feel.

“Shh, sweetheart, hang in there. I’m gonna get the nurse.”

My father’s voice and the gentle stroke of his hand on my forehead do little to soothe me.

Drugs, I need drugs, and lots of them.

I’m sure my face is a grimace, and tears run down my face in rivers.

Fuck, this hurts so damn much.

Thankfully, Dad reappears with Heather in tow, who smiles reassuringly and pushes some more painkillers through my IV. The relief isn’t instant, but moment by moment the pain starts to recede. I’m left feeling warm and cozy, and even manage to smile at my dad.

Wow, I’ve had a doobie before, but this? This is much better.

“Sweetheart, what happened? Can you tell me?” he asks, his voice gentle, but I know it’s more of an order to report. I try to talk and am surprised at how alien my voice sounds. It's like someone dragged a belt sander down my throat.

"Take your time," Dad encourages.

I let my mind drift to the beating that bastard gave me in the cell. Instinctively, I reach up to touch a dressing over my eyebrow. *Huh, stitches, maybe? Meh, couldn't care less.*

"They came, handcuffed us, made us walk to the station wagon. You found it?"

I look up at Dad, who nods and holds out a glass of water with a straw. Without hesitation, I suck down the blessed nectar, cooling my sore throat.

"They shoved us in the trunk," I continue. "Thanks to Ferret, I had a key to the handcuffs. I freed Ellie first. She helped me, and as soon as I got free, I asked for a pit-stop. Once they opened the trunk, Ellie stabbed one of them in the side. Two others came at me. I grabbed my gun and shot their asses, but they obviously returned fire and shot me.

"Last thing I remember is Ellie shouting 'Watch out,' another few shots, none of them mine, and then Caleb taking his shirt off and pressing it to my stomach. After that, everything is blank until I woke up here."

Once I finish speaking, my breaths are sawing in and out, and the machine next to me begins to beep faster. Dad reaches over to stroke my hair.

"It's okay, sweetheart, I've got you. You'll be fine. Everything will be okay. We had to call an ambulance for you, hence the 5-0 hanging around, asking questions. You got Benito. We removed him and sent him to old man Cabal."

He nods his head toward a gigantic bouquet of white flowers. There's a card attached, but I know without reading it who it is from.

"Cabal is happy that you took care of his problem," Dad continues. "The boys in blue only know about one corpse. We kept Benito out of the picture. Remember that when they question you. They are outside, waiting for the doctor to determine whether you're fit to be interviewed."

I nod at him, my eyes tracking the beaker of water. He holds the straw up to my mouth again. Exhaustion takes over, and my eyes begin to droop.

"Sleep, sweetheart. Rest is the best medicine for you now." Dad smiles warmly at me, and his reassurance lets me give in to sleep once more.

◊◊◊

Opening my eyes feels laborious, but the cold washcloth on my face is hard to disregard.

When I glance around the room, I realize it is Ally who's sitting next to me, washing my face as though it's the most normal thing in the world to do.

"Hey, friend, welcome back." She smiles at me.

"How bad is it?" I rasp, my voice still rough.

"Put it this way. I'm enemy number one right now. Your dad, Raven, Sparks… I am without doubt the most hated person around the club. Sparks hasn't spoken to me in days."

"How long have I been here?" I ask.

"Two days and one night," Ally replies. "They shot you up bad, hon. One in the thigh and one in the abdomen, but they stitched you back up. You'll be like new in no time." She grins at me, then continues, "Listen, I can't help but notice the tensions between you, the Souls, and the Slayers. Must be awkward. Are you sure you want to come on board as enforcer for the Wild Pixies WMC? Neither Jules nor I would blame you if you wanted to back out."

What the hell is Ally up to now?

"Of course I want to be your enforcer. Ally, that isn't even a question. I so need to get out of the Restless Slayers' grip. The MC is moving in a direction I don't want any part of. Too much backstabbing and just bad vibes. If you ask me, Fury is only holding on by a thread. Mark my words, the implosion is coming, and I want to be as far away from it as possible when it happens. I love you and your girls, and I love the Slayers' old ladies, too."

My eyes stay trained on hers, trying to show that I'm serious. It's the best decision I've made in a long time. I'm finally putting me first. Yes, I'll have to leave Meghan and Dad, but I can still visit them, or Meghan can visit me here.

"Okay, hon, if you are sure?"

My answer is instant. "I'm sure, Ally. Are you sure I can stay at Debs' Haven until I find a place of my own?"

"Absolutely. Ellie, Amy, and Darcie have got a nice room ready for you. You can move in as soon as you want. Also, I moved your bike to Debs' Haven. Hope you don't mind. I thought you might want it at your convenience ASAP. Nothing like a nice hard ride to clear out the cobwebs."

"Thanks, Ally, I appreciate this more than you can imagine." I sigh.

"Ha, you might appreciate my next actions even more." She winks at me and pulls out a box of goodies from the local bakery from under her top.

"What? I had to smuggle it in. Mom tried to bring you home-cooked food, and the staff told her no, so I got creative."

"As long as it doesn't taste of armpit… beggars can't be choosers, I guess."

I smirk at her and reach my hands out to the box of deliciousness. I am surprised to note my IVs have been removed and I can now move my arms. Apart from the pain burning through my body, I can even shuffle in the bed. My stomach growls and I'm a slave to its need. Ally holds the box closer. I grab a Danish, and my God, the flavor explodes in my mouth. Better than orgasms, I swear.

Just as I go to take a second bite, the door opens, and I almost choke as a hunk of a doctor enters the room. Men this hot should come with a warning sign! My ovaries are doing a happy dance right now, and despite my pain, moisture gathers between my legs. Ally stares at him, her tongue lolling out. I snort, watching her. Damn, this guy has us all in a fluster.

"Miss Frost?"

God, even his voice is like honey.

"Yes, that's me."

"Could I talk to you in private, please?"

"It's okay, Doctor…"

"Sorry, I'm Doctor Ritter," he quickly introduces.

"Okay, Doctor Ritter. Anything you have to tell me, you can say in front of my friend here. I give you permission to share any information necessary with her," I tell him.

Ally's eyes go as round as saucers.

"Are you sure, Tanya? I can get your dad, if you'd rather?"

I shake my head.

"Nope, Ally, it's all good. So, go on, Doctor Ritter, what did you want to talk to me about?"

"You were brought in with gunshot wounds to your thigh and your abdomen. The operation we did was a success. We repaired the torn vein in your thigh, repaired the damage in your abdomen, and removed the bullets. You are healing well, and the nurses tell me you're doing fine. You are both fine. But obviously, we won't be able to give you stronger pain relief anymore. That's why I removed the IV this morning."

I regard him and my brain stutters to a halt. I don't understand.

"What do you mean, you can't give me stronger painkillers? My pain is a one hundred out of ten right now?"

Something is nagging at me, but I can't put my finger on it.

"And of course, Ally is fine. She wasn't the one who was shot," I add.

I watch the hot doctor's facial features change from confusion to understanding.

"Err, Miss Frost, when we did all of our blood tests, we also did a routine pregnancy screen. I take it you don't know. Miss Frost, you are almost three months pregnant."

I feel as though my bed is being sucked into a vortex.

"That can't be right. Please repeat the test," I croak, helplessly staring at Ally, who takes my hand.

"I assure you, Miss Frost, the results are correct. You are ten weeks along. I've made arrangements for our in-house OB-GYN to come and see you before your discharge. They can do the exact dating and the first ultrasound to confirm everything is alright. Congratulations, Miss Frost."

What the hell is going on? I can't be pregnant, I can't! Pennywise made it abundantly clear he wants nothing to do with me anymore. It was always meant to be a one and done.

Stunned, I watch as the door closes behind the hot doctor, all feelings of arousal shocked out of me. I turn my head towards Ally and let the choking tears flow.

5 — PENNYWISE

"Quiet!" Raven bellows into the packed church meeting. "Dawg, the floor is yours!"

"Right then, ladies, updates on the businesses. Zippy's Tattoos is raking it in. We still need to find an assistant for the front desk and a new artist. Financially, Zippy's is solid. As is Leather and Lace. The ladies' nights are making a fortune. Who knew that ladies love their dollars in male G-strings?" Dawg shudders. "The private rooms remain fully booked out, and that goes for normal nights and ladies' nights. Membership is on the up. Let anyone say the bar business is dead. I dare them.

"Stormy Customs and Lightning Security are doing well enough. No issues there. Actually, Ferret, we had great feedback about the new guy, Chris. He's popular with the customers."

Ferret nods. "That he is. A good guy who doesn't take any shit but has a diplomatic side, defuses a lot of crap rolling towards him. Still think he'd make great brother material; I'll keep working on him. The security business is going great. We've had a lot of inquiries for personal security, might be something we wanna look into, help broaden the business base. The more income streams, the better."

Slender speaks next.

"The club is secure. No threats from anywhere right now. Pennywise and I have concerns, though, that we need to discuss with the officers after the meeting."

Nodding my head, I stare Raven straight in the eye. Now's the time to discuss the bad vibes everyone is getting from the Restless Slayers. The Stormy Souls is a small club. We don't have chapters in other areas of the United States yet. Affiliation with the Restless Slayers MC ties us to them. But this could change the way things are going.

Which means safety suddenly becomes our number one concern. There is no obvious threat yet, but my gut is telling me that could change on the turn of a dime.

Lost in my own thoughts, I only half listen to the ongoing discussions. I know I should concentrate, but my brain refuses to cooperate.

All I hear is "Cops… blah, blah, blah… Cabal… blah, blah, blah… Prospect… blah, blah, blah."

As hard as I try to pull my completely fritzed brain together, it's not working.

Shit, I really need to sort my life out.

In my mind's eye, a slew of images flash like a movie reel. Bikes riding at each other, bullets flying, cops leading bikers away in handcuffs.

I know it's my imagination running riot, but I can't seem to stop it. Slender glares at me and slaps me round the back of the head.

"Oi, dickhead, get your shit together!" he hisses at me.

I rub my stinging head, attempting to tune out my mindfuck movie and focus on what's going on in the room.

"Okay, that's all for now, ladies. Meeting adjourned." Raven bangs the gavel.

The room empties, leaving just the officers. Raven, the Prez; our VP, Vegas; Dawg, as Secretary; the club's IT guy, Ferret; our Road Captain, Clusseaud; our SAA, Slender; and myself, the club's Enforcer.

Slender gets up and walks out to the bar, returning moments later with a bucket of beers and glasses for the bottle of whiskey Raven pulls out from his desk drawer.

"I think we all need this, boys. The last few months have been irritating to say the least," Raven declares to the men. The only sound in the room is the sloshing of large helpings of whiskey into glasses.

I can't take my gut stabbing anymore.

"Okay, I'll play. What the fuck is going on? The Restless Slayers spend way too much time at our compound. It makes my skin crawl and my brain itch.

"Ever since the incident with Slender and Ellie, something seems wrong." I look Raven straight in the eye when I make my statement. Suddenly, the tension in the room seems to deflate.

"I know we have to play nice with them, dominant club and all that malarky, but hell, enough is enough. My gut is screaming at me, telling me something isn't right. What the hell are they playing at?" Panting hard, anger rolls off me in waves as I clench my fists, trying my hardest not to slam them onto the table.

"And Tanya, Masher's daughter? Enforcer for the Wild Pixies? What the ever-loving fuck? They are a party club, nothing more!"

"Sit your ass down and shut the fuck up!" Raven growls. "Before I forget you are my enforcer and instruct Slender to take you outside and beat some sense into you! You've been a grade-A asshole for a while now, Pennywise."

I hate the way he uses my full name and the ice-cold tone it rolls off his tongue with.

"Get your act together. I've had enough of your shit. Consider this a warning! Don't make me repeat myself!"

His glare makes me shrink into myself.

What the fuck? Have I really been that bad?

Shit, I've let myself and the club down here, and worst of all, I've let Mom and Dad down. They taught me better.

"Sorry, man," I grumble, only now realizing I'm standing and leaning towards Raven. *Fuck.*

Sitting my ass down in my chair, my eyes travel round the room. Dawg shaking his head at me and Slender and Ferret glaring, tells me I overstepped big time.

"Okay, now that we've got that settled, let's move on," Raven speaks up. "I hear your concerns, Pen, and I'm sure the others agree. I certainly do. However, our hands are tied. They are our dominant club, and we have to play nice. *For now.*

"That said, I don't want to hear anymore gripes about Tanya and her new position. That's a matter for the Wild Pixies, not us. They are not a party club, Pen; they are an MC in their own right. I've worked with Ally long enough to appreciate that. You should too. The Wild Pixies are their own entity, and their club business isn't ours.

"However," Raven continues, "I completely get your gut instincts regarding the Slayers. Something is off. I've spent enough time over there to notice there are tensions within the club. Fury isn't popular, for reasons unknown to me. I won't stick my nose into their business, but what they did to you, Slender, was way off the mark. I hate that we have to work with them regarding the sex traffickers, but it is what it is. They have all the connections, so we're dependent on them, in more ways than one."

"I don't like it," Feret pipes up. "I've spent a lot of time with Ghost lately, coordinating the searches, establishing contacts with the Cabals, etc. Don't get me wrong, Ghost is a nice guy, knowledgeable and well connected. But as soon as the topic of conversation comes around to Fury, he shuts down. It's like a mask goes down and the teeth grinding begins. It has me on edge."

"Ferret, do you think you could discreetly look into what's going on? They clearly have something to hide, and we need to find out what it is." Raven looks at Ferret expectantly.

"I can try, man, but it's difficult with Ghost watching over my shoulder all the time. If you ask me, it's time they all went home. Give me some space to dig," Ferret replies.

"Now, Chloe mentioned to me that Amy, you know, the blonde we rescued and who is now at Debs' Haven, went catatonic again as soon as she saw Fury. I put it down to what she'd been through, but Chloe's convinced there's more to it. Her gut is seldom wrong," Raven says.

And as he does, alarm bells ring in my head.

"What do you mean?" Ferret asks.

"I'm not sure what I mean, man, just saying that Chloe's gut instincts are usually solid, which worries me. What do we know about this Amy chick?" Raven raises a good point.

"Not much, really. Want me to dig into her?" As he speaks, Ferret's fingers click over his keyboard at speed.

"Sure, that might help," Raven agrees.

"What has she to do with the Restless Slayers?" I ask.

"Not a clue." Dawg shrugs his shoulders. "If there's a connection, though, we'll find out. Could be a rat? Stranger things have happened."

"That it for now?" Raven asks. "Everyone clear on how we play this?"

"Yeah, crystal," Slender tells him.

"Let's get out of here then." Raven stands, and everyone else follows his example and piles into the bar. I make a beeline for the kitchen, where Mom holds court.

Opening the door, saliva floods my mouth when I'm hit by the delicious aroma wafting through the kitchen. Mom smirks at me, knowing full well that the way to bikers' hearts is through their stomachs.

"Yes, Noah, I made brisket, with all the trimmings. Meat is just resting, so hands off. Dinner will be ready in thirty minutes."

I know better than to steal a piece. She'll beat my fingers with a meat tenderizer. Instead, I walk over to her, wrap my arms around her, and hug her tight.

"Love you, Mom."

"Love you too, Noah." Her muffled reply puts a rare grin on my face. She's the only one who calls me by my given name. And I love it.

"Mom, have I been a pain lately?"

"Yes, dear, you've been a complete dick. I don't like it, pack it in. You're not too old for me to spank you. You'll fit across my knee, I promise."

I love it when she mocks me. Although, I wouldn't put it past her to make good on her threat. Time to sort myself out.

I let her go as the door opens, and the two prospects come in. They grab stuff to lay the huge dining table, directed by Mom. I smile, watching how tightly she controls those two hoodlums. And how much the prospects adore her. She has that effect on folks. Her strength, fairness, and empathy shine through everything she does. I can't put into words how proud I am of her.

The way she handled Dad's death, bringing not only fatherless me up but also Slender and, for a large part, Raven, Ashley, and their younger brother Nathan.

"Chow's up!" Greg shouts into the bar, and within minutes, the table is packed with brothers and old ladies. Talk flows as everyone makes their plate.

Man, I love this club. As much as I love my amazing mother.

6 — TANYA

My eyes sting terribly and a hollowness consumes me. I feel dead inside. How could this happen? I've been so careful; never missed a pill in my life.

Pregnant! It's a catastrophe!

Ally, bless her, stays next to me, holding my hand. Her gentle, rhythmic strokes soothe me a little. I hiccup and grab the tissue she holds out to me. Blowing my nose and wiping my tears, I'm sure I look a sorry sight.

"Hey, hon, are you okay? I know, stupid question, really. I can see you're not. Damn, I just want to hug you, but I can't." Ally points towards the hospital bed. "Do you want to talk about it? If you don't, that's okay too, though. I'm here for you. All the girls will be. No matter what."

"What am I gonna do, Ally?" My voice comes out a mere whisper, and Ally leans in closer.

"I've no idea, hon, not a decision I can help you with, I'm afraid. How do you feel? Do you want to keep it?"

"I've no clue, Ally. I'm so confused. How did this even happen?"

Ally snorts. "Well, I can draw you a diagram if you like. Or tell you a bedtime story. Cast your mind back to three months ago…"

I snicker.

"What's your dad gonna say? He won't be happy that one of his brothers is your baby-daddy."

"Oh God, he's gonna kill me," I groan and bury my face in my hands, my cheeks burning as though on fire. "If he finds out, we're toast. It's gonna cause so much trouble between the clubs."

With that admission, I daren't look Ally in the eye.

"What do you mean cause trouble between the clubs? Tanya, what's going on?" Ally's concerned eyes lock with mine.

I take a deep breath. It's now or never. If I want to come out of this in one piece, whatever happens, I need allies, and I need to be honest, at least with Ally, my friend and my Prez. God, she might kick me out of the club before I've even started.

"Do you remember the Restless Slayers rally?" I ask her.

"How could I not? All that shit with Rusty, Meghan, Prez, and Chloe, it's one for the history books."

"Well, I got extremely drunk and had a one-night stand. That one and done turned into a several-nights stand. But it wasn't with one of the Restless Slayers…"

I watch as Ally's eyebrows shoot up in sudden understanding. She watches me like a hawk.

"Who?"

Her stern voice unsettles me. There's nothing for it. I've got to tell her.

"Pennywise," I whisper, my eyes roaming everywhere in the room. Everywhere but Ally.

"You've got to be fucking kidding me?" Ally yells.

Feeling like a scolded child, I draw my head lower in between my shoulders. Let's face it, if I can't face Ally, I stand no chance with Dad or Pen.

"Tanya, are you out of your ever-loving mind? Jesus, that's gonna cause major drama."

My anger gets the better of me.

"Don't you think I know that?" I hiss. "It's not as though I planned this, is it? It's a clusterfuck. How do you think I feel? Like a piece of shit for causing nothing but trouble. I may be a bit psycho, but I ain't stupid."

My hands shake, and my whole body vibrates with anger.

"Tanya, if you want to step back from me being your enforcer, that's okay. I'll understand completely, but don't give me any more shit than I'm already giving myself."

"Sorry, hon, it's just such a shock," Ally replies contritely. "I'll have to speak to Jules; see what she thinks. Let me talk to her. In the meantime, is there anything I can do for you? No matter how pissed I am, you're still my friend, always will be. So, speak up." She smiles at me between clenched teeth.

"Thanks, Ally. Nothing I can think of now. Unless you can smuggle me a burger and onion rings?" I wink at her.

Ally, being Ally, clicks her heels and salutes before she turns and walks out the door. When she leaves, she speaks to Caleb, who's stationed outside my room, guarding me. I can't hear what she says, but Caleb nods, so I take it as a positive sign.

A knock on the door announces my dad's arrival, with the nurse in tow. She helps me use the bedpan and allows me to sit on the edge of the bed for a few minutes. My head spins like a disc in a player.

"Come on, sweetheart, that's enough." My dad gently lifts my legs and turns me back into the safety of my bed. "Would you like me to get you a coffee, sweetheart?"

"No thanks, Dad, but could you get me some orange juice, please? I hate the water here. It tastes like old socks."

Dad, the mountain of a man SAA, turns around, howling with laughter.

"Like what? Old socks? When have you ever tasted old socks, darlin'?" He walks to the door, still chuckling. "I'll be back in a moment," he says as he closes it.

Pulling the call bell, I pray the nurse will be back before he is, otherwise the situation could turn into a disaster sooner than I know what's hit me.

Luckily, it only takes the nurse a minute until she enters.

"How can I help you?"

"I have a request. My father is not to be told of my pregnancy. In fact, from here on out, you and the team will only discuss my medical conditions with me. No one else. Please add that to my notes."

She nods at me, turns on her heel, and leaves. That was easy. Hopefully, it will give me time to think about my situation without everyone knowing. Ally will keep her lips zipped. There's no worries there. I trust her implicitly.

I've never felt so empty and drained in all my life. I need to sleep and have a chance to collect my thoughts without being woken up during the night for checks. Not only did that fucker shoot me, but I've also had to tell my story to relentless cops and put up with Dad being with me just about every waking moment. Now this curveball landing straight in my lap, and me juggling it like a hot potato. All I want is to sleep and to get out of here.

The next time the door opens, my dad steps back in with a bottle of orange juice.

"Thanks, Dad, you're a lifesaver."

He just nods and sits down in the chair by my bed.

"Hey, sweetheart, need to ask you something. Were you serious when you spouted off that you'll become the Wild Pixies' Enforcer? Not asking as SAA, asking as your dad. I wish your mother was here. I'll be straight up with you; I have no clue how to handle this."

His honesty amazes me, and suddenly, I'm overcome with shame for keeping things from him. I grab his hand and don't wanna let go. He's been my hero, my superstar. When Mom died, I was only four months old. I don't remember her. Between him and the club bringing me up, I've never wanted for anything, always felt loved and protected. I love my life in Grand Forks, but it's time to live my life on my own terms. Especially under the current circumstances.

The Wild Pixies are a national ladies' MC, so it won't matter where I end up. Whether in Grand Forks, New York, or Timbuktu. Admittedly, I like it in Duluth and Superior. I love the women here. The only wrench will be being so far away from Meghan, my sister from another mister, and Dad.

"Dad, yes, I'm as serious as a heart attack. I'm honored they asked me, and old enough to start out on my own. Can't live with you and the club forever." I smile at him, trying to soothe the sting my words leave behind.

"My little girl is all grown up."

His glassy eyes really tug at my heart strings.

"Well, my little bird, you need to learn to fly. Now is as good a time as ever. When you get out of here, I go back and pack your stuff. I'll bring it down to you. You can always ride up to visit, or I'll visit you and bring Meghan." Dad puts on a brave face, but I know this hurts him badly.

"I'll be fine, Dad. You've been the best teacher and parent growing up. I love you, Dad." Tears roll down my face.

Damn it, I'm turning into a crybaby!

Dad sniffles, leans over, and hugs me carefully to him. It hurts, but there is no way I'll tell him to let go. No way in hell.

"Sweetheart, your mother would be so proud if she could see you now. Not only do you look like her, but you are fierce, loving, and the best daughter any father could ask for. Well, aside from your bloodlust, skills with a knife and gun… You get the gist." He smirks at me.

The mention of my mother has all the fight draining from me. I hate lying to Dad. It makes me feel cheap and worthless. But I've got to get my head around all of this first. So far, I have no idea what I'm gonna do. As soon as I do, so will he, even though his disappointment will sear me to the bone.

All I can hope is that he doesn't disown me. With his position in the Restless Slayers MC, it is a distinct possibility. First though, I have to make up my mind. There is a baby growing inside of me. Since the recent law change, abortion isn't an option.

However, adoption is. This tiny life deserves more than a fucked-up mother and it's one-and-done father. It deserves loving parents, a safe place, and a different life to the one Pen and I lived as kids.

Could I be that? A loving parent? Even with the clubs, or rather, within the clubs? And how would it affect

Pennywise? Is it even fair to put this on him? One and done. Does he even need to know?

"Hey, sweetheart, you seem tired. I best leave you to rest, honey."

Crumbs, I forgot Dad was even here.

He stoops, kisses my forehead, walks out, and softly closes the door behind him.

7 — PENNYWISE

Alone at last. I can't help but breathe out a sigh of relief when Masher and Ghost ride out of our compound.

Masher took the news of Tanya's new appointment relatively well, which came as a surprise to me. I would have wagered that he'd blow a fuse, but no, he seems supportive as far as I can tell. But hey, what do I know?

Getting together with Dawg, Dougal, Ferret, and Slender, we discuss the goings on at Lightning Security.

"Man, I really want Chris to come on board permanently," Ferret states. "But I have a feeling Neil will kick my ass." He laughs.

"I concur on both counts," Dawg adds, smirking.

A loud crash has us all jumping out of our skin. It announces that Dougal, who's been rocking on his chair, finally went over. I can't help but howl with laughter.

"Your mama never told you not to rock on chair legs?" Dawg shakes his head at him. "Such a child."

Groaning, Dougal picks himself and the overturned chair up off the floor.

"That was my artistic component. Scores please." He snickers, taking a deep bow.

Slender slaps him round the back of his head. "Idiot, don't make me tell Sarah," he threatens. "How is she, anyway? Haven't seen her at the clubhouse for a while."

"Sarah's real busy with work, Leo, and Jade. She's finally got Jade into counseling and enrolled at the local high school. Leo is being funny, but not in a ha-ha kind of way. He doesn't deal well with change because of his autism, so Jade moving in with us has been a challenge." Dougal sounds serious now.

"She has to put up with a lot of crap at work. She and Ashley are constantly moaning about it. Though, Ashley is due to go on maternity leave soon, which means Sarah will whine about her job even more. I love her with all my heart, but sometimes, I wish she had an off switch."

Dougal grins, shrugging his shoulders. We all know he'd throw himself in front of a runaway train for her. So, we don't take his gripes seriously.

Slender sits forward in his chair, grinning at us. "Talking about maternity… Have we got a book going on Vegas acting insane when Ashley gives birth? He told me last week that they are going to birthing classes. He was so smug about it. I reckon once Ashley goes into labor, he'll lose his shit."

"Fifty dollars that he'll get kicked out of the delivery room," Dougal says.

"I think he'll pass out instead," Slender adds.

"Nope, I think he'll be on the gas and air," Dawg counters.

"You're all on," Ferret says, waving a small notebook in front of us. "Tell the others the book is open. And in the event there's no winner, the money will go towards a college fund for the baby."

We all give Ferret the thumbs-up and open our wallets.

"Who's next? I think that'd make an interesting bet." I smirk, congratulating myself on my foresight. "Fifty dollars on Raven," I add.

"Na, put fifty on Slender." Ferret smirks and immediately receives a "No chance in hell" reply from Slender.

Dougal points his finger at me. "Gotta be Pennywise."

I ignore his goading and silently shake my head, grinning. I'm not stupid enough to be caught in that trap. Instead, I pull out another fifty and hand it to Ferret.

"Expensive meeting, boys."

Not that I mind. Turning our betting practices into a college fund is a great idea, and I'm more than happy to support it with my hard-earned cash.

We pull ourselves together and finish the rota for the next month. By the time we're done, it's late, and all I want is to get to the bar. It's a party like atmosphere in the common room. Some brothers are playing pool. Two of the club girls, Ebony and Tequila, are dancing with each other, trying to catch a brother's attention, but failing. They have been with the club for a while.

In fact, Tequila's been here since I prospected, which was a few years ago now. She's looking her age and well lived in. Time for some fresh blood on the club girls' front.

Dougal walks straight over to a table, where Sarah and Chloe are sitting. Sarah's red mane is a great indicator of her fuse. She absolutely has a redhead temperament. She fits right in with all the other old ladies.

Ashley is absent; so is Vegas. Caroline stands with Dawg at the bar, her arm draped possessively around his waist.

Slender taps me on the shoulder.

"I'm off, brother, got to pick Ellie up from Vegas and Ashley's. Girly catch up and all that crap." He rolls his eyes.

"Okay, catch you later, bro."

I slap him on the back as he turns to leave.

◊◊◊

I can't believe my eyes! We're all ready and in line, waiting for Raven to start the ride out. Next to me is this massive dog, wearing a leather cap and goggles, his tongue lolling, tail wagging, in a sidecar attached to Slender's bike. He has Ellie on the back and Tucker in the sidecar! I swear, that dog is laughing at me. He reminds me of a cartoon dog, whose name I can't quite recall.

Clusseaud's planned the Highway 61 to Gunflint Trail, so it should be an enjoyable ride.

The gate opens, and another group of riders joins us. I do a double take as they ride past me to join the back of the ride. It's the Wild Pixies, with six bikes. Ally, Jules, Tanya, Caroline, Greta, and to my utter surprise, Chloe is with them, wearing her 'Property of' cut. Can't believe Raven allowed that. He must be going soft. Pussy-whipped, definitely.

Tanya must be nuts! She only got discharged from hospital two days ago. Now she's on her bike, preparing to ride a four-hour round trip? No way should she be riding!

What can I say? She's a special kind of crazy. Once a nutter, always a nutter. Irresponsible chick!

However, it's not my business. If she were mine, there's no way she'd be riding. Just goes to show, yet again, that the Wild Pixies are not an MC I can take seriously.

Raven circles his arm, signaling we're setting off. For the whole ride, Tanya doesn't leave my mind. Why the hell do I even care? One and a few times more and done. She ain't my problem.

Since the shooting, we've hardly crossed each other's path, never mind spoken to one another. So why is she occupying so much of my in-short-supply brain space? Those eyes… those legs… that voice moaning my name... That laugh—a contagious, full-on belly laugh—drags me in every time. And let's face it, laughter has been in short supply lately.

I glance across to Slender but the only thing I can see is Tucker, who gazes at me, grinning his doggy ass off from under his cap and goggles. Despite the ridiculousness, I try and fail to hide my smirk. At least we don't have the Restless Slayers hanging around us like flies on a dung heap.

We pull into the parking lot at Grand Marais Artist's Point, overlooking the sea, woods, and the lighthouse. Gotta give props to Clusseaud; this place is beautiful.

Dismounting our bikes, we wait for the support vehicle to arrive with the prospects, who'll set up a barbeque and the tables and benches we brought, along with a cooler filled with sodas of every description. Drinking and riding isn't our deal.

I plonk myself down on the grassy verge overlooking the sea and take a deep breath.

Man, I had no idea how much I needed this. The sea calms my frayed nerves and settles my overwrought mind.

Ignoring the brothers' noise, I just sit and breathe in the sea air. Man, I love these times of calm. Unfortunately, they're usually the precursor to a raging storm.

The back of my neck tingles, like someone is staring a hole into it. I turn and see Tanya looking straight at me. She moves from the table and strolls towards me, her expression unreadable, yet I get that sinking feeling again. Can't help it, my intuition is on high alert.

"Hey, can I sit?"

I point to the verge beside me.

"It's a free world, lady. You can sit wherever you like," I reply nonchalantly.

"Don't be an ass! We need to talk."

Oh, how I hate those four words. Nothing good has ever come out of "We need to talk," and the whole male species dreads hearing them. Not that I have anything to worry about, since we're not a thing.

"What about? Didn't think we had any reason to? Do you need anything? How can I help?" I try not to sound like a cave dweller but am struggling.

I shudder, watching her take a deep breath and exhale slowly. Here it comes.

"I'm pregnant. And before you ask, it's yours. I'm not a club slut; I don't fuck around. So don't insult me. You can save your breath on that one."

"Come again?"

"I'm pregnant, you goddamn oaf! You knocked me up!"

Laughter bursts out of me.

"Haha, haha, good one…" I can hardly breathe as I start howling like a hyena.

When she doesn't reply, I sober immediately.

"You.. are… joking… right?" I take a moment or two to take in her serious face, and as sudden as it started, all my humor is gone. *Puff.* Instead, all the blood leaves my brain, and darkness encroaches on my vision.

Fuck, I can't pass out, not in front of the brothers.

“Holy shit, you are serious.” Only a croak comes out after my vision stabilizes.

“Yes, Pen, I’m deadly serious. Don’t worry, I expect nothing from you. But I’m telling you now, I’m keeping it. I’m three months gone, didn’t even realize. Only found out while I was in hospital. Pregnancy tests are standard, apparently.

“The only one who knows is Ally. She was there when the doctor told me. Well, her and now you. Don’t ask me how this is gonna work, I don’t have a clue. My head is messed up, and I’m struggling to think straight. I just wanted to tell you first, before I tell anyone else. As I said, I have no expectations of you. I’ll have this baby, with or without you, and it’s up to you how much you want to be involved. Anyway, I’ll leave you to your thoughts.”

Tanya gets up and walks back to the Wild Pixies as though she didn’t just drop the atom bomb on my head.

Fuck. My. Life.

8 — TANYA

"Here are your papers, Miss Frost." Nurse Heather passes me a bunch of paperwork, which I promptly give to Ally, while Heather helps me into the wheelchair.

"I've got this," Ally says, chucks the papers in my lap, grabs hold of the chair, and whisks me down the corridor at lightning speed.

"Slow down, girl, I'll throw up otherwise," I groan.

Ally, heeding my warning, pushes the elevator button. As we exit downstairs, I spot Ellie with Amy.

"Finally! I thought we'd have to come and break you out." Ellie chuckles at me. "Your dad and some prospects have been and gone, dropped your boxes off and sorted what they could. He bought you a brand new flat-screen; he also set up your laptop. You literally have nothing to do but to walk in and get settled."

I grimace as I heave myself as carefully as possible out of the wheelchair. The pain in my stomach is excruciating. There are stitches left in the wound, which won't come out until the day after tomorrow. Ellie and Amy help me into the front seat and buckle me in, while Ally gets behind the wheel.

An hour later, after a stop off at our favorite fast-food chain, we roll into the parking lot at Debs' Haven. It takes Amy and Ellie to help me out of the car. Ally throws Amy the keys.

"Thanks, Amy, I appreciate it."

Amy just nods and pockets her keys. She's a quiet one and generally keeps herself to herself, but who can blame her?

"Right," Ally says as she opens the front door, steps through, and leads me down the corridor. "I thought it best if you were on level ground and don't have to worry about stairs."

She pushes open the door to my new abode. It's a huge, beautiful room, full of boxes, with a lovely new flat-screen, a comfy-looking couch, a small coffee table, and a king-size bed. It's very inviting and homely, and I can't stop the tears that well in my eyes. These women must have worked their butts off to get this room ready. I'm not used to being cared about like this.

"Now, stop with the waterworks already," Ellie states, hands on hips. "You'll set me off."

I sniffle once or twice, swallow hard, and wordlessly hug Ally so hard she coughs.

"Thank you, guys. I didn't expect any of this. Nobody has ever done anything that nice for me." I sob, surprised that I can't stop the tears from falling. I'm not normally a crybaby.

Ellie shoots me a strange look; Amy grins knowingly, and while no one is looking, Ally silently mouths *hormones*. Good to see she kept my secret.

"Guys, I'm sorry. I need to get into bed. Would you mind if I call it a day?"

Pain sears through my abdomen. I need to lie down and take one of those ridiculously weak pain killers they gave me at the hospital.

Ellie pulls back the comforter. Ally and Amy guide me to sit on the bed; they help me get undressed and comfortable. Then, Amy tucks me in.

"There now. I've put a baby monitor on your nightstand. If you need anything, just shout."

Amy's kind smile makes her look beautiful. I hardly recognize the woman in front of me. She looks healthier. Her long, light-blonde hair, now with a glossy shine, frames her face; her cheeks are rosy, if still a little drawn, but her inner beauty makes up for that ten times over.

I am safe, warmed by their care. With a relieved sigh, I close my eyes as tiredness overwhelms me.

◊◊◊

Having spent the last two days resting, I finally get my stitches out and am raring to go. I can't wait to get back on my bike.

I know, I know, I'm pregnant and all that, but luckily, no one is trying to wrap me in cotton wool. I am the captain of my ship, and I need this ride out. It will be my first chance to ride with the girls in my new position as enforcer and have the opportunity to finally feel like I'm part of the club.

I've spent time with Ally and Jules over the last couple of days, and they caught me up on all things Wild Pixies WMC club business. Let's just say, it was a steep learning curve, and I'm itching to get to work properly. I have a list three foot long of things to do. However, today, I intend to push it all to the side and focus on the ride. Oh, and the looming talk with Pennywise. Not looking forward to that, for sure. But it has to be done. This baby will not just connect us, but the two clubs as well, as I fully intend to bring my little girl up in the Wild Pixies.

Hopefully, it'll be a little girl anyhow. A little girl, who will grow up wearing leather, feeling safe and loved. I don't expect Pennywise to co-parent with me. In fact, I expect nothing at all of him. It's my choice to have this baby, so it's my job to parent her.

I'll do it on my own. If he wants to be involved, then fine, but if he doesn't, my little girl will not suffer for it. I've decided not to tell Dad who the father is, unless Pen wants to be involved in our princess' life. If he doesn't, I don't need the aggravation from Dad, which undoubtedly will come my way once he finds out.

Grabbing my bike gear and brand-new Wild Pixies cut, which Ally dropped off this morning, I gingerly walk outside, my wounds still smarting. Ally and the girls are waiting already.

I put my helmet on, swing my leg over my bike, hissing with discomfort as the action pulls on my not-quite-healed thigh wound, pick up the kickstand, and press the start button. My sweet ride rumbles into life. I pull up behind Ally and Jules, nodding at Ally's questioning look, and before I know it, she's given the signal to roll out and we're on our way to the Stormy Souls' clubhouse—our meeting point for the ride.

The run to Gunflint Trail, well planned by Clusseaud, is great. The stunning scenery allows me to relax into the ride, and I love the comfort of my riding position. I missed this—me, the bike, and nothing else.

Bit by bit, my brain drains of all the unwanted and unneeded extra stresses and concerns, leaving me in a much more peaceful and collected state of mind. My face nearly cracks with the smile, which unbeknownst to me, has crept across my cheeks. I feel like the Queen of my world. As it should be.

We pull into Artist's Point and park up, all in one line. It feels amazing to be part of something bigger than me. Truly part of it, not just on the periphery.

"Are you alright?" Jules asks, and I nearly drop my helmet. How did she sneak up on me like that? Note to self: must be more aware of my surroundings.

"Yes, Jules, I'm fine. A bit sore, but much better mentally than before we set off."

"I get that. It's the magic of the rumbling two-wheel vibrator between a lady's legs. Does it to me every time." She smirks at me with a wink.

"Have you told him yet?" Ally whispers in my ear.

Jeepers creepers! I squeal and jump at least three feet up in the air.

"Ally, are you trying to kill me off?" I ask, breathless and with my heart pounding like a machine gun in my chest. I have to lean over my bike for support, while Jules bends over laughing, slapping her thighs while she's at it, howling like a coyote in heat.

"Now now, don't pass out on me, girl, or else folks will think you're soft," Ally giggles in my ear.

“Holy shit!” It’ll take me a moment to calm my racing heart and get my breathing under control.

Jules, still chortling, moves to Caroline and Greta, chitchatting, leaving Ally and me standing to one side.

“Ally, don’t do that. Scaring me half to death. I’m in a delicate condition,” I joke.

“And it’s your condition I’m talking about here,” Ally says, all joking forgotten now. “Tell him, Tan. You must. Now is as good a time as any, since he’s sat on his own. Best not to put it off any longer.” Ally nods at me and walks over to the other girls.

I sigh.

She’s not just my Prez and friend, but also very right. I swallow hard. Let’s get this over with.

Mustering all the courage I have, I make my way over to Pennywise, who’s sitting on the grass verge, deep in his own thoughts.

“Hey, can I sit?”

He points at the verge beside him.

“It’s a free world, lady. You can sit wherever you like.” His nonchalance tells me that I’m not welcome.

“Don’t be an ass! We need to talk.”

“What about? Didn’t think we had any reason to? Do you need anything? How can I help?”

He sounds like a caveman, and it rubs me up the wrong way. I was gonna do this gently, but since he's being a dick, I'll rip the Band-Aid right off.

"I'm pregnant. And before you ask, it's yours. I'm not a club slut; I don't fuck around. So don't insult me. You can save your breath on that one."

"Come again?" Shock, disbelief, and a whole host of other emotions play out on his face with only two words spoken.

"I'm pregnant, you goddamn oaf! You knocked me up!"

"Haha, haha, good one…"

I'm not sure what exactly I expected, but laughter wasn't it.

"You.. are… joking… right?"

Looking him straight in the eye, all signs of laughter disappear from his face in an instant. He goes deathly pale and, for a second, I think he's gonna pass out on me.

"Holy shit, you are serious," he croaks at me, the gravity of the situation finally sinking in.

"Yes, Pen, I'm deadly serious. Don't worry, I expect nothing from you. But I'm telling you now, I'm keeping it. I'm three months gone, didn't even realize.

Only found out while I was in hospital. Pregnancy tests are standard, apparently.

"The only one who knows is Ally. She was there when the doctor told me. Well, her and now you. Don't ask me how this is gonna work, I don't have a clue. My head is messed up, and I'm struggling to think straight. I just wanted to tell you first, before I tell anyone else. As I said, I have no expectations of you. I'll have this baby, with or without you, and it's up to you how much you want to be involved. Anyway, I'll leave you to your thoughts."

With that, I get up and walk across to Ally and the girls.

9 — PENNYWISE

What the hell?

My mind reels, jumping from one emotion to the next. Realizing I'm rubbing my head incessantly, drawing looks from Slender, I kick myself and stop.

What the ever-loving fuck just happened? What does she mean, pregnant? She said she was on birth control and clean; I trusted her. No way can this be true.

Even if it is, I don't want another life dependent on me. I'm everything a parent shouldn't be. How is this even going to work? She says she doesn't want or expect anything from me, but she's a woman. Women say things like that and then hang you upside down by your balls. What. The. Fuck.

"Hey, man, you alright?" Slender has me jumping six feet in the air with fright. Sneaky bastard. He plonks himself down next to me, staring straight ahead at the jaw-dropping scenery.

"Watched your little exchange with Tanya, man. What's going on? You look like you've seen a ghost."

My chortle sounds bitter even to my own ears. "She's pregnant. Says I'm the father. What the hell?"

"Holy crap," Slender chokes out. "No doubt or anything?"

Weirdly, his comment rankles me.

"No, dumbass, no doubt. At all. If she says it's mine, it is." I shoot daggers from the side-eye I give him.

Slender holds his hands up, trying to calm me down. "Hey, I didn't mean it like that, Pen. Just meant, has she done a test?"

"Yeah, the hospital did one when they admitted her. It's true. She wouldn't lie."

"Jesus, what are you gonna do?"

"No clue, Slender. I've only just found out, and my ass is hanging so low, it's dragging on the ground. She says she expects nothing from me, that I can be as involved as much as I want or not at all. She'll do it on her own. Slender, I'm not father material. What the hell am I gonna do?"

"First, you gotta tell Raven. Shit could fly low. Especially once Masher finds out, and find out he will, eventually. Wouldn't like to be in your shoes there."

"He can fuck off as far as I'm concerned," I growl and mean it.

"Simmer down, asshole, I'm not the enemy here," Slender gripes back, sounding pissed.

Jeez, I'm behaving like an asshole.

"Sorry, man, just all a bit much at once." I try to sound contrite.

He nods at me in acceptance but continues, "No matter what, Pen, you must tell Raven. And it might help if you speak to Vegas too. He's in your situation. Okay, so they wanted a kid, and you don't. But he'll know how it feels to doubt being father material."

I look at Slender as though a second head is growing out of his armpit.

Despite nodding, everything inside me rebels against his suggestion. I certainly won't bring this up to anyone else right now. We're all stressed enough as it is. I'll keep it to myself for now and try to get my head around it. Everyone else can wait. I am numb from the shock of this revelation. It feels like I'm outside of myself.

I've never wanted kids. I understand what it's like to grow up in an MC, and certainly wouldn't wish it on anyone, less so a kid of my own. The constant danger, the rough play, flying bullets. Trying to protect my brothers is all I can do. I sure as hell can't protect another life as well.

"Come on, man, let's join the others." Slender nudges me with his shoulder.

Taking a deep breath, I explain, "Slender, I'm not gonna tell Raven now and spoil the ride out. There's time enough when we're back."

His expression toward me is unreadable, but after a few moments, he nods, and in sync, we push up off the ground and join the others.

The prospects have lit the barbeque, and my stomach growls from the delicious aroma wafting over at us. I square my shoulders and concentrate my attention on the brothers, joining Sparks and Zippy who are playing ball, and try to forget about the nuclear bombshell Tanya just dropped on me.

◊◊◊

Back home, we make our way into a late church meeting, beers in hand and still stuffed from the cookout at Artist's Point. The prospects outdid themselves. Greg and Caleb are doing well and are proving to be solid brother material.

"Settle down!" Raven bellows and bangs the gavel several times.

Slowly, the chatter ceases.

"Thank you, Clusseaud. That was a fantastic route. Well done," he says, nodding to our road captain. As usual, the ride out went without a hitch.

After the usual business updates, Ferret stands.

Oh, this can't be good.

"Right, boys, listen up. I've done some digging. First of all, Amy. She's a ghost. Her records only begin two years ago; there's no documentation before then, at all. Looks extremely fishy to me. I picked her trail up two years ago with customs and immigration, but nothing whatsoever before that. I tried multiple ways, even asked Ghost for help. Neither of us can find a trace of anything at all on her. Only that she came in on a British passport. That's it. The whole thing makes my brain itchy. Is she a snitch? Unlikely, given the circumstances we found her in. But can we rule it out for definite?" He doesn't even notice he's pulling his hair.

"Next, Chris spoke to me the other day. A young guy in his twenties approached him, asking for contact with the club. Told Chris he wants to prospect. I gave him permission to give out Slender's details. Would you mind checking him out if he gets in touch?"

Both Raven and Slender nod. They know by the antsy demeanor, hair pulling, and quick eye movements, that it's better not to interrupt Ferret. It's obvious he's struggling to keep it together. As if on cue, he takes a long drag from his beer bottle. Everyone's noticed his growing alcohol consumption recently. His PTSD is in full swing, and we have to watch helplessly while he struggles. We learned a long time ago that we can only help him if he asks for it. And right now, he isn't. Doesn't stop us worrying about our brother, though.

"Last but not least, I've put some feelers out with our nomads and other clubs. I didn't like what I heard. Raven, we need to have a serious meeting. It's become obvious they aren't passing on any knowledge they have, even if it's important and affecting us directly. I'll catch you after the meeting about this."

Raven nods at him, brows in deep furrows. A clear sign that he's not liking what he's hearing.

"Now then, the info I got by going round the houses is shocking. Be prepared to be floored, brothers." After a dramatic pause, Ferret continues, "The Restless Slayers are up to their eyeballs in with the Cabal Cartel, and it seems they are supporting Benito Lacasa's replacement. Dawg, will you tell them what you found out, please?"

"Okay, ya'll know I'm still driving for Digby Haulage. Good job too, since Jules is still in the office and feeds me info. Looks like Digby hasn't learned his lesson yet. Still got people in and out of his office who leave without signing contracts. I believe Jules is keeping a diary. But here's the kicker. I've seen Fury walking in and out of that office one too many times. What is he doing there? If not having his fingers in Digby's rotten pie?"

Dawg stares around the room. Speechless, we stare back at him in utter disbelief.

"Are you sure, Dawg?" Raven asks.

"Absolutely positive about him coming and going. Jules has to hide every time his bike runs into the yard, which is at least once a week. He can't make her. That would put not just us, but also the Wild Pixies at risk, and from what I heard from Jules, they have enough shit going on without having to contend with the Restless Slayers."

"Anything we need to worry about from that direction?" Raven cuts in.

"Don't think so, Prez, but it might pay to have a chat with Ally, find out what's going on. Jules was understandably cryptic," Dawg replies. "Overall, I think the greatest risk comes from the Slayers. I know quite a few of them, and I'm aware Fury's popularity is dropping through the floor. This could be the reason. Most of the guys are alright, with a few exceptions. Masher, Ghoul, and Ghost are one hundred percent anti flesh trade. They'd never agree to any of this."

Everyone looks shell-shocked.

Raven's eyes, hard as granite, scan the room, taking in our reactions, before he thunders, "Fuckin' bastard! I knew something stank but couldn't put my finger on it. I wonder whether his other chapters know. Shit, fuck, damn, I want to shoot that fucker."

Vegas' agitation is palpable. He rolls his shoulders and clenches his fists. Slender has his knife out, sharpening it in front of everyone.

"All the officers stay; everyone else, out!" Raven bellows.

Looks like my little problem is gonna have to wait, considering all this.

As everyone else leaves, Slender stomps to the bar and picks up the office cooler, already filled with beer. He adds a bottle of potent stuff and carries it back into church. Everyone gives him a wide berth. No one wants a confrontation with our pissed as hell SAA.

He closes the door behind him, plonks the cooler in the middle of the table, grabs the shot glasses out of it, and pours the whiskey.

He shoves a glass at each of us, raises his, and proclaims, "To the Stormy Souls, the only sane club in an area of five-hundred square miles!"

His toast rings true. Even I smirk, but then he says, "By the way, Pennywise has something to tell you all."

God, I could kill him right now. Jumping to my feet, I turn, and only Dawg grabbing my arm stops me from planting my fist in Slender's face.

"What the fuck, man? Settle down. If you need to blow off some steam, do it outside!" Dawg bellows at me.

It leaves me feeling incredibly insignificant. I'm sure my dick has shrunk inside of me, as have my balls.

What the fuck am I doing? I'm a fucking idiot.

I exhale slowly as I observe pissed off faces all around. Hell, might as well make it a full house.

"Tanya is pregnant. I knocked her up. It wasn't planned, and I've no clue what to do or how to react. She told me earlier, at Artist's Point. And before you say anything, I know how fucked up this is."

"Are you fucking shitting me?" Raven roars, his face beet red, bordering on purple. I'm sure steam is coming out of his ears as he jumps up, rounds on me, his fist raised, ready to attack.

With a loud crunch, my nose gives way and blood pours from my face. I don't even bring my hands up to protect myself; I simply let it happen. I deserve it.

10 — MOM

I've watched my son closely over the past few days. Hell, I've watched him closely ever since he entered the world with his determined wail. He'll always be my baby, but even I must admit, he's grown into a man. A valued brother and enforcer for the club, his daddy would be so proud of him if he could see him now. He's much like Derek. Strong, caring, protective, but he grew up way too fast.

The day his father died, he became a man. The man of the house. As much as I wish he hadn't, there was nothing I could do to stop it. Trying to give him guidance wasn't always easy, but he got there in the end.

Recently, though, I've noticed a stubbornness about him I dislike. I'm not sure what's caused it, but he's turning into a jackass of a human being, not recognizing or controlling his emotions. My time is largely spent in the kitchen and at the bar, giving me a perfect vantage point to observe the brothers discreetly. And I don't like who he's turning into.

Now, making sure everyone's settled with a drink, I watch in horror as the church door opens and my boy more tumbles than walks out, his nose streaming with blood and his face looking like someone used him as a punch bag.

I know Raven wouldn't allow this if something wasn't seriously wrong. I step out from behind the bar, waving at Tequila to take over from me, and make my way to my son, who's curled up on the floor in front of the church door.

"Come on, get up, let's sort you out. When we're done, you'll tell me what the hell is going on." I grab him by his cut, pull him up, and march him into the kitchen, where the first aid kit on the wall makes itself useful.

Certain his nose is broken, I clean his face, none too gently, ignoring his hisses.

"Now, tell me what the hell is going on with you? You've not been yourself for a while now. Don't try to talk your way out of this. Remember, I know when you're lying," I warn him.

I'm not quick to anger, but when I am, you better tread carefully, or I'll tear strips of you and flay you with them. Noah, aware of this, looks everywhere but at me.

"Get it over with already. You're not too old for me to put you in timeout or give you a red ass. I'm sure you'd not like either right now. But mark my words, if you don't tell me yourself, I'll badger Slender and Raven. You know they'll tell me. I'd rather hear it from you."

He knows he's out of options and visibly shrinks into himself in capitulation.

"Mom, really?" He sighs then stares at his boots. "I fucked up, Mom, badly. I got a girl pregnant. She wants nothing from me, but it could cause a major hassle. I don't know what to do. I'm so angry with the universe and everything. Can't even put my finger on why. Never in my life have I wanted a kid. Growing up in the club has shown me that this is no environment for a child. Death and hurt follow us around, so does other… drama. The last thing any kid deserves is being brought up here. Or should I say dragged up?"

Wow, he didn't just spout that shit, did he?

Not trusting myself, I take a step back from him, before I beat the shit out of him with the rolling pin laying on the kitchen counter within my reach.

"You what? Would you care to repeat that? I'd think long and hard about it, Son, if I was in your shoes, cause Momma's reaching the end of her tether with you!" I shout at him. "Are you trying to tell me, in all honesty, that I've dragged you up rather than brought you up? You ungrateful little shit! Your father and I did everything we could to make sure you had the best life possible. You always had everything you wanted, needed, and more.

"Your father was a good man who'd have given his last shirt for you. Yes, it's unfortunate that he died when and how he did, but neither he, nor I, deserve your ire and skewed view of the world. Don't you EVER talk to me like that again, you hear me? Or I'll break your nose myself!"

Panting, trying hard to keep my temper in check, I watch him pale. Deservedly so. The arrogant, self-centered little shit.

"And why, pray tell, would you knocking up a girl cause hassle for the club?"

Having watched him sneaking around the past few weeks, I have a reasonable idea of what's coming, but insist on him spitting it out, taking some responsibility for his actions at least. God, I'm so incensed, I'd like to grab a meat fork and stab it through my idiot son's hand.

"Jesus, Mom, calm down will you?"

Oh, he didn't just...

"Spit it out!" My hands shake as I struggle to calm my temper.

"Okay, okay, Mom. It's Tanya. I got Tanya pregnant."

"You stupid, stupid boy. I brought you up better than this. Do we need to have the bees and the birds talk again? Or how you should always wear a raincoat to protect yourself from fallout? What the hell, Noah?"

Tanya. I knew it! I mentally high-five myself for knowing my son better than he knows himself.

"Mom!" protests the silly boy. Can't see much of a man here in front of me, just a scared little boy.

With a sigh, I let him have it.

"You know what, Noah? I've been watching you two sneaking around for a while. So has Masher, by the way."

Noah's face couldn't possibly pale any more at that revelation. He has the look of white bed sheets right now.

"You weren't as discreet as you thought. I won't tell you what Masher said. It's up to you to man up and speak to him. But I can tell you how disappointed I am with you. Not for sneaking around with Tanya. She's a brilliant girl; I'd be proud to call her family. But for the self-absorbed way you carry on, with your head so far up your own ass it's not even funny anymore. You'll get no sympathy from me, Son. Just a well-deserved kick up your butt. Now, either pull your head out of your ass and do what's right, whatever that may be, or stay out of my sight if you don't want me to kick your ass any further."

Noah gets up, shoots me a look that screams *'mother you just don't understand,'* and trudges out of the kitchen like a scolded five-year-old. Well, I guess if he behaves like one, he'll get treated like one.

Grabbing my tobacco, papers, and filter-tips, I walk out onto the back porch, flump onto the decking boards, roll up, light my cigarette, and take a long drag, sucking blessed nicotine into my lungs. I wish I had a joint right now. The Devil knows I could do with one to calm myself down. But since I've not partaken for many years, the nicotine will have to do.

Instinctively, I grab my cell, open my messages, and start typing.

Me: Hey, it's me. How are you doing?

I watch and wait as three little dots appear almost instantly.

Mommasboy: Hey beautiful, I'm fine thanks, busy, but fine. Wish I was with you, though.

Me: Me too, just had a run in with my son, could do with one of your hugs right now.

Mommasboy: Do I need to come over and beat some sense into him?

Me: You can come over, but not to beat him. I've other plans for you. LOL.

Smiling, I shut my phone off and simply enjoy the tranquility of the back porch. I know I'll have backup if I need it; however, I can easily handle this myself. Still, it's comforting. After so many years on my own, to finally have someone being there for me is a novelty I hope won't ever wear off. I never thought I'd be interested in another man after Derek. Derek was the love of my life, my other half. His death devastated me beyond belief. If not for Noah and the club, I doubt I would have survived his loss. I threw myself into taking care of everyone else, to help me move forward and not shrivel up in hatred.

Derek never kept club business from me much. I knew how much he hated the direction the club was going then, and how much he hated Rusty.

I hated Rusty; it was him who started the shootout, and him who Derek protected, paying for it with his life.

But all that is by the by now. Derek would want me to find someone else. He loved me fiercely and only wanted happiness for me.

Happiness sometimes comes out of left field. It sure did for me this time. I've seen enough and experienced enough in my fifty-odd years to stay grounded, and taking things slow is just fine by me. It gives us a chance to get to know each other better and see where this is going. There's no rush. I don't mind keeping it on the down-low, prefer it that way, actually. It's what's best for both of us right now. We're both busy people, with hectic lives. Others depend on us, so sometimes it's difficult to make time for us. But that's okay. We're still new and feeling our way into this.

My cell vibrates in my back pocket. I open it up and read his message.

Mommasboy: Hm, sounds intriguing. How about you show me tonight? I've just finished up and could be with you within the hour.

As much as I want time with him, tonight is not the time. There's too much going on.

Me: Sorry, big man, tonight is no good. I have a few days off next week. How about we get away for a couple of days?

Mommasboy: You're on. I'll take a few days off. Send me the dates, beautiful, and we can escape the chaos together.

I smile as I send him the dates. The club can do without me for a few days. It's time to live for me and take some chances.

Who knows where it'll lead.

11 — TANYA

Sitting away from the Stormy Souls, the Wild Pixies hold court. It's our version of church. Since we're a national club, it's difficult to get all the members in one place regularly, so since Covid, we have resorted to online meetings and find this works very well. Or so I'm told, since I'm the newest fully patched member. Today, though, most of the officers are present, and we all have our phones out so the remaining members can join the meeting.

"Hi, everyone, thanks for dialing in to join us. Just a real quick meeting today. I wanted to introduce Tanya to you all. Since she's our new enforcer, it's vital for all of you to understand who she is."

Ally nods at me, and I wave at my cell screen, full of faces I haven't seen before. A little shocked, I realize how big the Wild Pixies really are. There are at least fifteen unfamiliar faces on my screen, and I don't even try to remember everyone's name. I'll ask Ally for a meeting later to get some information about everyone.

Huh, we even have an IT girl?

Surprised, I realize I've underestimated the Wild Pixies completely.

"Our little Psycho here…" my eyes nearly pop out of my head as Ally casually drops me a road name I hadn't expected "…is pregnant, so be gentle with her," Ally continues, while I mouth *Psycho? Really?* at her. A cacophony of "congratulations" breaks out, turning my face tomato red. I hate being embarrassed in front of others like that.

"Okay, our next church is mandatory for everyone. Sturgis is coming up soon, and I need everyone there. No ifs, no buts, no coconuts. Fail to turn up and you'll face a heavy fine. A thousand dollars for non-attendance, which will be payable to Debs' Haven. Right, Chicas, you know where I am. Get on with the rest of your day and have a great weekend." Ally closes the meeting, and my screen goes dark as everyone disappears.

"Psycho? Seriously?" I round on Ally, who just laughs at me.

"Rather fitting, don't you think? You are a bit of a psycho when push comes to shove. I've seen what you are capable of, and trust me, I won't piss you off in a hurry." She laughs at me.

Lost for words, I just grin and shrug my shoulders at her. My smile fades as quickly as it appeared, though. Ally watches me like a hawk.

"Stop it, Tanya. Psycho or not, you'll be a great mom. Your psycho side has no bearing on your ability or value as a parent. It doesn't make you more or less worthy as a person. It just makes you, you."

With that, she wraps me in a tight hug. My eyes burn with unshed tears. Within a couple of sentences, Ally summed up most of my self-doubt and fears.

"Deep breath, sister, you'll be okay. We'll look after you come hell or high water," Ally whispers, holding me a moment longer before letting me go.

◊◊◊

Sitting at my small coffee table, I nearly jump out of my skin as someone hammers on my door.

"Hold your horses," I shout, nearly fainting when I open the door and my dad stands in front of me, an evil grin plastered across his face.

"Hey, sweetheart, thought I'd drop in and see how you're doing?"

"Dad, you just fricking took ten years of my life." I slap his chest before throwing myself at him, clinging to him like a monkey as he steps in and closes the door.

"Everything alright, sweetie? Didn't expect that kind of reception."

He eyes me up and down as he sets me back on my feet.

"Yes, Father, I am fine." I try to stay serious, putting on my most proper choir girl speaking voice. Doesn't last longer than a few seconds though, before I bust a gut laughing.

"You look well, girlie." The bear of a man smiles at me, his love permeating deep in my bones.

"What are you doing here, Dad?" I ask

"Oh, just out and about, club business and all that, so I thought I'd drop by and see you, take you to dinner. How about it? We can catch up?"

"Sounds like a brilliant plan. Let me grab my jacket and we can go." I wink at him.

Throwing him the keys to my car, he shoots me a questioning look but says nothing. I'm gonna have to fess up. My leather trousers are getting too tight to button up, and I'm starting to show. At the moment, I can hide it with a long jumper, but that won't last long. It seems my tiny bump is growing every day.

So best get it out of the way.

We drive to a restaurant in Superior, walk in, get seated, and wait for the server to bring the menu. It's a relatively upmarket place. Dad draws frowns from most patrons. He cuts an imposing figure with his new buzz cut, leather clad frame, and tattooed neck and fingers. He has more, but they're not visible. We look through the menu and place our orders.

Dad sips his beer, whereas I have iced water.

"Dad, we need to talk." I open the conversation I've been dreading since I left the hospital.

"Okay, shoot, sweetheart, I'm all ears."

Nothing for it, but to be straight up.

"I'm pregnant, Dad, I found out in the hospital, and I've decided to keep the baby. The father may or may not be involved, and that is fine by me. I didn't plan this, but hell, few people do nowadays, not that it matters. I'm happy, and I hope you'll be too." Rushing everything out on one breath, I daren't look into his eyes.

After a beat of silence, my eyes fly up to his as he coughs and almost chokes on his beer.

"Dad, you okay?" I ask, leaning over and patting his back.

"Yup, I'm okay," he croaks out. "You just surprised me, sweetheart." His tone is as even as can be after his choke attack.

He clears his throat.

"I knew something was up, but also knew you'd tell me in your own time. If you're happy, sweetheart, then I'm happy. Just tell me this much. Is there someone

I have to kill for this? Do I need to get my shotgun out and chase someone?"

Laughter bubbles up from deep inside of me.

"No, Dad, nothing like that."

"Who's the father?" I expected that question and prepared for it.

"Not important, Dad. I had some fun, now I'm dealing with the consequences. It's likely I'll be doing this on my own, so…" I let my voice drift off but pull out the ultrasound scan I keep in my pocket and hold it out to him.

"Oh wow, I'm really gonna be a grandaddy," he breathes, holding the scan as though it's the most precious gift, his smile a mile wide.

Huh, I didn't expect that reaction. Shows, even after all these years, the old man can still surprise me.

"Are you alright, Dad? I thought you'd fly off the handle. Certainly didn't expect you going all mushy over my little princess."

"Princess? I think you mean biker," he replies. "Look at the way he's laid in there, arms out like he's riding a chopper."

I take the picture back and stare at it, trying to see what he does. Nope, I only see a mass of black and gray with some whitish streaks.

Turning my attention back to Dad, I study him a little closer. The strain around his eyes is obvious. He's smiling, but it doesn't quite reach his eyes. His knee is in constant motion. So much so, the table wobbles with it.

Our food arrives. We eat and talk for a while before I broach the subject.

"Dad, seriously, are you okay? You seem tense. Is it because of me?"

"No, sweetheart." He sighs. "Nothing like that. Just club business has been busy, and I've not had time to breathe yet. Don't worry about me. I'm doing great. Just need a break, is all. I'll be right as rain."

Sensing a lie, I decide not to press him further.

We pay the check and drive back in amicable silence. Dad opens the door for me and walks me to my front door, handing me the keys.

"Okay, sweetheart, I have a motel booked for the night. I'll ride back at the crack of dawn."

He steps up and hugs me tight, kissing my cheek.

"Bye, Dad. We must do this again soon. Thanks for the lovely meal and for not being angry with me."

"I could never be angry with you, sweetheart. Now, look after yourself and my grandbaby," he throws over his shoulder as he walks over to his bike.

I wave, turn, and unlock the door. As I enter my room, I hear his bike start then pull out of the parking lot.

Well, that went better than I expected.

Feeling a sense of relief, I sit back on the sofa and grab the pen and paper I dropped like a hot potato when Dad arrived. I look at my list.

Job
House
Pixies update
OB/GYN appointment
Meet with Ally

Most pressing are the first two. Much as I appreciate having a place at Debs' Haven, there are others who rightfully need it, and with a baby on the way, I need more space. I still get a healthy support payment from Dad every month, but I don't want to be beholden to anyone. I need my independence, and that means securing an income, paying my bills, and making sure my little one has a safe place to land.

Note to self: take leather trousers to the local alterations place and make them fit for pregnancy.

I am aware some people think that riding is dangerous, especially if you're pregnant, but I want to have the option. Riding is no more unsafe than driving a car, as far as I'm concerned. I wouldn't let anyone else wrap me in cotton wool, so I sure as hell won't do it myself.

12 — PENNYWISE

My healing nose does not detract from the glares I get from my brothers. Raven barely speaks to me; Vegas talks only when absolutely necessary. Slender keeps to himself more, and Dawg mostly ignores me. In short, I'm an outcast in my club, and I hate it.

Mom's tirade plays on repeat in my head.

Am I really that much of an asshole?

She hasn't mentioned the total fiasco again. In fact, she seems brighter lately, smiles more. I even caught her singing in the kitchen. She just seems… more balanced.

The other night, she even got her saxophone out and played in the clubhouse, jamming with Dawg on his guitar. It was outstanding. An oasis of peace in crazy times.

Maybe that's what I need to sort myself out. An oasis of peace. Time away, just by myself, to clear my head. Hmm, I'm not sure. Though, I know I've gotta do something before my ass swallows me whole instead of just having my head up it, as everybody's recent reactions have clearly shown.

I've thought of nothing else but Tanya and the baby. What do I do? Do I claim her and take responsibility? Would she even want to be claimed? Do I like her enough to make her my old lady? Can I deal with the responsibility of having a child? All I've got are unanswered questions. Instead of dealing with them, though, I push them aside. Denial is a beautiful thing.

My cell ringing diverts my attention. Ferret.

"Hey, shithead, come to my office."

What does he want now? To be honest, I'm tired of the name calling. Not taking much more of their shit.

I open the door to Ferret's room. He's sat at his laptop, as usual.

"Look at this," he says, pointing at the monitor.

"Oh my fucking God, is that the Restless Slayers' system?! My eyebrows hit my hairline, and my eyes pop out of my head as I take in what's on screen.

"Jesus! And we had them involved with busting up the human trafficking ring on our turf? Oh, fuck me sideways, that could have ended in an all-out shitstorm!"

"You see the same thing I do, then?" Ferret asks.

"Absolutely, man. Fury is knee deep in this shit. Fuck my life, this could turn into an all-out war with them, and they're our dominant club. Does Raven know?"

"Not yet," Ferret replies. "But he will do in a moment."

He picks up his cell and dials.

"Hey, boss, sorry to disturb you. You better come to my room; we've found something. Yes, ASAP would be best. Thanks, man."

I stride to the door, open it, and just as I look around the corner, Raven jogs up.

He steps in, and I close the door behind us.

"What's going on, Ferret?"

"Have a look yourself, Prez. See if you come to the same conclusion we did."

"Hell's bells, how did you get into their system? Never mind, forget I asked. Now, let's see. Are these accounts? Oh fuck, what? Please tell me I've got this all wrong. Those payment days coincide with us finding Debs and the other girls. I knew about the payment for Ellie and Tanya. That was agreed to draw the traffickers out. But the first one? Shit, shit, shit!"

Raven begins pacing the room.

"Those fucking bastards, why would they do that, knowing we're trying to stop this? Unless it's to get one over on us? They're our dominant club, for Christ's sake! Jesus, that puts us into a near impossible position!" Raven pins Ferret with a glare. "Who else knows?"

"Only you, Pen, and me so far," Ferret answers, lighting up a joint.

"Keep it that way. I'll send out a group message calling an emergency officers' meeting tonight. We can bring everyone up to date then and start making a plan on how to deal with this shit that just dropped right in our lap."

Raven turns and storms out, slamming the door behind him. Ferret jolts and pales. His PTSD is never far from the surface.

"Share, man," I tell him, holding my hand out for his joint.

He passes it to me, and I take a deep drag. Man, I need to calm down. A second and a third drag has me feeling better. I hand it back to Ferret.

Ferret serves me with a long, hard stare.

"Pen, I'm gonna give you some advice here and now. Whether you take it is completely up to you. Let me tell you, I understand completely how you feel about Tanya and the pregnancy. When I was your age, I found myself where you are. Stationed abroad, I lived the high life, had a lovely old lady, even married her. Then I went to Iraq and came back a different person. Drinking my life away, literally. All I saw was my bike, my club, and booze, so I pushed her away. And when I say booze, I'm talking a bottle of whiskey and about ten beers at least, every night.

"Even now, I hardly remember those years. My wife tried to be there for me, but I locked her out. Long story short, we divorced. But we had this connection. So, one thing came to another, and she ended up pregnant. We tried again, but just after my son was born, I ran for the hills. I couldn't deal with myself, never mind a baby. She never held it against me, even encouraged me to have contact with my son. I disappeared in the end, back to the States, and left the military."

He pauses, taking a deep drag from his joint, blowing out the acrid smoke.

"Now I have an almost thirty-year-old son, somewhere on this goddamn earth, who I don't even know and who doesn't know me. I was fine with it when I was twenty. Now, not so much. I'd give everything I have to turn back time and do things differently. It's impossible, though. Pen, be smart, don't make my mistakes, please. If you gotta make some, make your own. Don't repeat mine. Lecture over. Now get out."

Staring at Ferret as though he's lost his mind, I stand and shake my head at the unbelievable story he just told me. No one knows anything about his past. Other than he's ex-Marine Corps and presumably saw and lived through some serious shit.

Ferret? With a grown-up child and an ex-wife? Wow, the thought blows me away. It sure puts my problem into perspective.

◊◊◊

After a hectic couple of weeks, I've concluded that life is just messed up. The club is reeling from the news regarding the Restless Slayers. Tempers were frayed at the last church meeting, which ended with Sparks turning one of the tables over in frustration and fury.

I get it. Ally, Jules, Hazel, Tanya, and Caroline were all put at massive risk, and that's on us. We shouldn't be behaving like one percenters anymore. Fair enough, we're not choirboys, not by a long shot, but we run our businesses clean and try to protect what's ours and our community. What's come as the biggest shock to us is how much Fury seems to be so deeply involved, even when his daughter suffered a sexual assault and he meted out rightful justice, alongside us. Not that he wasn't right to do so, it just seems so contrived. He did it in style, too. None of us guessed what he was up to.

Next question is: Who else is in on it? One thing is for sure, we're gonna keep our distance and make contingency plans, so we won't get caught up when the shit eventually hits the fan. And it will hit. It's just a matter of time.

"Noah!" Mom's voice takes me by surprise; I didn't see her walking across the yard.

"Hey, Mom." I walk over to her and wrap her in a tight hug.

"What are you up to today? Have you spoken to Tanya yet?" she asks.

"No, not yet, Mom, I'm just about to finish up here. Then, I'm getting on my bike and riding over to Superior. Don't worry, I won't put it off any longer."

"Good boy," she says, patting my cheek, then leans in and kisses me before walking away.

With a sigh, I walk up to my cabin, peel off my clothes, and jump in the shower. Thinking about Tanya always has the same effect on me. My dick thinks it's his birthday, stands up and celebrates. He just can't help himself.

"Down boy."

"Yeah, as if you didn't fancy yourself some more of that."

Am I really having a conversation with my cock?

Darn it, I must be going mad, but okay, I'm game. Let's play.

"You can't have it your own way, big boy," I look down and tell him.

"You're a fool. I only want what you're already hot for. What can I say? It's a magic pussy. It hugs me so tight, so right."

"Yes, and look where your stubborn head has gotten us. A bun in the oven. Hello? Pen to Dick, pay attention, would you?"

"Don't care, dumbass, and if you were honest with yourself for one second, you'd admit that you have a connection beyond my baser needs. So, stop blaming me and enlighten yourself, asshole!"

What the hell? Now my dick is giving me crap. I need to lay off the booze and sure as anything, off the weed. It obviously sends me loopy. That's my excuse anyway, and I'm sticking to it.

Disturbed about my dick convo, I jump out of the shower, dry myself, and throw on some clothes. Well, I have to smell them first, haven't done my washing in a while. Mom would kick my ass.

God, this place is a pigsty.

Grabbing a hamper, I throw all the washing that's on the floor into it, walk out, lock my door, hamper in hand, and find Tequila.

"Hey, Pen, what can I do for you?" Her suggestive, teasing smile leaves her face as quickly as it appears when I hand her the hamper.

"Be a dear, Tequila," I say in my sweetest voice, "and do my washing." Her face falls at my request, so as an afterthought I add, "Please."

Her shoulders drop, resigned.

"Oh, and leave it in front of my door. No need to iron anything, just shove it through the drier," I throw over my shoulder as I walk out of the door.

Getting on my bike has the same calming, settling effect it always does. The rumble of the engine starting beneath me always makes me smile, washing away all my worries and invigorating me unlike anything else. Okay, like almost nothing else does. Tanya's eyes and tight body being the next best thing.

Huh? Where did that come from?

Note to self: Her pussy isn't golden, her pussy isn't golden, her… okay, so it is golden. Never mind the person said pussy belongs to. She's brave, strong, a little psycho, all wrapped up in a fabulous package.

Did I just use the word fabulous? I had no clue it was even in my vocabulary.

Man, I'm getting a sinking feeling that I'm well on my way to being fucked, and not in the way I like.

13 — MOM

Feeling refreshed after a few days away with my man, I suppress the giggle wanting to bubble up. I've not had a fun, dirty little secret for a long time. In fact, I can't even remember ever having one. The more stolen time I spend with him, the more I miss him when he's not around. We talk every day, send messages back and forth, but I miss his calming influence on me. His strength, understanding, the look in his eyes as though he wants to eat me alive. I've not had stirrings in my lady parts for many years. They stopped with Derek's death. So them now roaring back to life has caught me by surprise.

I thought long and hard about whether to give in to them, but hell, I'm only human. Also, I'm in my fifties and not getting any younger. I need to grab life by the balls and live it while I can. It's not a dress rehearsal after all. I'm falling for my man, hard and fast. Falling for the second time in my life, and I welcome it.

I'm so ready to embark on a new adventure. Just thinking of him, I sense the ghost of his touch burning a trail down my body, igniting my need all over again. Shaking my head, I try to clear my mind. Blast his talented fingers.

Walking across the yard, I eyeball Noah, lost in his own world.

"Noah!"

"Hey, Mom." He smothers me in a bear hug.

"What are you up to today? Have you spoken to Tanya yet?" I ask, although I don't expect an answer. Not a sensible one, anyway.

"No, not yet, Mom, I'm just about to finish up here. Then, I'm getting on my bike and riding over to Superior. Don't worry, I won't put it off any longer."

"Good boy." I try not to let my surprise and elation show, so I pat him on the cheek and let him get on his way.

It's about time he stepped up. I'd just about given up on him. I planned to call Tanya and invite her for breakfast at Ally's coffee shop, but that will have to wait now. Give Noah a chance before I speak to her. Probably easier to get a sensible answer that way.

The sound of my ringtone pulls me from my thoughts. Plucking my phone out of my bra, I check who's calling me. I can't identify the caller by the ringtone. It seems Noah got Ferret to play with my ringtones again. Now a rooster crows incessantly, and I can't switch the darn thing off. As I look at the caller ID, I see it's my guilty secret.

"Hey," I answer the phone. "Are you bored, or do you miss me already?"

"Missing you, boo. Why? Is that a problem?"

"Nah, not at all, but boo? Seriously? How old are we? Twelve?" I cackle.

"What's wrong with boo? You don't like it? Okay, how about pumpkin, cupcake, sweet cheeks… hang on, hang on, I've got another one… peanut, or how about babycakes?"

Howling with laughter, tears run down my face as I drop onto one of the picnic benches outside.

"You're killing me here, stud," I choke out, struggling to form audible words.

"Stud? Well, I'll take that." His self-assured tone just increases my laughter attack.

It's been a long time since I've belly laughed like that, or God forbid, giggled like a naughty schoolgirl. He makes me *feel*. I experience a sense of beauty with him. His eyes and lips show me his adoration. No words needed.

"Hey, I meant to tell you something, stud, but you made me completely forget what it was."

My scolding loses its fierceness with the giggles suffusing it.

"I'm sorry, ma'am," he replies, trying his best to sound contrite.

"Oh, stop it." I cough, trying to catch my breath and stop giggling.

"Okay, I'll behave. What's so important you actually forgot?"

This man.

"You are such a pain in my ass. Now shut up and don't make me regret I just said that."

He's the expert in twisting the meaning of my words into something dirty.

"I'm gonna be a grandma!" I shout in his ear.

Take that! I giggle again.

"Wow, Helen, that's awesome! I'm so happy for you. Tell me, what do you know?"

"Not a lot yet, only that my son got his girl pregnant. Unfortunately, he's been behaving like a dick about it. He's heading over there today to talk to her. I wish he'd get his head out of his ass. He'll make a great dad."

"Helen, give him time. I remember when it was me. Being confronted with a baby can be quite a shock. Don't get me wrong, as soon as she arrived, I fell in love with her and wouldn't change a thing. But when you're young and dumb, you sometimes can't see the wood for the trees. He'll come round, I'm sure."

"What have I done to deserve wise old you?" I ask him, my face cracking with a huge smile.

"It's that sexy saxophone of yours. I watched you play it and thought, hell, I need those lips on my—"

"Don't you dare say it!" I screech at him.

"Okay, okay, I won't. Hey, I gotta go now. Just thought I'd give you a quick call between jobs. Helen? Love ya, girl."

My heart stops for a second before it restarts, double beat.

"Aw, love you too, and I'll show you how much next time I see you," I whisper into the phone.

"Bye, love, see you soon," he says, and the line goes dead.

Wow, I never thought he'd say it first. Those three words that mean so much.

I walk into the clubhouse as if floating on clouds. Looking around with a sigh, I pick up some dirty glasses, wash them, and then head into the kitchen to start the evening meal.

Tequila catches me as I open the refrigerator door.

"Your son treats me like his maid," she whines.

"You know exactly why you are here, Tequila. You are here to help and service the brothers who want to be. Doing washing, cleaning and tidying is part of your job. That's why you have free room and board. Now stop whining and start peeling potatoes for mash."

Sometimes the girls need putting in their place. They forget their station. Over the years, I've seen many come and go. They think they'll make it to old lady, but who wants a woman who spreads as easy as soft butter? Not the brothers, that's for certain. They'd bathe in bleach before they'd go down that route.

While a grumbling Tequila peels potatoes, I get everything together to make my special fried chicken and homemade biscuits and gravy. Working quietly, my thoughts wander off, thinking about my sneaky hotel break. We only spent three days together, but Chicago left a lasting impression on me.

The SkyDeck and Millenium Park were amazing. I guess the company colored my perception of Chicago. The Waldorf Astoria has to be the poshest hotel I've ever stayed in. I felt every inch the small-town girl in a big city.

I also saw a side of my man I didn't expect. Romantic dinner, jazz club, signing me up to a jam session all surprised the hell out of me. The whole three days centered on what I wanted. He insisted. We didn't do a single male activity. When he booked me into the hotel spa and treated me to a massage and facial, he completely bowled me over. He treated me like a princess. Like a precious treasure. I felt loved, cared for, and safe for the whole three days. He literally wrapped me in cotton wool. My every need attended to.

And not just seeing the sights. In the bedroom, he made me feel prized, sexy, all woman, and revered. He devoured me time and time again. Just remembering his muscular body, veins standing out like ropes on his arms, his tight ass, cut thighs and abdomen still have me swooning.

The salt and pepper of his beard and hair suit him. He turns me on just sitting with his arm over the back of the sofa, watching me intently.

I want to jump his bones every time I see him. But it's all still newish, still fresh. We're taking it slow, seeing where it goes.

Who am I kidding? I'm a goner for him, and I don't feel an ounce of guilt. Derek would have wanted me to be happy, to live my life to the fullest. For many years, I tried to deal with my grief and bring Noah up to be a decent man. That's what I concentrated all my energy on. Now it's time for me. I don't want to spend the last thirty years on my own, wondering why life passed me by.

I've been given another chance at happiness, and I intend to grab it with both hands.

14 — TANYA

"Hey, thanks for that, Ally. I'll give Zippy a call just as soon as I come off the phone with you.

"Yes, Ally, I'll be at church on Sunday. In the meantime, Keep me up to date. We can't take shit like that lying down. And I know I'm pregnant. Doesn't mean I can't do my job.

"Okay, see you then. Bye Ally, and thanks again." I blow out the breath I don't realize I'm holding. This is the first lead of a job I've come across, and honestly? I need one ASAP. I hate to depend on Dad. As much as he doesn't mind, I have to take responsibility for how I make a living. A baby isn't exactly cheap. I stroke my palm over the tiny bump.

"Hey, Peanut, how are you doing in there? It's Mommy. Your father is an ass. I'm sorry. We'll be okay, though, just you and me, Peanut. Your grandad will love you, and you'll have lots of aunties and uncles who'll always take care of you. Now, concentrate on growing into a strong girl. I can't wait to meet you."

For the first time in weeks, a happy smile creeps across my face. I'm physically well; the pain I've experienced over the last few weeks is finally absent. I even started gentle exercises. My leathers are back from the alteration's lady, and I can now do the button up. I know it sounds silly, but to me it's a tiny victory in the battle to keep or rather, bring my life together. Being in control is important to me, when I've had so little growing up.

Tough men dominated every aspect of my life and ruled my world. I learned early on to stand up for myself. Giving up that control I worked so hard for is not on the agenda. Ever.

I grab my cell and call Zippy.

"Zippy's," a deep voice growls at me. Wouldn't want to cross that one in a dark alley, for sure.

"Hi, it's Tanya, Ally said to call you. She thinks you might need an assistant for bookings and front desk."

"I do. You got any experience?"

"No, but I'm a quick study. And I'm available to start immediately."

"Okay, that sounds good. No going psycho on the customers, though. I find you alienating them. I'll kick you to the curb sooner than you can say dick."

Man, Zippy is a growler. This is gonna be fun. *Not.*

"Come see me tomorrow morning. I open at eight, so be there at seven, so I can walk you through what needs doing. I'll let Ferret know to do your background and add you to the payroll. Until your background comes back, you are on probation. We clear?"

"Crystal. See you tomorrow at seven," I reply before hanging up, a shudder running down my back.

What the hell have I let myself in for?

A thumping on my door almost makes me jump out of my skin.

As I open it, I nearly pass out. *What the hell?* The last person I expect to see is Pennywise.

"Hey. We need to talk."

What an opening line. Laughable, but he's right, talk we must.

"You gonna be civil for a change?" I snipe at him.

"I will if you will," he answers calmly, staring at my obvious bump.

With my free hand protectively covering my little Peanut, I open the door and let him in. He takes one look around, making me feel judged as hell.

"Look, if you don't like it, we can go for coffee," I grouse at him.

"Sorry, didn't mean to come across like that. Here is fine. At least we can talk privately."

Pennywise surprises me as he walks towards the couch and folds his lanky frame onto it, making the room appear tiny.

"Look, I'm not trying to be an asshole or anything," he says, looking anywhere but into my eyes, "but this place is too small for you and the baby. Never mind all three of us."

"All three of us? Are you on crack, Pennywise? You've been clear from the start about how you don't want a child. What's changed? Do you really think you can waltz in here and decree we'll live together and bring up Peanut together, like a responsible couple? Are you messing with me?"

Disbelief is only one of the emotions streaming like lava through my veins. Anger is another. Right now, I want to hit him around the head with a cast iron frying pan!

He sighs.

"Sorry, Tanya, let me try this again. I'm no good at this kinda thing. Talking and making sense is not my strong suit."

He finally looks me in the eye, letting me see he means his apology.

"Apology accepted," I answer before sitting down on a chair, settling in to listen.

"Tanya, I don't know how to even start. I'm sorry for the way I behaved. I was stunned. An asshole, but a stunned asshole. It took me a little while to get my head around it. I realize you didn't plan this, and I know you don't wanna trap me. I realize that's the furthest thing from your mind."

He takes a deep breath as I nod in agreement.

"I still believe I'm not ready for a child, but I want to take responsibility. It is my son or daughter you are carrying and growing inside you. I want to be the best father to him I can be, but I'll probably fuck up a few times along the way."

He stares at his feet, avoiding my eyes again. I'm confused and don't understand what he's getting at.

"What do you mean, Pen? You'll have to explain. I don't get it."

"For starters, I want to claim you at the table."
All breath leaves me, and it seems I've entered an alternate universe.

"You wanna do what?" I need to make sure I heard that right. Maybe there's something wrong with my ear-to-brain connection. "Did you just say you want to claim me? Are you out of your ever-loving mind?"

"Hear me out," he says. "I want my son to be born having my last name. I want to give him and you the best life I can. Your father will go nuts at both of us. I want to claim you because of what I just said and to avoid more trouble between the clubs. I'm trying to be practical and do the right thing for you and my son."

"Your son? Don't you mean daughter? No way will I breed another version of you. I'd have to be an enforcer more than I could be mom, no way, Jose. It's a girl," I argue.

Despite the crazy he's spouting, I admit he has a point. My dad will go apeshit and the situation between the clubs is strained enough as it is. I don't need to add fuel to the fire.

"If you think I'll ever wear your cut, you have another think coming!" I snark at him.

He holds his hands up in defeat.

"I know, Tanya, I don't expect you to." He sighs.

"Okay," I tell him, determined to wrestle control back into my own hands. "This is how this is gonna go. First, you prove to me you really want to be involved. That starts with attending medical appointments and ultrasounds. Get to know our little Peanut. Second, we are gonna get a house together ASAP. Peanut needs somewhere to live and grow up safely.

"Once we know where we'll live, you can claim me at the table. Don't get me wrong, this is gonna be an equal partnership or nothing."

I watch as he pales a little, but nods.

"Pennywise, don't even think that ours is going to be a normal relationship. It's not. You hurt me badly. So any thoughts of sex is off the table. At least for now. Trust is a fragile thing, and you need to build that. I'm not saying never, just not now. Also, while we are together, we will both be faithful to each other. I ever find out you've strayed, that's it. No second chances."

Pen cuts in, "Tanya, I wouldn't do that to you, ever. Let me show you how serious I am. Will you agree to live at the compound? I have enough money saved up to build us the house of your dreams. All you have to do is agree the plans." He holds a business card out to me, one for a contractor. The same one who built Ashley and Raven's house, and those are spectacular.

"Okay. You build the house, I'll furnish it. I won't be a kept woman, Pen, I will contribute equally," I tell him.

For the first time since he arrived, a small smile plays around his lips.

"Truce?" he asks me.

"Truce," I reply, feeling like a ton of weight is lifting off my shoulders.

"May I?" He points at my bump.

"Sure, Peanut is yours to love too." I grin at him as we both stand.

He lifts my top and caresses his palm over my bump. The hairs at the back of my neck stand and liquid heat shoots between my thighs. I bite my lip to keep the groan in.

"Hello, Peanut, it's your daddy here. Sorry it took me so long. I promise to love you always, teach you how to ride a bike, buy you your first cut, and take care of you and Mommy. Can't wait to meet you." At his mile-wide smile, warmth creeps into the darkest corners of my soul, warming me.

Maybe everything is gonna be alright.

My dad took the news well. The question is, will he take the news of the father just as calmly? Pennywise guessed at his reaction. Little does he know that Masher, the SAA beast, went all mushy over his little 'biker.'

Sorry, princess, I mean. I'll keep that to myself for now. For starters, I don't want to worry Dad any more than necessary, and plus, it'll be fun to watch Pennywise squirm at the prospect of telling my dad. Yes, I admit, I have an evil streak.

They don't call me Psycho for nothing.

15 — PENNYWISE

I expected Tanya to come in hard. So, I prepared myself to be shot down in flames. Admittedly, I deserve it, and I'm grateful she lets me off easy, What I didn't expect, though, was the jolt of lightning shooting up my arm when cradling her bump. Nor the words leaving my mouth, nor that I mean every single one of them. I've heard of parental insta-love, but it hits me right in the feels, unprepared for the overwhelming urge to protect Tanya and my little Peanut from anything and everything the world will throw at them.

Her eyes going all soft, watching me interacting with Peanut, gives me hope that maybe we'll be able to do this after all.

I agree with everything she says. Not for the sake of it, but because it's fair. The no-sex rule will kill me. I love her riding me like she's in a rodeo, but she's right. If we want to make this a lasting relationship, we need to start at the beginning and work for it. Both of us.

I don't want to leave her and Peanut, but I must get back for a meeting with Slender, Raven, and Ferret. To not draw Tanya into my arms and kiss her senseless is the hardest thing ever. Memories of her lips on mine plague me every night. I just can't seem to shake her. So instead, I hold onto hope that committing to her will ease my sleepless nights.

◊◊◊

"Let's get this over with." Raven's oddly robotic voice cuts through the general conversation. I've never heard him like this before. We stare at him as though he's grown a second head.

"Fury is up to his neck in the sex trafficking. Digby Haulage is their main, but not only way of moving their freight. The Restless Slayers are in uproar and at each other's throats.

"Jules and Dawg are at risk because Fury knows them, and so does Digby now, thanks to Fury." Raven takes a breath after rattling off this substantial list of facts.

Through it all, the room remains in absolute silence.

The door flies open with such force it bangs into the wall as Dawg enters, snarling like a rabid dog.

"That fucker! He made me watch while he escorted Jules off the premises with a gun to her head and gave me a message. '*Stormy Souls are not welcome and will be shot on sight*,'" he rants. "I knew something was dodgy. I knew it! Fury is a dead man. I don't care whether he's the King of England. I'll end him!"

"Sit the fuck down and shut up," Raven grates out, "before I make you!"

He shoves Dawg's notebook and pen towards him, as Dawg folds himself onto his chair, still foaming at the mouth.

Ferret raises his hand, and Raven nods at him.

"I've been pulling information from several sources. I've got an old army pal at the Bureau, and he did some digging. They have extensive knowledge of Rigby and the Restless Slayers. They've been on their radar for quite some time. Us getting involved, scuppering their efforts, put us on *their* radar as well."

"Fuck!" "What the ever-loving shit?" "Oh hell, no!" are some of the shouts going around the room.

"Quiet!" Raven bellows before chaos takes over completely.

Ferret slams his palms on the table to gain our attention.

"Calm down. Ray, my contact, has promised to keep us out of it, as long as we assist the Bureau. This is way too big for us. Best thing we can do is cooperate. You never know when one needs brownie points. We are legit, but since we've drawn the Bureau's attention now, we have little choice in the matter."

Slender runs his hands through his hair until he looks like a mad professor.

"Jesus, we don't need this shit. We have enough going on as it is. How do we separate from the Restless Slayers? Surely, that's got to be the first step?" He looks around the room, drawing all of our attention.

Raven, Vegas, Slender, Ferret, Dawg, and I look at each other. This is gonna cause a shit ton of problems. We cannot afford for this to escalate into an all-out war between the clubs.

"If that ain't enough"—Raven sighs—"I've just had an interesting call with Masher."

We all sit forward, waiting for the other shoe to drop.

"He's told me he wants out of the Slayers, doesn't agree with what they are doing, doesn't agree with Fury, neither do a lot of their officers. Fury rules with an iron fist, so their hands are tied behind their back. Too many vote with Fury, come hell or high water. He mentioned Ghoul and Ghost as the other ones who want out. They have to tread carefully. It seems Fury suspects something. Masher will keep me abreast of what's going on there. At least we'll have inside information. Could be useful if we're working with the Feds."

All eyes are trained on Raven; the silence is deafening.

Dawg clears his throat.

"We need to bring this to church, have a full meeting, and vote on the Feds and separating from the Slayers. Honesty is the only way forward, without dropping us deeper into the shit."

Around the table, heads nod in agreement.

"Ferret, get in touch with your man, see what's needed. Slender, no one rides out alone, we have to step security up. All women belonging to the club will have a shadow from now on. Slender, set up extra training in the gym and on the range. Put all the women through their conceal and carry permits, if they haven't already got them. Not that they'll need it, but until this is solved, we need to prepare for anything." Raven closes the meeting, stands, nods around, and walks out, back slightly bowed from the pressure he's under.

Holy shit, I expected something, but not this. It seriously throws the cat amongst the canaries.

"You alright?" Ferret asks. "Nose all healed?"

I want to wipe that smirk off his face with my fist, but I deserved Raven's punch, so I let it slide.

"Yes, I'm fine. Cleared the air with Tanya, too. We're gonna try to make a go of it."

"What took you so long?" Slender's eye roll makes me chortle, and Dawg whistles the wedding march.

"Fuckers," I grumble. "I'll claim her at the table in the next full meeting. Or at least, that's the plan. Looks like I may have to juggle some raw eggs, given the current situation."

"Well, at least our sons can grow up together," Vegas throws in the room. "Congratulations, by the way, and be prepared for tears, hormonal Bedlam, late night excursions to soothe cravings, and lots of sex." Vegas smirks and I groan, thinking about our no-sex-rule.

"I'll be glad when it's over," Vegas adds. "Only another couple of weeks to go."

He winks at me as if I know what he's talking about.

Don't get me wrong, I love seeing my brother happy, but despite everything, I struggle to identify with his bliss.

◊◊◊

The next fortnight passes in organized chaos. Everyone is aware of our link to the Feds, and at least our meeting agreed that our involvement is necessary to keep the ship steering straight.

The brothers have a mixed reception for my claiming Tanya, given the current circumstances, but I got the go-ahead.

Tanya has completed the plans for our house on the compound with Paul, Slender's friend of old. I left this entirely to her. It's not that I don't care, but I've been so busy with the extra training, security, and running of the businesses, I've been unable to find any more time in my day, since even mine has only twenty-four hours.

With the foundations done, the build makes good progress. Paul reckons we can move in within the next two months. I can't wait for the day Tanya, Peanut, and I are finally in the same location. It will make life so much easier, especially since Tanya now works for Zippy and his new apprentice, manning the reception.

Neither Tanya nor I have told Masher about us. Keeping Masher's asking for a patch over from Tanya is hard. It feels like keeping secrets, which I guess I am. But with Tanya being the enforcer for the Pixies, I guess our ranks are gonna clash sometimes. How Dawg and Sparks manage the situation, I do not know, but I'm not going to open a 'Stormy Souls Old Lady Officers Anonymous' either.

Chips aren't my thing.

All I do know is that every day, Tanya and I grow closer, and being away from my pregnant old lady is much harder than I thought. I love our little Peanut; would lay my life down for either of them. I've never known a love so all-encompassing. It rushes through my veins as soon as I lay eyes on Tanya and her growing bump. Just can't keep my hands off it. She laughs at me when I lay my head in her lap and talk to my little Peanut, reading stories or singing lullabies—the same ones I remember Mom singing to me when I was little. But the process has brought us closer. There is a connection, a warmth spreading between us.

Tender, gentle care. Unexpected, but welcomed by both of us. The way we interact is changing, too. With the hindsight of a fortnight, I agree that no sex is the best thing for us at the moment. But, man, it's getting tougher every day.

16 — TANYA

The stress of the last few weeks has been unreal. I feel like I've been chewed up and spat out. I try to eat healthy and sleep, but hell, I struggle on all fronts, to the point of doubting my decision to join the Pixies. The levels of tension and strain are insane. My first church meeting was a rude awakening. Not that I didn't expect to be busy, but not like this.

Things between me and Pen improve every day. We're as open with each other as we can be, giving our positions and sometimes split loyalties to both clubs. It's difficult not to bounce some things we're dealing with off Pen, since they involve both clubs.

Some of the big one percenter MCs really don't like another MC consisting of women. Misogynistic attitudes and actions are rife, and their ripples in the MC pond far-reaching.

With a sigh, I roll out of bed. Nothing for it but to face the day head on. Another meeting with Paul, to complete the second fix, then a trip into town to order furniture. My dad has not been in touch for a while, which worries me. Especially since he called me a week ago, asking if we could meet and talk. He never just drops off the face of the earth.

After a shower and breakfast, I grab my helmet, swing my leg over my baby, and head into town. The meeting with Paul only takes a few minutes, and Ally is ready and waiting for me at the furniture store.

"Girl, you shouldn't be riding!" Ally admonishes me.

I ignore her concern for me, knowing it comes from the best of places, but if I don't ride, I'll go quietly insane. And no one wants that.

We traipse through the store, and with Ally's help, I pick out a fitted kitchen with all stainless-steel appliances, reduced to half price, a large sectional, dining room table and chairs, as well as rugs, cushions, and other bits and pieces. Bedroom furniture, we already have between us, and Peanut's room can wait for a while longer.

"Ally, stop," I protest. "I'm exhausted."

"You look like shit, girl," Ally replies. "Let's go sit, grab some food, and chill for an hour," she suggests, and I'm happy to oblige her.

Crossing the street to the diner, my legs suddenly buckle, and I'm overcome by darkness.

◊◊◊

The bleeping of machines slowly filters through my consciousness.

What the hell happened?

I open my eyes and try to sit up, only to be pushed back onto the hard trolley underneath me by Pen and Ally.

"What's going on? Where am I? What happened?"

"You passed out in the middle of the road; gave me the fright of a lifetime," Pennywise tells me, his hand on my chest to stop me from sitting up.

Completely shocked, I stare at him, his face a mirror of his worry.

"Peanut," I whisper.

"Peanut is okay; you are okay, but you need to take it easier." Chloe steps out from behind Ally and Pen. "No more riding, either. Your cervix has softened and opened a little. They'll take you into the operating theater in a short while to put stitches in; they should prevent you from going into early labor," she explains to me, her scolding eyes never leaving mine.

"I'm releasing you off your duties until the baby is born," Ally announces, with both Chloe and Pen nodding in agreement.

The door opens, and the doctor and a nurse walk in.

“Are you ready?” Their question needing no answer as they grab hold of the trolley and push me out of the room.

When the procedure is over, all I want to do is go home. Chloe decrees she’s staying with me; so does Pen. It’ll be a tad cramped in my room, but hell, anything to get out of here.

They roll me out to Chloe’s SUV in a stupid wheelchair. I could have walked, but the hospital insisted. Pen and Chloe help me into the backseat, Pen gets in next to me, and Chloe gets in the driver’s seat.

“Caleb and Greg are picking up the bike,” Pen tells me, and I know better than to argue.

Trying to get comfortable in the backseat, I snuggle into Pennywise, who wraps his arm around me. I feel safe in his arms, as though nothing can touch me. I guess trust is developing between us; well, at least with me. The way he looks at me right now makes my heart melt. Full of worry, pride, love… yes, love shines clearly out of his eyes, like a beacon.

The more time we spend together, the deeper we connect.

I take a moment to realize that Chloe’s turned left towards the Stormy Souls’ compound, rather than right towards my room in Superior. Again, I don't argue. At least Pen's two-room cabin makes things easier.

Chloe stops the car outside Pen's, opens the back door for me and, together with Pen, supports me into the cabin. I make myself comfortable on the couch, kick off my boots, and breathe a sigh of relief. This pregnancy is kicking my ass. It makes me more tired than I've ever been, and all I want to do all day is sleep. It makes up for the lack of morning sickness.

My boobs are tight and ache; I can't drink coffee unless it's decaf, no alcohol, and now, no more riding, either.

Peanut, you better be worth it, girl. I won't be doing this again.

Not to mention the thought of labor and giving birth. Pushing the equivalent of an American football out of my hoo-ha is not something I'm looking forward to. And it's all Pen's fault.

"You!" I round on him. "It's all your fault! I'm uncomfortable and getting fat. Soon I'll be waddling like Ashley. I can't drink, can't ride, and if you think your dipstick is coming anywhere near me again, ever, you've got another think coming."

Pen's head shoots round, eyes wide, mouth hanging open.

"Come again?"

"You heard," I snipe at him.

He rolls his eyes and looks up to the heavens.

"He's not gonna help you. He's on my side," I grumble.

Pennywise just huffs, turns on his heal, and wordlessly storms out of the cabin, slamming the door behind him. Chloe winces at the loud bang.

"You know you are being a prize bitch, right?"

"I know." Tears fill my eyes, and my brain has a hard time catching up with my emotions as I sit on the couch, blubbering like an idiot.

What the hell is going on with me?

Have aliens taken over my body? Or worse, my brain?

"Hey, shh," Chloe attempts to comfort me. "It's your hormones. They send you haywire. It will pass."

Her soothing hand stroking my hair calms me a little.

"When?" I hiccup.

Chloe shrugs. "After the baby is born."

She laughs straight at my horrified face.

I'm gonna be a nutcase for the next six months? Shoot me now.

"Go to bed and rest." Chloe draws me up off the couch and shoves me towards the bedroom. I huff but follow her orders. I'm too tired to argue. My eyes close as soon as my head hits the pillow.

◊◊◊

Refreshed, I wander down to the clubhouse, the sleep having vastly improved my mood. I can't wait to be in our own house. Not that I mind being in Pen's cabin, but there's a constant in and out of club officers. Privacy is nonexistent, which makes me grouchy. Especially since, thanks to my hormones, I'm constantly horny. It sounds funny but it's more of a curse than a blessing.

Jesus, the caterwauling coming from the clubhouse hits me before I even open the door. Screaming and cussing. It sounds like someone is being taken to slaughter! I rip open the door and run through as though my hair is on fire. The image in front of me stops me dead in my tracks.

Ashley, on top of the pool table, legs akimbo; Vegas pacing, pulling his hair, looking like a mad professor ready to pass out. Mom by Ashley's side; the office door wide open, revealing Raven shouting on the phone. Chloe strolling out of the kitchen with Tequila in tow.

What the fuck?

Chloe takes charge immediately.

"Everyone out!" she hollers. "Vegas, where are you going? Not you! Hop on the table, help Ashley sit up and sit behind her, supporting her back. This baby is coming, ready or not!"

"I want an epidural," Ashley yowls.

"Too late, missy. You'll never make it to the hospital in time. I can see the baby's head crowning." Chloe suppresses a snicker.

"You bastard, your dick is never gonna get near me again! I'll chop it off first!" Ashley yells at Vegas, who flinches, but wisely says nothing.

I sneak next to Mom.

"What happened?" I whisper.

"Ashley had breakfast with a side of contractions. She wouldn't listen, though, saying they were Braxton Hicks. Until her waters broke when she stood. By that time, her contractions were about two minutes apart, and when Chloe checked, she was fully dilated. She's having this baby now, whether or not she wants to." Mom grins. "Serves her right, too. If she'd listened to me, she'd be in the hospital now, with a nice epidural."

Unnoticed by us, Pennywise has walked into the bar, and is now staring at the pool table from behind us.

"Take your eyes off my old lady before I rip them out of your head!" Vegas growls at him.

Pennywise turns green, then white, before he crumples to the ground.

Oh, holy mother of God, is that what awaits me?

Dawg, Dougal, and Caleb appear next to him, pick him up, and carry him off into the office.

As they pass me, I just catch Dawg saying, "The pool is open. Fifty bucks he'll pass out when it's his turn!" followed by laughter and nods all round.

Men, they can be such children sometimes.

17 — PENNYWISE

Well, I'll not live this one down in a hurry. My still fuzzy head is trying to make sense of what just happened. Walking into the clubhouse is something I do every day. I've come across so many weird sights in there that nothing surprises or shakes me anymore. Or so I thought.

The sight of Ashley on the pool table, Vegas behind her, Chloe, Mom, and Tanya hovering, and the unobstructed view of a sight I never in a million years wanted to see, threw me for a loop. No, it not only threw me, but my blood drained to my feet, and within a second flat, I passed out.

"Hello, young lady, are you back with us?" Dawg wisecracks, curtseying.

"Be you next." Dougal laughs at me.

"Man, you best not do that with Tanya. She'll cut off your balls," Caleb teases.

"Prospect, don't get lippy, or I'll cut yours off and you can carry them in your purse!" I gripe at him.

Raven is pacing the room.

"Shut up, you morons, that's my sister out there, and I can't stand much more of her wailing before I go out there and stab Vegas in the balls for putting this on her!"

Striker gets up and closes the office door.

"Better?" He smirks.

That's when it hits me. Six more months and it will be us. Not on the pool table, mind. I'll make damn sure my old lady is in hospital and has access to all the epidurals in the world. Not only that, but no way in hell would I want to watch her bringing our child into the world. Not at the foot end of the bed, anyway. There are some things a man just doesn't need to see.

Even through the closed door, we can hear Chloe's command.

"Push, take a deep breath, chin on your chest and push down, the head is right there! Right, that's it. One… Two… Three… Four, that's it! Keep going!" Chloe shouts at Ashley. "Okay, take some deep breaths. You're doing great, Ash. On the next one, you push again hard. That's it! One… Two… Three… Keep going…"

Ashley's screams can be heard out on the road, I'm sure.

"Yes! The head is out, Ash. One more big push and it's done!"

In the distance, the wailing sirens of an approaching ambulance brings some comfort to our stretched nerves.

"Go on, Ash, one more! Yes, like that…!"

A wail breaks through the silence in the office. A thin newborn cry makes its presence known, literally screaming the clubhouse down.

We rip the office door open and race into the bar, just as Mom hands a towel-wrapped bundle to Ashley.

"Congratulations, you've given birth to a strapping little boy! Well done, Ashley, he's huge. Must be at least ten pounds!" Chloe declares, smiling from ear to ear.

"Everyone, meet my son, the next generation of the Stormy Souls MC!" Vegas smiles, his voice vibrating with pride as he cradles Ashley and his son. No one begrudges him his joy, the tears running down his face.

Ashley turns her head and smiles at him, teary-eyed, waiting for Vegas to nod at her.

"Meet Alex Carl Vincent Albright."

Even I have to wipe my moist eyes. They named him after Carl, aka Flakey, a former member and Ashley's best friend who died a year ago. Just like Ashley and Vegas to do him that last honor.

Not sure whether Alex agrees, but his screams drown out every other thought.

The EMTs walk through the door, assess Ashley, and get a handover from Chloe, before they load Ashley and Alex onto a stretcher and transport them, with Vegas following, to the hospital.

Walking up to a stunned Tanya, I wrap her in my arms.

"Can I change my mind?" Her jittery voice reaches me.

"Nope, babe, too late for that now. But I'll make sure you won't give birth on the pool table. We'll have to throw that out now." My reply earns me a sharp jab in the ribs.

"Seriously? That's what you're worried about?" Tanya hisses at me. I know I shouldn't smile at her right now. She's a little vexed, but I just can't wipe the smirk off my face. It's just too much fun to wind Tanya up and watch her go.

Smiling down at her and kissing her nose, I tell her, "Settle down, my little psycho. It's all good. Main thing is that both mother and baby are alright, and that I won fifty bucks. Vegas did me proud!"

I chuckle, wrapping my arms around Tanya, pinning hers to her side so she can't jab me again.

"Now, we just need to provide Alex with a little playmate and best friend. Next year, both boys will run around together, best mates."

Tanya cuts me off, "You mean Alex is gonna stare at our daughter, who will follow him around like a shadow?"

"Don't even joke about that!" I clip. No way are we having a little girl, no way in hell! My poor heart can't cope with boys loitering around a little girl of mine. I'll end up in the pen before she hits ten years of age.

No, just no. It's a boy. I'll teach him to ride, to shoot, and take him fishing, just like my dad did with me. Little girls are not allowed. I daren't voice my thoughts, though, as Tanya would call me out, and a chauvinist would be the kindest name she'd call me.

"Hey, babe, Paul called me. The work is progressing faster than he expected. He wants us to have a look. First fix is done, and the second fix will go in next week. He needs to plan where you want sockets, paints, tiles, all that kind of stuff," I relay Paul's conversation without a clue what any of it means.

I throw my arm over her shoulder and guide her out of the clubhouse, up the road where the houses are being built. Raven's and Vegas' are finished. But ours, next to Vegas', has me stunned. I can't believe what I'm seeing. A gorgeous double-fronted log cabin, with a half-up double garage, sits in front of me. Last time I was here, the foundations were in, and the first walls started going up. But this looks finished. Apart from the garage and landscaping.

"Wow, Tanya, this is amazing." I gasp, staring at her in disbelief

She grins at me, pride shining out of her eyes.

Paul strides towards us, handing Tanya a set of keys.

"There you are, Tan." He winks at her. Unsure whether it's his familiarity with my old lady or him ignoring me, I want to punch him right in his smirking visage.

"Thanks, Paul, this is beautiful," she tells him, unlocks the door, and pulls me inside with her, Paul following on our heels.

Within twenty minutes, she completes the plans for electric sockets, gas outlets for the kitchen, with no help from me. I'm useless at it. Give me a bike. I can fix and modify that any time, but houses? Electrics? Not my thing. Tanya talks dates with Paul, and I'm stunned when they arrange furniture delivery for the week after next. We'll be in in two weeks? I can't wait, nor help the smile on my face.

Once we return to the clubhouse, we grab Mom and take one of the club's SUVs to the hospital. After a quick stop at the local toy shop, we enter the waiting area with the biggest stuffed bunny you can ever imagine. Not only that, but he's wearing a cut, with tags that read *Alex, Sergeant at Arms in training* on the front, and a smaller version of the Stormy Souls patch on the back. A bunch of blue helium balloons tied to the bunny's wrist complete our baby gift.

The waiting area is packed with bikers carrying toys and hampers, smiling and laughing, pride gleaming out of everyone's eyes. Our noise draws the attention of others in the waiting area as well as the disapproving stare of the reception lady.

"Hold this for us?" Tanya asks Chloe. "Got an appointment with the OB/GYN."

"Sure, no problem, See you soon," Chloe answers, before she takes the balloon and bunny from us as Tanya draws me to the elevator bank.

"What's going on?" I ask her.

"Ashley couldn't have timed it better. I've an appointment upstairs for an ultrasound." Her smile almost blinds me.

We step out of the elevator and walk to the reception area.

"Tanya Frost. I have an appointment," she tells the receptionist.

"Ah yes, you can go straight through." The receptionist points at the door to the side of her desk.

Tanya grabs my hand and leads me through the door into the doctor's office.

"Hi, Tanya, nice to see you again. How have you been? I saw in your notes that you were admitted yesterday after fainting."

"Yes, I was. I think I did too much. I feel fine now," Tanya answers obediently, which makes me snort, and earns me another jab in the ribs. I'll be bruised like a peach at this rate.

The doctor eyes me speculatively.

"I guess keeping her in check is difficult, huh?"

"No, no, I keep an eye on her, and she'll be good now," I answer. *Ouch!* Another jab.

"Now then, let's see what's going on." The doctor smiles kindly and leads us into the next room, where Tanya climbs onto the examination couch, pulls her yoga pants underneath her bump and her T-shirt up.

It's the first time I have seen her swollen belly in all its glory. Amazement and wonder rush over me. The beauty of a life we made growing in my woman's tummy, safe and sound, brings forth feelings of love and protectiveness, at a depth I've never known before.

My mouth is as dry as the Arizona desert as the doctor squirts gel onto Tan's skin and grabs a probe, running it over her abdomen. Then I see it.

A tiny but fully formed body appears on the screen with a black dot pulsing at a rate of knots.

The sound of our Peanut's heartbeat makes me weak at the knees, and I drop onto the chair next to the couch, still holding Tan's hand, tears streaming down my face.

"Everything looks fine." The doctor's voice breaks through our stunned silence. "Would you like me to tell you what you are having?" She smiles at us.

"Yes!"

"No!" we both shout simultaneously.

Tanya glares at me.

"Stick your fingers in your ears if you must. I want to know the sex of our baby," she growls at me.

Not gonna argue with her.

The doctor runs the wand across her abdomen a few more times, then smiles and says, "Congratulations, it's a baby girl."

Darkness closes in on my vision again, and the next second, I'm out cold.

When I come around, I'm on the floor, with Tanya sitting on the examination couch, looking down at me.

"I'll enter the pool Dawg has going. I'm gonna bet fifty bucks you'll pass out at least five more times before the birth." She smirks at me, while the doctor takes my blood pressure and helps me to sit up slowly.

Holy shit, we're having a daughter!

18 — TANYA

The door opens to the buzz of tattoo guns. Sounds like Zippy is busy already.

I stick my head around the door. "Hi, I'm here. Need anything?"

"Nah, we're all good." He nods at me, and my mouth drops wide open as I spot the stunning blonde pin-up-style girl watching over his shoulder. Must be the new apprentice. She's young, can't be older than eighteen. Her portfolio is on the reception desk. Eve scrawled in beautiful script all over it. I open it and am stunned at her beautiful artwork. If she tattoos as good as she draws, I might get her to do my next one.

Yesterday, we spent mainly at the hospital with Vegas and Ashley. Alex is such a cute baby. Pennywise had to take him off me and hand him back to his glowering mother. Vegas loved the bunny with the cut.

We duly showed off our ultrasound picture, and Vegas howled with laughter at Pennywise passing out. We were the last to leave and spent the rest of the evening talking about names for our little princess. It's early days still, but I think we settled on Becca, after my mum, Rebecca.

We agreed to tell my dad when he next visits. Together. Not looking forward to that, I must admit. He knows about the baby, but not about Pennywise. Since we're living together and are moving into our new house in two weeks, we can't keep it quiet any longer.

I spent ages last night trying to squeeze information out of Pennywise. Something is going on. Every time I bring the subject to my father, he clams up and his eyes shutter. I'm worried that Dad is in trouble. I know he's more than capable of looking after himself, but Pennywise's reactions concern me. Clearly, he's not sharing what he knows. I don't blame him, though; club business isn't my business, same as Wild Pixies' club business isn't his.

Despite Ally giving me time off until our princess is here, I'm more than aware of difficulties cropping up left, right and center. One of the big male clubs, the Devil's Wings MC, has been running a campaign. They hate all female MCs. Ally and Jules both had funeral wreaths sent to their houses, and Hazel had a prospect parked outside her house. They clearly would like us to cave, but none of us are. If they think they can intimidate us, they are sadly mistaken.

The Stormy Souls and the Restless Slayers know nothing of this, and that's how it'll stay. We fight our own battles.

My phone chimes, and when I check, it's a text message from Dad.

Dad: Hey, girl. How are you and my grandbaby doing?

Me: Fine, Dad. Everything is peachy. Had an ultrasound yesterday. We're having a little girl.

Dad: We?

Me: Yes, the father and I are going to do this together, so baby has a mum and a dad

Dad: You gonna tell me who it is, or what?

Me: Sure. When are you next visiting?

Dad: I'll be down on the weekend. I have a meeting with Raven.

Me: Okay, we'll meet you for dinner at the Steakhouse in town. How about that?

Dad: Sounds good, baby. Love you. See you on Saturday.

Me: Great, see you Saturday. Love you too, Dad.

There's nothing for it. Best to face the music as soon as possible. Maybe Dad will take it as well as he did the news that I'm pregnant. My hopes aren't high though. I fully expect an earbashing.

The buzz of the tattoo gun stops. Zippy, Eve, and the happy client walk into reception. Ringing up his tattoo, I take the client's money, booking him in for the next session at the same time.

"Same care instructions as always. See you in two weeks." Zippy shakes the guy's hand and watches as he leaves.

My eyes remain glued to the back of the guy's thick thigh and the amazing ink he now sports, even as the door slams shut behind him.

Eve's pealing laughter rips me unceremoniously out of my admiration.

"Gorgeous specimen, isn't he?" she asks with a wink.

I have to clear my throat before I answer.

"The skull is awesome." I cough, my cheeks burning with embarrassment. I'm sure I've just turned beet red.

Zippy holds out a glass of water to me.

"What's the matter? Want to book Pennywise in for one?" he teases mercilessly.

Then, he looks Eve up and down.

"Okay then, let's see what you can do." He takes off his shirt, and instantly, I'm drooling. Must be the pregnancy hormones. Or something in the water, maybe? Who came up with that no-sex rule? Was that me? Well, there's no way that's carrying on.

"Excuse me, I'm gonna take a long lunch. You have no appointments until three P.M. I'll be back by two!" I shout after Zippy and Eve, turn on my heel, and strut out the door, their laughter following me until the door closes behind me.

As I get in the car, I fire off a message.

Me: You better be home and ready when I get there. Just leaving work.

Pennywise: Huh? What do you mean?

Me: I'll be back in ten minutes. Get naked and be ready for me to jump your bones.

Pennywise: Has my ship come in?

Me: I can change my mind, Pen. No worries, I'll go get a massage instead.

Pennywise: Don't you dare. See you in ten.

I'm never gonna admit to him I need his dick so badly I'm leaving a wet patch on my car seat. That's for me to know and for him to never find out.

Parking the car outside the cabin, I head inside, wasting no time, drawing my T-shirt over my head as I lock the door. I turn, and the picture that greets me makes my already wet pussy gush. A very naked Pennywise, reclined on the sofa, stroking his thick, rock-hard cock, grinning at me, waving me closer. The saliva pooling in my mouth has me licking my lips.

Without further thought, I drop my jeans and panties, leaving them where they fall, and go down on my knees in front of Pen. I love his taste. It drives me wild. So, with a moan I can't contain any longer, I lower my head and swallow him whole.

Sucking him in hard has him hissing, his cock throbbing in my mouth. The salty taste of his pre-cum turns me even hotter. With one hand firmly around his root, my other hand squeezes his balls, just the way he likes it.

"Baby, stop," he groans, "I'll come too soon. My balls are churning already. I want to make it good for both of us."

He lifts me off his cock, and reluctantly, I release him with a pop. Then, he hoists me into his arms and carries me into the bedroom. I bounce a few times as he throws me on the bed. He follows me instantly, spreading my legs wide, and diving straight into my fluttering pussy, licking through my folds, his tongue playing with my super sensitive clit. My whole body bows off the bed. I can't stop my back from arching. My thoughts fray, trickling out of my head like sand in an hourglass. Unable to tell when or how it happens, I explode into Pen's mouth with a scream, literally seeing stars, my brain electrified as though shocked. It still isn't enough.

Panting, I sit up, grab Pen, and throw him onto his back. I straddle him, his eyes as dark as coals. I grab his hands and pull them above his head.

"Don't move," I whisper in his ear, sucking on the lobe.

Leaning back, I lift and impale myself onto Pen's gorgeous cock. He slams his eyes shut, trying to stay in control as I bury him deep inside me until he bottoms out. His cock throbs inside me, unbelievably hard, and my pussy answers in rhythmic contractions I can't seem to control.

Having him seated so deep inside me drives me crazy. I start to move, gentle and slow at first, lifting myself up and sliding all the way back down. Relishing the feel of him being so impossibly deep.

As I increase the speed with which I impale myself on him, my need rises. Pennywise's teeth clench and with a sudden move, he flips us around until I am on my hands and knees. He knows my body so well. He plays it like a finely tuned fiddle.

"You need my cock, baby? You'll get it."

I know he'll make it good for me, he always does.

"Harder, Pen, I need it harder."

"Won't it hurt the baby? I don't want to go too hard, just in case."

"Pennywise, I swear if you don't fuck me harder, you won't fuck me again for the next twenty years!" I threaten, and at that point, I mean it. I desperately need to come.

Every nerve in my body is stretched tight, like wires on a thread board, just waiting to ping off with the next stroke.

"Please, Pen, harder." I'm not beyond begging.

With that, Pen loses control. He slams into me in one hard thrust, and that's all it takes. Fireworks go off in my brain as my pussy squeezes around his throbbing dick. My jaw clenches, stifling my scream, as wave after wave of pleasure crashes over me. Pennywise's loud groan breaks through my fog as he fills me with ream after ream of his cum.

I drop onto my back, fighting to catch my next breath. Pennywise drops down beside me, his arm over his eyes.

"You're gonna kill me one of these days, Tan." He chuckles, rolls onto his side, and pulls me into him. I snuggle into his chest and experience safety, love, adoration, and what's likely a first-time-in-my-life feeling of true happiness.

19 — PENNYWISE

Sitting in the office at an officers' meeting, discussing the trouble with the Restless Slayers MC, my phone dings.

Tanya: You better be home and ready when I get there. Just leaving work.

What the fuck? Has she lost her ever-loving mind? Are her pregnancy hormones running rampant again? She's driving me nuts, I swear!

Me: Huh? What do you mean?

Raven stares at me, watching me reply.

"Sorry, boss, it's Tan, gotta answer this. She's at work."

Raven, not happy, nods in my direction.

Tanya: I'll be back in ten minutes. Get naked and be ready for me to jump your bones.

What? I read that line at least ten times before I shoot off a reply.

Me: Has my ship come in?

Tanya: I can change my mind, Pen. No worries, I'll go get a massage instead.

Me: Don't you dare. See you in ten.

"Sorry, boss, she has an emergency." I add air quotes to not worry the others. "Gotta go, I'll catch up with Slender later. He can put me in the picture."

Not listening to the protests thrown at me, I strut out of the room and up to my cabin, quick smart. I'll have a surprise for her when she gets in. My cock is hard as steel and dancing a happy dance behind my zipper, which is less than comfortable since I went commando this morning. Within seconds of entering, my clothes are off, and I recline on the couch, waiting for her to make an entrance, stroking my weeping dick.

Ten minutes later, on the dot, I hear her car pull up outside.

When the door flies open, our eyes meet, and hers mirror my need for her.

I wave her closer, watching her tongue shoot out and lick her lips, with her eyes glued to my hand stroking my dick.

In a flash, she's dropped her jeans, pulling her panties off with them. The large wet patch on the light fabric betrays her arousal. Her pussy is soaking for me.

I groan as I watch her drop to her knees and with her eyes on mine, lower her hot mouth around my weeping cock, taking him in all the way, sucking hard. She has no gag reflex. I know she loves my taste, she's told me so, and when she sucks me in hard, I see stars. Panting, I struggle with control. It's been weeks now, so I know I won't last.

When she secures one hand firmly around my root and the other sneaks to my balls, squeezing and rolling them, I'm done for within seconds.

Unable to form a coherent thought, I only manage to groan, "Baby, stop. I'll come too soon. My balls are churning already. I want to make it good for both of us."

It takes all my willpower to lean forward and lift her head off my cock. I stand, stoop, lift and carry her to the bedroom. Throwing her onto the bed, I watch her delicious body bounce, her tits bigger than I remember. I follow her, kneeling between her legs, spreading her wide open for me. Her glistening folds and her unique aroma act like a magnet, drawing me in.

With my hands holding her thighs, I dive in, licking straight through her folds, her moans spurring me on. Her pussy is so needy, it flutters even with the slightest tonguing I give her. Paying attention to her swollen clit, her body bows off the bed, and with a guttural scream she explodes, her pussy gushing her release straight into my mouth.

Holy hell, she's always been responsive to me, but now? If that's what pregnancy hormones do? Bring it on, just bring it on!

I'm wholly unprepared when she jackknifes up, grabs my waist, and throws me onto the mattress. Sometimes I forget her physical strength and skills are equal to mine. Finding myself unceremoniously thrown onto my back, my need ramps up a thousandfold, as I watch her trim body with baby bump straddle me, grabbing my wrists and pulling them up above my head.

"Don't move," she whispers in my ear, causing shivers to erupt all over my skin, leaving goose bumps in their wake, as she sucks on my earlobe. She has the most extreme effect on me physically, always has, and I wonder whether I'll ever get used to the power she has over me.

She leans back, lifts, and slams down her hungry pussy over my weeping, throbbing cock. I slam my eyes shut, and it takes all my effort not to blow this second. The ripples of her pussy around my pulsing cock as she bottoms out on me are almost too much to bear. A deep groan rumbles up from my chest when she starts to move. She sets a gentle, slow pace, driving me nuts, but it's not what either of us needs.

Unable to take much more, I grab hold of her hips, flip us around so she's on her hands and knees, managing all the while to stay seated inside her. I know what my little wildcat needs.

"You need my cock, baby? You'll get it," I hiss through clenched teeth.

"Harder, Pen, I need it harder," she begs me.

"Won't it hurt the baby? I don't want to go too hard, just in case." The thought has been on my mind this whole time and is the reason I've held back.

"Pennywise, I swear if you don't fuck me harder, you won't fuck me again for the next twenty years!"

Her threat has the desired effect. I shove into her hard. I can feel her whole body tighten around me. My hands hold her hips steady as I hammer into her from behind.

"Please, Pen, harder," she pleads, her voice cut with a desperate edge to it.

Slamming into her harder, I lose my last inch of control and fuck her like a possessed man.

I can't stop the boiling in my balls; the tingle at the bottom of my spine turned into a fizzing bubbling volcano a while ago, and as her pussy strangles my cock with her orgasm, I follow her scream with an almighty rumble from deep within my chest, erupting and filling her with reams and reams of my cum, while her pussy still convulses around me.

It's so intense, my vision darkens at the edges. Sex with Tanya has always been fantastic, but this, this is something different. It's soul deep.

I fall onto the bed next to her, taking care not to crush her and Peanut, covering my eyes with my arm, trying to catch my breath and make sense of what just happened.

"You're gonna kill me one of these days, Tan." I can't help but chuckle, rolling onto my side and pulling her into me.

The way she snuggles into my chest, facing me, her bump touching me skin to skin, I can't help but let the happiness spread through me. I feel it deep in my bones.

"Hey, Tan." I look into her soulful eyes. "I love you and Peanut."

What the fuck? Where did that come from?

"Hey, Pen." She grins at me. "We love you too, regardless of your asshole ways."

Huh, I feel as though I've just been gut punched, but in the best of ways.

"Turn over, baby," I cajole her.

As she does, my arms close around her, my hand resting on her bump, caressing it gently. Until my hand nearly gets batted off.

"What the hell?"

"Looks like our daughter is gonna be a footballer." Tanya laughs.

"That was Becca?" I'm stunned. That little lady has her mama's strength, that's for sure.

I move down and lean over, kissing my daughter through her mother's skin.

"Hi, Becca, it's Daddy. I love you and your mama so much. Please be a good girl for her, grow fast and strong. We can't wait to meet you."

It might be silly, but I think I can feel an answering movement against my cheek, which gently rests against Tan's bump.

Tanya's giggles draw me out of my reverie.

"What? This is a private conversation between me and my daughter," I huff with a grin a mile wide.

"Don't you mean *our* daughter?" Tanya smirks.

"How long has she been moving like that?" I stare at her belly in wonder.

"Oh, I could feel her move about two weeks ago, but nothing as dramatic as this. This was a first for me too. She's a strong little lady."

Tanya's smile lights up my world. I'd take a bullet for her any day, but in this moment, my love for my two girls overwhelms me.

"I'm sorry, Tan. Sorry for being such a dick to you. Finding out about Becca messed with my brain. I promise to make it up to you both."

My fervent apology drags a grin out of my beautiful beyond belief, old lady.

"Shower with me?"

Does she even need to ask?

Time flies while we enjoy a shower and a few more orgasms. Hey, I can't help myself. I need to take full advantage of her hormones while it lasts. My vixen is horny, and it's my duty to fulfill her needs.

We split outside with a long, lingering, sensual kiss, which has my dick jumping behind my jeans as I watch her get into her car and drive down the path to the clubhouse.

I follow her down on foot, knock on the office door, and wait until Raven calls, "Enter!"

As I enter and go to my seat, all eyes are on me.

"Sorry, emergency dealt with. What did I miss?"

20 — TANYA

Hell, did I just tell Pen I love him? Damn pregnancy hormones!

Nevertheless, it's the truth. I've realized that Pen is it. He's the one. No matter how much I tried to fool myself that we were casual, I fell in love with him hard and fast at the rally, and the alcohol did not put enough of a haze on my brain to avoid losing a fraction of my heart to him.

The way he handled Rusty and the Restless Slayers in the months that followed, only drew me in further. His jaded soul speaks to mine in the same language. I'm a tough chick, brought up by tough men. I can turn control freak within a blink of an eye. My partner needs to be my equal and know how to handle me, or I'll railroad him into the ground.

Pen is everything I ever wanted in a man.

The death of his father scarred him, causing his hard shell to form. But glimpses of Pennywise, the man rather than the enforcer, gleam through his rough exterior.

The way he looks at me when he thinks no one is watching causes my knees to become weak, and the pure love shining out of his eyes makes my heart pitter patter.

Not to mention his long, lanky but muscular body, defined in all the right places.

Phew, is it getting hot in here? I can't help it; I want to jump his bones all the time.

The way he talked to Becca was too cute. It warmed my heart, filling me with love for both of them to the brim. If I could take a still photograph of that moment and keep it in my heart and mind forever, I would.

The chime of the doorbell rips me unceremoniously out of my thoughts.

"Hi, Tanya, didn't know you work here." Caleb smiles at me. He's the cutest prospect I've ever seen. He'll break hearts, probably already does.

"Hi, Caleb. What can I do for you?"

"Got an appointment with Eve, for my first tattoo." He winks at me.

"Okay, let me go grab her. You booked a two-hour slot, right?"

When he nods, I cross him off the list and walk into the back, where the artists are working.

I stick my head round the door of the coffee room. "Eve, Caleb's here."

"Thanks, Tan. Are you ready for this?" Zippy smirks at Eve.

"Ready as I'll ever be," she sighs, gets to her feet, and follows me to reception.

"Hi, Caleb, thank you for making an appointment with me. Full disclosure: you are my first,"

Caleb can't suppress a snicker.

"First tattoo on human skin, asshole. Be nice or I'll tattoo a dick on your back!" Eve threatens, glaring at poor Caleb. I almost feel sorry for him.

"Prospect!" Zippy thunders at him. "Staff get treated with respect here, and the ladies most certainly do. Don't like it? I'll get Tan to hold you down and tattoo a dick on your forehead!"

"Sorry, Zippy. Sorry, Eve, no offence meant." Caleb's shocked but sincere apology has me turning away from them, hiding my smirk.

Eve brings out her portfolio.

"None taken. Do you know what you want? And where you want it?" Eve is all business now.

Zippy watches her like a hawk.

Caleb pulls a crumpled piece of paper out of the inside pocket of his cut and hands it to Eve. Zippy looks over her shoulder and whistles through his teeth.

"Who drew that for you?" Zippy sounds impressed and takes the paper out of Eve's hand, whose chin about hits the floor, eyes glued to the paper.

"I did," Caleb answers, standing taller. "I've always loved art. Can't paint for shit, but I can draw. It keeps me balanced."

Twisting around, I snatch the paper out of Zippy's hand, and all breath leaves me in a *whoosh*. In front of me is an intricate design of a stunning woman, half portrait, half sugar skull, surrounded by a heart of barbed wire with intertwined roses. The name underneath reads *Anya*.

"You sure you want a name on you?" Zippy smirks while Eve watches.

"It's my sister. She passed, so it's a tribute to her," Caleb answers, swallowing hard.

"Okay, let me get this ready for you, Caleb. I'll be back in a jiffy. Do you mind Zippy watching me do your ink?" Eve throws over her shoulder while walking to the special copier to create the stencil.

"No, no problem," Caleb replies as he follows Zippy through to the back to Eve's station.

Two hours later, a buzzing Caleb steps out, his chest bare, proud as punch, showing me his new tat. It's on a spot over his heart.

Man, if I wasn't with Pennywise, I could seriously be interested in Caleb's chest. He's broad shouldered, with a very defined six pack standing out on his light brown skin. Well, I can't eat out, but I can look at the menu. I try to wipe the lecherous smirk off my face and stop ogling his body, concentrating on his tattoo.

"Wow, Caleb, that's amazing! That was all Eve?"

The portrait portion of the designs looks scarily real. The skeletal part is done so fine, it looks almost fragile.

"Yup, all Eve's work. I only watched for thirty minutes. She's a pro with the gun already," Zippy chimes in, standing behind a very red-faced but proud Eve.

"We can open her books for morning slots; afternoons she'll be with me," Zippy states, and Eve's face almost cracks with her blinding smile.

I ring up Caleb's tat, take his money, and hand Eve the twenty bucks Caleb tipped her.

The next client walks in and disappears with Zippy. Eve, as if by magic, produces two cans of soda, handing me one.

"Wow, that went better than I thought," she chirps, still grinning.

"You did great, girl. Fantastic job."

◊◊◊

The weekend comes sooner than I'd have liked. Today is D-day. We're getting ready to meet Dad at the Steakhouse in town. I spotted him earlier, but he disappeared into

Raven's office at the speed of light, so there was no chance to even say hello, other than a nod.

Becca has been very active all night, pulling somersaults or something. She doesn't have the day-night thing down yet. Seems to be like me—a night owl. My hand rubs my belly more often than not.

Now, at the six months mark, my bump is substantial, and every time I see Ashley with Alex, I want to just grab him and snuggle him. When he cries, my boobs leak, and Pennywise is more than intrigued with my ever-growing milk containers. All he needs to do is touch my nipples and he gets a taste.

He talks to Becca every day. Mom has taken to reading Becca stories in the evening; her voice seems to calm my active little acrobat.

Other than that, things are great. Pennywise and I have fallen into a comfortable routine and can't wait to welcome our little princess into the world.

The scan today showed she's grown by quite a lot, and everything is just as it should be. We paid for a 3D scan, and I can't stop staring at my daughter's beautiful face, nor the shock of dark hair on her head. Looks like she's taking after Pen.

Spending time getting ready, I talk to Becca.

"Hey, little lady, are you gonna give Mommy a break tonight? We're going to see Grandaddy. Him and Daddy are probably gonna use bad words. Don't listen to them. They are men, and most men are fools. Little tip from your mom. Stay away from boys, they are smelly."

As though to answer, Becca kicks me and dances a tango on my bladder. Rushing to the bathroom to take care of business, I sigh. The constant peeing isn't something I'm gonna miss. Neither the swollen ankles, nor feeling like Big Bird from *Sesame Street*.

"Are you ready, babe?" Pennywise sneaks up on me, wrapping his arms around me from behind.

"As ready as I'll ever be. Promise you won't turn asshole psycho on Dad?"

"I promise to behave and be civil. Same goes for you though, no psycho. Don't want my girl to develop bad habits even before she's born." He chuckles.

"Her language will be colorful enough as it is," I agree, turning in his arms, pulling his head down to me, and kissing him with a passion I always carry just under the surface for him.

"Love you, Pen," I whisper against his lips.

"Love you too, Wildcat." His smile warms the coldest recesses of my soul, opening my heart wide to him.

"Let's go, before I ravish you," Pen mumbles before he steps back, grabs my hand and the car keys, and drags me through the door.

Parking outside the restaurant, I note Dad's bike is already in the parking lot.

Here goes nothing.

Forcing a smile to mask my anxiety, I hold Pen's hand as we enter, and the server seats us at my father's table.

His eyes shoot thunderbolts at us, his face a mask of fury.

"Oh boy," I whisper to Pen.

"Yup, this is not gonna go down easy," he whispers back, both of us aware this will go down like a lead balloon.

21 — PENNYWISE

We don't even get all the way to the table before Masher stands and his hand closes around my neck, making breathing extremely difficult. I'm not sure what worries me more: his tight squeezing fist, or the other hand balling, his arm pulling back, ready to punch me out.

"Stop it, Dad, you're making a scene!" Tan's hiss reaches through the roaring in my ears.

"You will not hit or choke out my baby daddy! You dare and it's the last you'll see of me or the baby. Now, take your hands off him and sit back down!"

Her steely squinting eyes make not only my balls shrivel to the size of raisins, it seems, as Masher's grip loosens around my throat and he steps back.

I'm man enough to admit that I'll probably need a change of pants by the time we're through. Not sure who scares the shit out of me more: my psycho Old Lady, or her pissed-as-hell father. His eyes narrow to mere slits as he opens his mouth.

"Tell me you're fucking kidding me. Out of all the men in the world, you chose this asshole?"

"Hello to you too, Dad. Before you start spewing bullshit, let's just look at who's sitting at this table. A man-whore Seargent at Arms, who brought me up to be strong, to follow my instincts, be independent and stand up for myself. Despite more dragging me up than bringing me up. And no, Dad, discreet is not your middle name. We also have a reformed man-whore Enforcer, my old man by the way, who loves me as much as I love him. Not to mention myself, an Enforcer in my own right for an MC…"

"Fine fucking MC," Masher scoffs.

Tanya's knife hits the wooden table in front of Masher so hard it vibrates, missing his left hand by a hairsbreadth.

"Don't you dare. In all these years, I've never once disrespected the Restless Slayers, little as I liked what the club stands for. I've been loyal to you and them. I never got involved in club business and have been supportive of you through all those years, never said a word. Not to you, not to anybody. But if you disrespect *my* choices and *my* club, you will discover a side of me you won't like, nor want to deal with. This is *MY* life, Father dear. So you can either simmer down, or we part ways."

Jesus, my woman is as tough as they come. She loves her Dad, and losing him like this would shred her. I place my hand on hers, my thumb caressing the back of it gently, trying to soothe and calm her.

"Tan, calm down, sweetheart. No one doubts your intentions, sense, or loyalties. You are an amazing person, the strongest woman I've ever met, but getting het up isn't doing any of us any good. Let's try to talk this through."

Oh dear, all I get from her is a huff and her leaning back in her chair, arms crossed, eyes shooting daggers both at me and Masher.

"Masher, I know this may come as a shock, but I love your daughter. I'd take a beating from you if that'll make you feel better, but I'd take a bullet for her and my daughter, even take one for you. You are part of Tan's family—our family. I've claimed her at the table, and she means everything to me. You love her and would go to war for her. But I'm not the enemy. It's taken me a while to realize it. Was I an asshole? Yes, no doubt. She's my other half. She's it for me. So, I hope you'll understand when I tell you I'm not going anywhere."

Masher says nothing as he pulls Tan's knife out of the table, gets up, and walks out.

"Asshole," Tan hisses between clenched teeth and scrambles to follow him.

I know better than to follow them. This is a father-daughter thing, and I value my balls too much to even try to get in the middle of it. I've said my peace. That will have to do. Now it's up to them.

The server arrives with the menus.

"Leave them here, darlin'. They'll be back in a minute."

I flash my brightest smile at her. No way did she not notice the mark the knife left in the tabletop. I'll have to dig deep and tip her well. She just glares at me but says nothing. Instead, she returns five minutes later, putting a beer in front of me.

"From the gentlemen at the bar," she sneers.

When I turn towards it, I spot Dawg and Dougal sitting there; Dawg waving at me, making lovey-dovey eyes and throwing me kisses. *Assholes!*

Dougal is nearly falling off his bar stool, he's laughing so hard. How the fuck did those reprobates find out where we were meeting Masher? Nothing stays secret for long where those two are concerned. I shrug at them, pick up my beer, and down it in one go.

Jeez, I needed that.

Fifteen minutes later, Tan and Masher walk back into the restaurant, arm in arm. Tanya's still got tear tracks on her beautiful face, making me want to kill Masher.

"Damn hormones," she says to me, smiling brightly.

"Better get used to that, boy," Masher states. "She'll cry at the drop of the hat now for the next four months. Rebecca did."

That's the first time I've heard him even mention Tan's mother's name. I look at my old lady, and she smiles and nods.

"We'd like to name our Peanut Rebecca Helen, if that's okay with you?" I ask the six-foot something giant sitting opposite us and watch as his eyes become glassy, and tears roll down his face.

"I love that name," he croaks out. Then he coughs, picks up his menu, and says, "What's good in here?"

We realize he's hiding his emotions behind that card, and we don't mind giving him a moment to compose himself.

The sour-faced server returns to take our orders, and conversation flows easily between the three of us until we dig into our meals.

I can't help but think that something is off with Masher, though. Whether it's the shock of our announcement, or something else. He seems jumpy, and the dark circles under his eyes give away his general exhaustion and strain. It's not my place to ask. The way my wildcat keeps eyeing him tells me she's noticed, too. For now, it's best to not poke the bear, especially after just having mended fences.

Once we finished our meal, we wave Dawg and Dougal over, who grab seats and join us for a beer. Tan is stuck with the non-alcoholic stuff but doesn't seem to mind our drinking.

Celebrating our baby girl with the others, the evening turns into stories, laughter, and it seems our family bonds are knitting more closely together.

By the time we're ready to leave, none of us, baring Tan, can ride or drive, so Tanya herds us all to the club's SUV and chauffeurs us back to the club. Dawg and Dougal help Masher to one of the crash rooms, while Tan and I make our way to our cabin. I can't wait for the house to be finished.

"Something is off with Dad," Tanya says as she peels out of her clothing and disappears, naked and sexy as hell, into the bathroom.

I watch her and my cock stirs into action. Jesus, she only has to be in the room and like a bloodhound, he stands to attention. I watch her walk back into the room, lovingly stroking her considerable bump as she pulls one of my old T-shirts out of the drawer, which dwarves her as she puts it on and climbs into bed. I follow her example, brush my teeth, wash up, and stroll out of the bathroom naked.

"Yes, Wildcat, I noticed it too. Let's deal with this tomorrow, though. For now, let me make love to my beautiful Old Lady, like she deserves." I crawl onto the bed, pulling away the sheets as I go.

Leaning over her, I kiss her deeply, unhurried, tangling my tongue with hers as she opens for me. I can feel her smile against my lips.

Then, I make good on my promise.

22 — TANYA

Stretching like a cat, feeling my deliciously sore muscles after last night, puts a smile on my face, even before I've rolled out of bed.

"Hey, Becca, what are we gonna do today? Daddy is working. So, shall we drag your pops shopping? I think he owes you some pretty clothes after the way he behaved last night."

Her replying bladder tap dance makes me giggle.

"Yes, baby, we'll make him pay. He can help pick out your nursery furniture. Hopefully, we'll be in the house by the end of next week. I can't believe you are twenty-four weeks old now; only sixteen more to go and you'll be with us. So, let's get Pop's wallet out, shall we?"

After showering and getting dressed, I walk down to the clubhouse, preparing to find my dad hungover and suffering in the kitchen.

To my surprise, the place is quiet. In the kitchen, I find Chloe, Mom, and Tequila, one of the club whores, making breakfast. The smell of bacon and eggs has me salivating. I grab myself a plate and fill it, then get settled on a chair at the table.

“Has Dad been in? He might not stomach breakfast, though, thanks to Dawg, Dougal, and Pen last night.” I cackle at the girls, fully expecting their snorts and chuckles.

Instead, serious faces greet me.

“What?” This doesn’t feel nor look right. Worry courses through me like a wild river. I know something was up with Dad last night, but hell, I have no idea what.

“Masher is in the office with Raven, Vegas, Dawg, Slender, and Pennywise,” Mom answers, and I nearly fall off my chair, worry increasing tenfold.

Mom turns away from me, beating the eggs as though they deserve a thorough thrashing.

“Hey, Mom, how’s your paramour?” I try to lighten the mood.

“My para-what? Mom turns, spatula in hand, the other hand on her cocked hip, not looking amused at all.

“Well… you know…” I stutter, a blush of shame creeping over my cheeks. “Your paramour… secret loverboy… boy toy…”

The words die a death of embarrassment on my lips as I watch Mom’s eyebrows draw together before they hit her hairline. Then, her eyes shoot lightning bolts at me, reminding me of Lyssa, the Greek goddess of wrath I enjoyed learning so much about in high school.

Tequila snickers, drawing Mom's attention from me to her, and almost runs out of the kitchen as though wild wolves are on her heels. Chloe's eyes are enormous as she stares at me, shaking her head, trying not to smirk in front of Mom.

"You insolent child!" Mom bellows at me, making me shrink into my seat, wishing the ground would open up and swallow me whole. "How dare you stick your nose into my private life? If I have a love life, it's none of your goddamn business! It's mine! I've been living in and for this club for most of my life, had to bury a husband I loved with all my heart, and watch everyone move on with their lives. Pennywise included!

"I hope to God, for both you and my sake, that you never have to experience that kind of loss. Once you've walked a mile in my shoes, which I sincerely hope you won't ever have to, then and only then are you maybe permitted to ask questions. Until that day, you will show me the respect I deserve and stop your impertinent questions, trying to be funny and failing miserably, may I add!"

With that, Mom throws the spatula onto the counter, turns on her heels, and walks out of the kitchen, slamming the door so hard it rattles in its frame, leaving me shocked in her wake.

Chloe walks to the coffee machine, filling two mugs and fixing them before she sets one in front of me as she sits opposite me at the table.

"I'm so sorry…" I whisper, feeling crushed. I've never seen or heard of Mom blowing a gasket, so I must have really hurt her.

"Don't apologize to me, girl." Chloe sighs, "Apologize to her, and do it soon. Don't let it fester. If she's seeing someone, I can't blame her for keeping it under wraps. It's about the only thing she has that isn't part of this club. I hope it's bringing her the happiness she so richly deserves, my friend."

"I know." I swallow hard, my eyes stinging with tears. Not from hormones this time, but from my childish, obnoxious behavior.

"Give her some time to cool off first, though," Chloe suggests.

"Chloe, you are a wise lady. Thank you for your honesty and your sage advice," I croak.

"That's okay, Tan. I'll always give you the truth, whether you like it or not."

"How long have they been in there?" I ask her, nodding my head in the general direction of Raven's office.

"Oh, about two hours now. I'm just about to text Raven to offer to bring them all breakfast. They just grabbed coffee, and in Dawg and Pen's case, Tylenol." Chloe winks at me while she sends her message to Raven.

A reply pings within seconds.

I help Chloe, piling up a platter with egg and bacon. Grabbing some slices of bread and buttering them, I add them to the platter. Chloe holds it while I get plates and cutlery, and we carry it over to Raven's office, together with a fresh jug of coffee.

The atmosphere is somber, so thick you could slice it with a bread knife.

"Thanks, baby," Raven says, tags Chloe around the waist, and pulls her into his lap, landing a seriously X-rated kiss on her.

I run my hand through Pen's hair, who draws me in for a lingering kiss that has my core clenching, then move over to Dad and kiss him on the cheek.

"Jeez, get a room!" Dawg cringes, while Vegas barks a laugh.

"Hey, Dad, wanna go Becca shopping when you're done?" I whisper in his ear.

He looks at me as though I've asked him to scrape his eyes out, shakes his head at me, puts his hand in his pocket, and hands me his credit card. Pen, likewise, pulls his out, smirking at me.

"Max Masher's out first, yeah?" He chortles, while I salute him with Dad's credit card, click my heels, and turn to leave, their laughter following me.

"Hey, Chloe, wanna come baby shopping with me?" I throw over my shoulder.

"Hell to the yes! Let's get a prospect who can load and drive the van while we shop. We can go over to your house first and see which room you want as your nursery, so we can make sure we fit it outright." Chloe winks at me and dances out of the office. Groans and laughter follow us down the hall, even with the door to the office now closed.

"Hey, Chloe, any idea why my dad seems to occupy a chair in that office all too often lately?" I reckon it's safe to ask her.

"No, hon, I have no clue. It's club business, and Raven doesn't tell me jack. Not that I want to hear about any of it." She shrugs.

Climbing into the club's SUV is definitely easier for her than for me. I feel like a water buffalo on stilts. It's not a pretty sight, more crawling and heaving myself in than anything else. Dignity is fast becoming a foreign word. Fighting off the bout of dizziness, which isn't unusual for me, I shuffle around to get comfortable, much to Chloe's amusement.

Caleb drives as though he's got a carton of loose eggs in the back, not two grown women.

I release a sigh of relief once we pull into the baby shop parking lot and scramble out of the van before he can come around the side to open my door.

Walking into the store, we grab a cart and fill it with all the necessaries. It takes less than an hour and we have the nursery complete. I wipe the sweat off my forehead. It's unbearably hot in here.

"Are you okay, Tanya?" Chloe looks at me, her eyebrows drawn in concern.

"Yes, I'm fine. Let's just get out of here. I need some fresh air."

We pay, and I'm sure my dad will have a heart attack once he gets the bill, but hell, we splurged on Becca. Next is the maternity wear I need. For that, we need to go to the mall. That's where Pen's credit card will take a hit.

We walk to the SUV, leaving Caleb to push the trolley and stow away our shopping in the trunk. As I open the door, I have to crouch down as a wave of nausea overwhelms me. The edge of my vision dims.

"Chloe!" is all I manage to croak before darkness swallows me whole.

23 — PENNYWISE

We've been stuck in this office for hours. I can't believe what Masher is telling us. Looks like the Restless Slayers are sinking lower than even I thought possible.

He approached Raven weeks ago about wanting to patch over. Masher doesn't agree with the way the Restless Slayers are going. He knows they are involved in the skin trade, and he wants out. The only reason Fury would let him go without too much of a fuss is Tanya being my Old Lady and being pregnant. He can excuse himself with wanting to be closer to his family.

"You'd be coming in as an ordinary member. No officer position for you, man." Raven makes himself perfectly clear. "I don't want bad blood between us and the Slayers. We can do without that shit," he states, glaring at Masher.

"No problem, Raven, I'll keep a low profile. Don't mind being a member. I just need to be part of a brotherhood I can wholeheartedly support. Which is impossible where I am now." Masher talks openly, and his eyes convey his honesty.

"You ain't staying with us, Masher. No offence, but, no, just no." There's no way I'll allow Tanya's dad to live in our house. Over my dead body.

"Okay, let's take a break. Masher, are you sure?" Raven levels one of his signature glares at Masher that has the rest of us shitting ourselves half the time. "I'll make the call, but don't waste my fucking time. You got to be certain," he adds.

"I am. I need out of there before I do something I regret and get thrown out bad."

"Okay, let's get some food, a beer, and then I'll make the call to Fury." Raven stands, and we all follow him out and into the kitchen, grab a sandwich and head into the bar.

When his cell rings, no one pays attention, but as he spins on his heel, his face as white as a sheet, staring straight at me, the hairs on the back of my neck stand and an ice-cold shiver runs down my spine. I think someone just walked over my grave.

"What's going on?" My voice sounds like rusty nails, even to my own ears.

"Fuck!" he screams into the room. "Pen, grab your gear and head to the hospital. Something's wrong with Tanya. She passed out and is not coming round."

All the blood in my body races from my head straight into my feet. I'm out the door and on my bike, followed closely by my brothers and Masher, who has my mom on the back of his. How I don't stack the bike, I'll never know. If I'm honest, I don't even know how I get to the hospital. The next thing I properly realize is me running at lightning speed through the entrance.

"Tanya Frost," I bark out at the receptionist. "She's my fiancée, before you ask."

"She's in maternity, take the elevator to the third floor, then left…"

Not listening to her instructions, I belt down the corridor to the elevator bank and push the button about a hundred times before the door finally opens. My brothers catch up with me and we pile in.

As soon as the door begins to open on the correct floor, I sprint out and grab the nearest nurse I can find.

"Tanya Frost?"

She points me to the room closest to the nurses' station. I rip the door open and storm to Tanya's side, who is now conscious, but tears are running down her face.

"Pen, I'm in labor. It's too early," she sobs.

"Babe, you know what the doctor said. Hopefully, it's just a false alarm and you'll be home with me in an hour or two."

The door behind us opens, and Mom walks in, followed by a doctor, pushing an ultrasound cart.

His face is bland as bland can be.

"Now, Miss Frost, let's see what's going on," he says, smiling at Tanya, while he tries to usher me and Mom out.

"If you think I'm leaving her for even a second, you are in deep trouble, Doc," I hiss at him.

He lifts his hands as though trying to calm me, when nothing can calm me now. Facing off with people smugglers and traitors doesn't bother me. However, now though, I'm scared shitless. For my woman, and for my baby. I do not know what to do, so I just grab Tanya's hand and let the doctor go to work.

Stroking her hair, I can't seem to shake the sick feeling of doom surrounding me like a smokey cloud.

It takes the doctor a moment to get everything ready. The ultrasound wand moves across Tanya's bump, again and again. He gets out a microphone and places it against her belly, but it stays silent. He calls in another doctor and confers with him. They nod at each other, and my heart sinks.

"I'm very sorry." He turns to both of us. "We cannot find a heartbeat. Your baby, unfortunately, has died."

I fall to my knees next to Tanya, wondering who is screaming, until I realize it's me.

Masher, who must have stepped in behind me, holds Tanya, who sobs uncontrollably, and Mom is on her knees in front of me, cradling me in her arms, like she did when I was a child and scraped my knee. It made it better then. However, nothing can make this better. Nothing.

"We'll give you some time." I hear the doctor say. "I'll come back in a little while to explain what needs to happen next." He nods at Masher and leaves the room, taking his damned ultrasound machine with him.

I scramble to my feet, shaking my head at Mom, who tries to support me. Then, I stare at Masher, who simply looks broken. I gesture towards the door, asking him wordlessly to leave and tell the brothers what happened.

Needing to be close to Tan, the love of my life, I walk around the bed and wrap my arms around her, holding her tight, rocking her in my arms.

"They must have made a mistake."

God, her broken voice nearly kills me.

"What did I do wrong, Pen? Is this my fault? Did I kill our daughter? What happened? She was fine this morning, kicking and moving, and now, a few hours later, she's supposed to have died?"

The guilt in her face and voice breaks my heart.

"Baby, it's not your fault, or anyone's fault. You've done nothing wrong, sweetheart. All I know is, I don't have the answers. If I was a man of faith, I'd say God loved her so much he needed her with him."

It pains me to force those words out, because personally, I don't believe. If anything, maybe my little girl is paying fate's price for the lives I've taken. But I keep that thought to myself.

"God can go fuck himself!" Tanya curses. "I want my little girl. I want Becca."

As a flood of tears begin staining her beautiful face, I grab her tighter and turn her head into my chest. It's the only comfort I can manage right now, without crumbling myself. Tanya needs me to be the strong one.

This is the nightmare I can't seem to wake up from. My chest feels tight as if squeezed by an invisible vise; my eyes burning as though sprayed with acid. I grind my molars, trying not to get sucked into that black hole of abyss that just opened up right around us.

I'm aware of my fingers losing their grip on the unstable edge of reality, as sorrow and grief surround me like a dark, thickening cloud.

24 — TANYA

Once again, I wake in a hospital bed; an occurrence that has happened far too often for my taste lately. Chloe is sitting next to me, holding my hand.

"Jesus, girl, you scared the living daylights out of me," she says. "What's going on? One moment you were right there, the next you crumpled to the floor."

"I'm as clueless as you, Chloe. I felt fine earlier, but now? Ahh, shit, that hurts!"

I grind my teeth. Looking down, I see my belly tightening up, and I feel as though I've been kicked in the stomach by a cow.

"Fuck! What the hell?" My eyes search Chloe's, who jumps off her chair and walks out, returning with a nurse.

She puts straps around my belly and cold pads underneath them, watching the monitor, moving the pads this way and that way. Chloe's face turns more serious by the second, staring at the machine as if willing it to work.

"You are in labor," the nurse finally says. "I'm going to get a doctor to come and see you and do an ultrasound scan, to see how baby is doing."

Stunned, I stare at Chloe.

"How long was I out?"

"A good ten minutes. I've called Raven, and he's sending Pennywise straight here." Her face gives nothing away. I wouldn't want to play poker with her.

"Chloe, it's too early," I whisper. "I'm not due for another twelve weeks."

Fear clenches my heart. What if something goes wrong? What if Becca ends up in an incubator, attached to wires and tubes and I can't even hold her?

"I wish there was something I could say to make you feel better," Chloe says as she strokes my hair, "but I know there isn't, so I'm just going to be here with you. Let's wait for what the doctor has to say." She gives me a tight-lipped smile.

Another pain rips through me, and the sweat I break out in runs in rivulets down my back.

"Oh my God, holy shit!" I groan, grabbing Chloe's hand and squeezing the hell out of it. By now, tears are running freely down my face, no doubt smearing my mascara all over the place.

The door crashes open, and Pen rushes in.

"Pen, I'm in labor. It's too early," I sob.

"Babe, you know what the doctor said. Hopefully, it's just a false alarm and you'll be home with me in an hour or two."

The next time the door opens, Dad and Helen walk in, followed by a doctor I've never met before, with an ultrasound machine. Dad comes over to my side, while Chloe moves, pats Pen on his shoulder, and leaves him to stay on my other side. I'm bracketed by the two strongest men, who will protect me with their life, pick me up and make everything alright, so why am I so anxious?

"Now, Miss Frost, let's see what's going on," he says, smiling at me while he tries to usher Pen and Helen out.

"If you think I'm leaving her for even a second, you are in deep trouble, Doc," Pen hisses at him.

The cold of the gel hits my stomach, and then the wand squishes over my bump from left to right and in all different directions.

I'm strung as tight as a bow, waiting for the comforting swishing sound of Becca's heart. The longer it takes, the more desperate I get. I want to scream by the time the doctor asks a colleague in for a confer.

My heart is hammering against my chest, my vision is starting to gray at the edges, and my whole body feels tense and unwell.

Please, please let the machine be broken.

The doctor turns off the machine and faces us.

"I'm very sorry. We cannot find a heartbeat. Your baby, unfortunately, has died."

The most terrifying wailing scream echoes through the room as Pen sinks to his knees.

My heart shatters into a million pieces, and the overwhelming pain flooding me almost takes my breath away. Dad holds me close while I weep, my hands gripping his shirt, unable to cope with the anguish.

The panic and raging torrent of fear outweighs any physical pain I feel.

Then, the fucking doctor has the nerve to speak. I don't want to hear what he's got to say. Hasn't he devastated me enough?

"We'll give you some time." I hear his voice but find it difficult to concentrate on what he's saying. "I'll come back in a little while to explain what needs to happen next."

With a nod at Dad, the doctor leaves the room, taking his hopefully broken ultrasound machine with him.

I don't notice Pen getting to his feet, nor Daddy prying me loose and Pennywise taking his place. It's like a surreal out-of-body experience, being in this room, shredded from the inside out. It's only when Pennywise wraps me in his arms that I truly realize Dad and Helen have left the room. The rocking motion of Pen's arms around me does little to soothe me.

"They must have made a mistake." My broken voice sounds foreign to my own ears.

"What did I do wrong, Pen? Is this my fault? Did I kill our daughter? What happened? She was fine this morning, kicking and moving, and now, a few hours later, she's supposed to have died?"

A deep, wrenching sadness only amplifies the overwhelming guilt I feel. A guilt I cannot even begin to give a name to.

"Baby, it isn't your fault, or anyone's fault. You've done nothing wrong, sweetheart. All I know is that I don't have the answers. If I was a man of faith, I'd say God loved her so much he needed her with him." Pen's contorted features mirror my desperation. To hear him say those words, though, knowing he is not a believer, flips my sadness into rage.

"God can go fuck himself!" I curse. "I want my little girl. I want Becca."

Pen turns me into his chest, holding me tighter, as if we could anchor each other. I take the little comfort it provides; though, it's not nearly enough to stop my cries. I know he's hurting as much as me, but right now I need him, need the warmth of his body to sustain my ice-cold soul.

Oh God, Becca, what did I do? Was it me?

Oh, honey, please be alive, please, please, please. I don't want to live without you.

Please let the doctor be mistaken.

As though my innermost thoughts conjured him, the door opens, and the doctor and a nurse enter the room.

"Is there any chance you are incorrect?" I ask. "You must be mistaken. She moved earlier, kicking just as normal."

We watch as the doctor slowly shakes his head, both of our worlds collapsing into a heap of rubble.

"I'm sorry, Miss Frost. You may well have felt the baby move earlier today, but it's not alive now. I wish it was different, but it's not. Please compose yourself so we can talk about the next steps."

I've just been told my baby has died, and he wants me to compose myself? If it wasn't so callous, I'd laugh.

Pen stiffens beside me. He's ready to explode. I grab his hand tight, wishing someone would wake me up from this nightmare.

The doc grabs a chair and takes a seat.

"Miss Frost, you're already in the early stages of labor, so we won't induce you. I'd advise you to get out of bed and start walking. Try the stairs. That should speed up the contractions and help with the dilation of your cervix. The sooner you are dilated, the sooner you can give birth and put this whole thing behind you."

Wait, what? Did he just imply I have to give birth to my dead daughter?

"Hang on there, Doc, let me just ask you, did you just seriously suggest Tanya is going to give birth to our…" Pen can't even bring himself to utter the words. "Give her a caesarian, knock her out and get our daughter out. You cannot seriously expect Tanya to deliver normally?"

He's standing up straight and with every word he utters, steps a little closer towards the so-called medical professional, drawing himself up to his full height and vibrating with fury.

The doc's eyebrows hit his hairline. "And you are?"

"I'm your worst nightmare if you don't start acting with a little compassion for my fiancée," Pen grates out.

"If you can't control yourself, I'll have to call security," the shithead of a doctor answers. Arrogant ass that he is.

“Pen, please, I need you here, by my side,” I croak, my eyes pleading with him. “I can’t do this without you.”

I stare at the horrible little man in the chair, not an ounce of compassion visible on his face.

“Please leave and send in a midwife or someone else we can talk to.”

The doctor nods, his face showing his displeasure only too well. But I don’t give a fuck. I need someone who is able to support me with kindness, before I’m swallowed up by the darkness taking hold in the depth of my soul.

25 — PENNYWISE

The fiery need to pummel that asshole doctor stutters my breath.

Trust my brave girl to keep it together better than me. But then she's always been better than me. She's the only one who can tame my inner monster, which right now is screaming to be let out.

"Honey, is it okay if I ask Chloe, your dad, and my mom back in?"

I absolutely don't want to leave her, but I need to speak to Chloe, and we both need our parents with us. Pressing my lips to her silky, sweaty hair, I await her nod in agreement.

"I'll be right back, sweetheart. Promise," I croak out and turn towards the door. Stepping through it, I close it silently behind me.

I wave to Masher, Mom, and Chloe, who stand by my side in an instant.

"Please, guys, can you be in the room with us? The doctor nearly got his head caved in by me about twenty seconds ago. We can't do this on our own."

I wipe my face with my sleeve, only now realizing that tears are constantly rolling down my face.

Without question, all three of them walk into Tanya's room. Raven pulls my sleeve and pushes me into a chair in the hallway, which is by now populated by all my brothers.

"I'm so sorry, man," Raven says. "Is there anything I can do to make it easier for you?"

"Yeah, shoot that fucking doctor. Right between the eyes. Make sure he knows I send my regards," I growl at him.

"Not what I meant, but I get why you'd want to. Overheard the asshole talking to the midwives in the corridor. I'm so sorry, man. Remember, I'm here if there's anything you need."

"Thanks, brother, I'll keep it in mind."

We man hug, and damn, if that hug doesn't mean so much to me right now.

"Prospect!" Raven shouts. "Get coffee for everyone and bottles of water."

Caleb salutes, clicks his heels, and is off down the corridor. If the situation wasn't so dire, I might have laughed.

I return to Tanya, who has Mom and Chloe sitting on one side of her bed, and Masher is holding her on the other. Strangled sobs leave her every so often.

If we thought a midwife would have been kinder, oh boy, were we mistaken. The woman is a veritable dragon. By now, I just feel numb all over.

The midwife confirms Tanya will have to give birth. In fact, she explains, "We can't just do a caesarean section just because you fancy it. If the baby was in acute distress, that'd be different. But this is not the case, so you won't get one. Get up and start walking to speed the process along, and you'll spend tonight in your own bed."

Tanya expels an audible breath, just short of a wail. She has shrunk inside herself during the minute it took for that evil woman to open her goddamn mouth.

With a deep, shuddering breath, Tanya pulls back from Masher, her face an emotionless mask, sits up ramrod straight, and drags herself to the edge of the bed.

"Okay, they want me walking, so, walking it is," she mutters from behind clenched teeth.

Just then, the door opens, and Raven walks in with coffees, followed by the prospect, holding more cups and some water bottles. He holds out a mug to Tanya, who grabs it, puts it to her mouth, and chugs it down in one.

"Oh shit, sorry, boss." Caleb turns to Raven. "I shouldn't have done that. Sorry." His stare hits his boots.

"Why? Not as if it can harm anyone now," Tanya scoffs, her sarcasm stinging as though she's slapped us all.

None of us knows how to react. It's Mom who acts. She shoves Masher out of the way, steadies Tanya as she sits on the edge of the bed, helps put her shoes on for her, then grabs her arm and guides her feet to the floor.

"Are you feeling dizzy, girl?"

"No, Helen, thanks for the assist. Mind coming for a walk with me?"

"Sure, Tan, let's get going. Corridor or stairs?"

"Don't care. As long as you keep me away from the elevator. I might just bolt."

It should be me walking with her, but I can't seem to get my feet to move. I'm glued to the chair, rocking back and forth, trying to pull myself together. It's only when Chloe and Raven pry my hands out of my hair that I notice I've been ripping and pulling at it. When I open my fists, a clump of hair drops to the floor.

Masher drags me up out of the chair and commands, "You're coming with me!"

He grabs my arm, throws Raven a chin lift and leads me to the elevator, pushes me inside and presses the down button. He's still gripping my arm as the doors open. Then, he drags me out of the hospital front doors.

What the fuck?

"Son, I won't pretend that I can imagine how you feel. This is the worst shit. But you need to calm down. My daughter needs you. More than anything, even more than she needs me. I know we haven't always seen eye to eye, and you think I was blind to what'd been going on between the two of you behind my back. Let me assure you, I was fully aware."

Masher grabs a pack of rolling tobacco out of his pocket, bends over and starts rolling. I watch as he sprinkles some weed into the mix, finishes the roll, hands me the joint and starts rolling one for himself. I know he hasn't finished whatever he wants to get off his chest, so I wait for him to continue.

Not that I know what to say to him. He lights his joint and throws me the lighter, and although I haven't partaken in weed for a long time, I light up and drag the acrid smoke deep into my lungs, coughing immediately.

"Look, son, I like you. You're good for my little girl. I've watched her blossom from afar and become more balanced. Thank you for that. But, man, if you don't help her through this, I swear by the Almighty, I'll kick your ass from here to hell and back. There won't be much left of you by the time you get to Satan. That's not a threat, it's a promise. Now smoke."

I wash the sweet, sickly taste down with my coffee and take another drag. Good job we're hidden around a corner, away from the entrance. Wouldn't want to get caught. Tanya would kill the both of us.

Once the effect of the weed hits me, I'm calmer. The joint is doing its job. But I'm entirely numb and disconnected at the same time. It's as though all of this is happening to someone else.

Masher stubs out his cigarette on his heel, looks me in the eye and says, "Let's go."

And like a sheep, I follow where he leads.

Back on the maternity floor, I watch as Tanya walks with Mom down the corridor. My heart breaking all over again as she stops, bends over, clutching onto the wall, swaying side to side, groaning. Mom rubs her back and mutters words I can't hear.

In this moment, I realize I can do this. I can share her pain and try to make it easier for her. So, I walk over to them.

"Mom, go get your coffee. I've got this," I tell her.

She stares at me for a moment but nods and goes back to the waiting area at the other end of the corridor, where my brothers are congregating. They surround Chloe, who I assume is putting them in the picture.

Tanya, clutching my hand, makes me look up at her. Her face is pale, her lips pinched, but she pulls on my hand and continues to walk.

I lose count of how many times we walk the corridor, which given the late hour, is now empty of my brothers. Only Raven and Chloe remain. We've climbed the stairs many times, stopping regularly when the next contraction hits. My hands are sore from all the massaging.

As we take a pause, the midwife appears out of nowhere.

"Miss Frost, please come back to the room. I need to check you."

We follow her back to the room in silence.

I help my girl back onto the bed, holding her hand as another contraction hits. My God, I'm sure she's just broken at least two of my fingers.

The midwife unceremoniously lifts Tanya's hospital gown, commands her to open her legs as far as she can, and I watch her arm disappear. Tanya's face contorts and a groan of agony escapes her lips.

"That's good. You are almost fully dilated. Not long now," the midwife says to no one in particular. In fact, she doesn't even look at us; she just gets up and leaves the room.

When she returns, she sets up a tray with all sorts of medical implements, a scalpel and a suture kit among them, and then leaves again.

26 — TANYA

My whole body is a ball of pain. However, because I witnessed Ashley's childbirth recently, I anticipated some of this.

Somehow, I'm still clinging onto hope against hope that Becca will be fine. I want her born, to hear her cry, and turn this terrible devastation into blinding happiness. However, right now, all I want is for the ripping pain to stop. It feels as though I'm being torn in two.

The midwife telling me I'm almost fully dilated is cold comfort. Being on this wretched bed is unbearable. I need to move.

Oh God, here's another contraction.

Pennywise reminds me to breathe, just like Chloe showed us, and it actually helps.

"Shit!" I shout as a stream of warm wetness gushes from me.

"What's up, babe? What can I do?"

God, I love this man so much. He's been my rock during the last few hours. He holds me when I need it, lets me hang off his neck, holds me close when everything gets too much, and takes a step back when I need it too.

"My waters just broke. Pen, could you go get Chloe? We need to change the bed. No way am I giving birth in this mess."

He nods and does as I ask. Chloe walks in with an arm full of fresh bed sheets.

"Could you help me to the bathroom so I can change and clean up a bit?" I grunt between harsh breaths as my next contraction hits.

"Sure, let's go."

Trusting Chloe with my life, I follow her into the small bathroom. I sigh with relief as I sit down on the toilet. The urge to pee is stronger than my need for dignity.

While I do my business, Chloe wipes down my legs with a soft warm cloth, dries me, and then gently washes my back and runs a damp cloth over my face. For the first time today, I appreciate the loving care she's giving me. Every touch is comforting.

Suddenly, the urge to open my bowels is overwhelming, and as I bear down, something slips from me. Chloe has been watching me closely.

"May I take a look at you?"

Nodding my consent is all I can do as pain like I've never experienced before tears me apart.

Chloe takes one look and pulls the alarm cord. Pen comes running into the bathroom.

"You need to pick her up and carry her to the bed," Chloe orders.

Pen cautiously moves his arms underneath me, lifting me, his face an undeterminable mask, and carries me to the bed.

Chloe is out in the corridor, the alarm bell still going off, shouting for help.

"I've sent Raven to drum on doors and get some staff in here," she splutters, trying to catch her breath. "Tanya, I'm sorry, the head is out."

Panic rises in me. With my chest unbearably tight, I feel like I can't breathe. All I can do is hold on to Pen for dear life. My limbs turn to jelly and spots dance in front of my eyes.

"Baby, breathe, you need to breathe." Pen's voice rips me out of my own head.

"Please, Pen, make it stop."

Somehow, he manages to climb on the bed and crouches behind me, my whole body bracketed by his, his strength flowing from his warm body, straight into mine.

"Oh, Tan, I would take all of your pain, if I could, and keep you from ever hurting again. I love you so much. Your strength and determination are incredible. I'm so damn proud of you. I love you so much it hurts," he whispers in my ear, his breath flowing over my neck, calming me.

"Where's the fucking doctor and the midwife?" he growls at Raven, who is stood at the door.

"I've been trying to find them, bud. The place seems deserted. I found a nursing assistant. She's paging the doctor and going in search of the midwife," he answers.

"Oh God, I need to push!" I scream.

Inhaling deeply, mirroring what I remember Ashley doing, I pull up my knees, press my chin to my chest, and push, despite the tears flowing down my face. At this moment, I don't care that Raven is in the room and Chloe is at the bottom end of my bed. All I care about is that I need to push.

I wish I could stop the inevitable, but that's impossible. So, I scream with the unfairness of it all, feel Pennywise behind me, my neck wet from his tears, and let nature take its course.

Suddenly the pressure and the pain are gone. Well, apart from the anguish rolling over me like a tidal wave.

The door opens and the midwife finally makes an appearance.

She stares at Chloe.

"What in God's name do you think you are doing?"

Raven steps in front of her.

"You will speak nicely to my wife, Nurse Ratched, especially since she's just done your job, delivering my brother's baby. I sent the nursing assistant to find you fifteen minutes ago. Where the fuck were you? And where is that incompetent imbecile of a doctor? I'm going to rip him a new asshole, and that is before I file an official complaint!" Raven's voice takes on that ice-cold, *I'm going to kill you* quality.

The midwife's eyes shoot glacial daggers at Raven.

"Here's some clamps. Since you've done such a marvelous job, you might as well continue." She scoffs at Chloe, throwing two plastic wrapped packages at her and slamming a pair of scissors on the table. "I don't have to listen to your threats, you street rat. No wonder it didn't make it with your lifestyle. Baby is better off dead, before you grow another biker whore."

Chloe jumps up, giving the midwife a resounding slap. Raven roars and steps towards the woman, fists balled, and Pen is trying to get out from behind me, white-hot rage radiating off him in waves.

"Please," I sob. "Pen, don't, I need you." My voice is hoarse from all the screaming and crying.

Where I was numb before, I'm hypersensitive now.

Why isn't she screaming? Why is Chloe crying? What's Raven still doing in here? Where is the doctor? What's going on?

Another harsh contraction rips me out of my thoughts, somehow even stronger than the last ones. At that precise moment, the door opens and the doctor struts in.

"Ah, I see you're just about done. One big push and the placenta will be out."

Pushing myself beyond my limits, I bear down as though my life depends on it. Then, the pressure eases, thank the Lord.

Chloe moves to the receiving station. The silence is deafening. It's the loudest thing I've ever heard.

Raven walks to Chloe and hands her a beautiful pink blanket. My eyes are glued to her as she gently and ever so carefully picks up my sleeping daughter and wraps her up, whispering to her. What, I cannot hear, but her care, her nurturing and loving tone, means more to me than a million dollars.

While the doctor checks the placenta, Chloe steps to my side.

"She's so beautiful, Tanya, with her dark wavy hair and those eyelashes. She's perfect." Chloe smiles at me with tears running down her face.

All I can do is hold out my arms while Chloe passes Becca to me. Pen wriggles out from behind me and climbs onto the bed with me. Becca is where she belongs—bracketed and guarded fiercely by her parents.

Dad leans over and kisses her forehead.

"Hi, baby girl, I hope you can hear me. It's Grandaddy. I love you so much and am missing you already. We'll be together again for real, and you can ride on my bike with me in heaven. But until then, enjoy being in heaven, little Becca."

"Have you decided whether you're going for cremation or burial? And what funeral home do we send the body to? Oh, I'll also need the name for the death certificate."

As one, our heads shoot toward the door, where unnoticed, Nurse Ratched has snuck in.

I start to wail, the pain and finality of this moment too much for me to bear.

Chloe marches over and hisses something I can't make out, then pulls her right arm back and punches the midwife in the face. Raven is behind her, wrapping his arms around Chloe, keeping her from lashing out again.

I can't help myself, suddenly my cries turn to hysterical, inappropriate laughter, and I shout, "Bullseye!" all the while holding my precious Becca's hand while Pen holds her other one, and the laughter just keeps coming. I try, but I can't stop it.

Everything changes when security appears in the room. Two burly, but milk-faced, spotty teenagers in uniform, insisting on Raven and Chloe leaving. They even chance a grab at Chloe's arm. Though Raven's death stare makes them drop their hands as though her arm is on fire.

Nevertheless, they march them out of the room, leaving us with Dad and Helen, who sit quietly in their chairs, their torment taking its toll on them both. And my tears begin to roll again as my fingers tenderly caress Becca's cheeks. This emotional rollercoaster is killing me.

Helen gets up, her red-rimmed, glassy eyes finding mine. "May I hold her?"

"Of course." I sniffle, wrapping my baby girl, who looks as though she's fast asleep, tighter into her blanket. I hate the thought that she's getting cold.

With shaking hands, I pass her to her grandma.

"Oh, sweetheart, Grandma is so happy to meet you," Helen coos, gently rocking Becca. "You are the prettiest little girl I've ever seen. I love you so much, and it makes me sad you can't stay. But I tell you what, when you get to heaven, look out for Grandad Bear. He'll take good care of you and love you until we're all together again. Until then, I want you to look after this for me."

Helen kisses Becca's tiny nose, smiling with tears running down her face, passes Becca into Dad's arms, and removes her bracelet. A gold chain wrapped around her wrist twice with a dragonfly charm. She lifts Becca's head and gently places it around her neck. It is miles too long and reaches down to Becca's hips, but I don't care. It's such a sweet, meaningful gesture.

Pen pulls me closer, wrapping me tightly in his arms, our tears never-ending.

27 — PENNYWISE

My heart breaks all over again watching my mom with Becca. That necklace was the last gift my dad gave her, shortly before he was killed.

Losing him was the worst day of my life, or so I thought. Eclipsed now by Becca's loss.

Masher stands with Mom's arm around his back, and they lovingly glance down at our beautiful baby girl.

I had no idea what to expect, but our little girl is perfect. Soon, we are going to say goodbye to her for the last time, and I don't know if I can. The thought of having to hand her over to the thoughtless, unkind staff fills me with dread.

Masher hands Becca back to Mom, nods at me, and motions to the door. I get his subtle hint.

"Hey, babe, I'm gonna take your dad outside and get us all a drink. Find out when you'll be released," I whisper in Tanya's ear.

The fear in her eyes stabs me straight through my already splintered heart. When she nods, I untangle myself from her.

Mom turns to Tanya. "Sweetheart, let's get you cleaned up and more comfortable."

Shit, I hadn't even thought about that. Once Becca was born, all I did was throw a sheet over Tanya and towels over the bottom end of the bed. *What a klutz!*

Before I follow Masher out of the room, I watch Mom carry Becca to the changing table, switching the heater on, and then turn to Tanya.

Closing the door to give them some privacy, I catch Masher's retreating form heading down the corridor. He stalks ahead of me to the elevator bank, and we go down to the cafeteria. He grabs two coffees and finds us a table in the corner.

"I'm so sorry, son." His red-rimmed, swollen eyes find mine.

I don't answer, because what can I say? Thanks? He gets it.

"Son, I know this is hard and life has dealt you both the shittiest hand imaginable, but despite all that pain and sorrow, you'll have to make some decisions. I'm here for you, as well as for Tan. Both of you have my support, no matter what."

The honesty, care, and unholy grief radiating from this big man almost brings me to my knees.

"I don't know what to do." It's not an easy admission.

"Would you like to talk it through with me? I might not be able to do anything, but sometimes having an ear to bend helps."

"Masher, as much as I loved it when Chloe punched that midwife, I understand choices must be made. It's not something I've ever needed to even think about before. My feeling is, I would like Becca to be buried so we have somewhere to visit her, but how can I talk to Tanya about all this? She's so broken. How can I hurt her even more by bringing this up?"

Sighing, I run my hand through my knotted hair, ripping my fingers through it in frustration.

"Pennywise, listen to me. All you can do is be honest with her. Talk to her, give her options. If I know my daughter, she will want the same as you do. A place to visit our little angel. Would you like me to make some calls and find a nice funeral home for Becca? And before you say anything, I'll cover the costs. Becca deserves the best, and so do you and Tanya. We all do. Please let me."

Today's events have made me see Masher in an entirely different light. This man has a huge heart. Sure, the tough SAA isn't an act, it's clearly from experience, but equally he'll go to any length for his family. How can I refuse him?

"Thank you, Masher. We'd be honored if you took all of that off our hands. One less thing to worry about for now. Thanks, man, I can't tell you how grateful I am." I clear my throat and still my voice is so hoarse, I struggle to get out the words.

We finish our coffee, grab Mom and Tan fresh ones, and head back upstairs. A new nurse is behind the desk. Must have been a shift change. I clear my throat, and when she looks up, her facial expression couldn't be more different from what I expected.

Warmth, empathy, and kindness radiate out from her, making me swallow hard, trying to suppress the hot stinging tears attempting to break free.

"You must be Noah," she quietly says. "I am so deeply sorry for your loss."

"Thank you." I look for her name tag. "Jennifer. I would like to introduce you to Tanya's father. I realize you will need information about which funeral home to send Becca to and all the other details. As you can imagine, we're devastated, and Mr. Frost has kindly offered to deal with all of those things."

"That's fine, Noah. I'll make arrangements with Mister Frost here. You take as long as you like with Becca. It's no problem at all."

“Thank you for your kindness and understanding. It is much appreciated,” I manage to get out between deep breaths and hard swallows.

Masher grabs my shoulders and turns me towards Tanya’s door. “Go on, son, look after our girls. I’ll be in soon.”

The sight that greets me as I walk into the room almost brings me to my knees.

Tanya is up and dressed and sitting in an armchair by the window, with Mom fussing about the room, changing the bed, and removing the chaos left in the wake of giving birth.

Tan looks up as I enter, the sadness in her soulful eyes like an arrow shooting straight through my heart. I sit beside her, getting as close as I can, and gaze at the little one, attired in pink and swaddled in a charming pink blanket featuring rainbows and unicorns.

Oh, Becca, I wish I could hold you longer, wish I could trade my life for yours. I love you so much, my beautiful princess.

“Hey, babe, I brought you coffee,” I tell my equally beautiful woman, holding out the take-out mug to her, and passing the other to Mom.

“Tan, I hope it’s okay, but your dad offered to take care of arrangements for us. He really wants to help, so I said yes. Do you mind? I can take over, if you'd rather?"

"No, Pen, it's fine. I'm grateful not to have to deal with any of that. I wouldn't know where to start, nor how I'd get through it. He'll do right by Becca and us."

Her eyes never leave our little girl as she speaks to me. Neither of us notice Mom leaving the room.

Tanya gets up, holding Becca tightly, and snuggles onto my lap, where I can wrap my arms around both my girls.

"Pen, I don't know how I can let her go," Tanya quietly cries into my shoulder.

"I don't know either, sweetheart."

I watch the clock on the wall, time ticking along as though nothing's happened, when all I want is for the world to stop turning.

It's been hours since we arrived, hoping to bring our baby girl home with us. Her car seat and Tanya's bag are still in the SUV in the parking lot, where the prospect left it. Darkness is closing in, not just outside, but inside me, and no doubt Tanya, too. Time loses its meaning as we sit there, trying to say goodbye to our baby girl, but can't.

Inside, I rail against the world, against God, against everything. On the outside, I try to project calmness, for Tanya's sake.

But being strong for both of us is the toughest thing I've ever had to endure.

28 — TANYA

It is almost midnight when I kiss Becca for the last time and hand her to the funeral director, who arrived ten minutes ago. He carefully takes her from me and cradles her lovingly in his arms, as he bows his head to us and solemnly moves away and out of the room, closing the door behind him.

He promised me Becca would not be put into those horrible carriers, that he'd keep her in his arms until they arrived at the funeral home, where they can put her to rest with the care she deserves.

Dad did good for our little star. Funny how I note Mom crying in Dad's arms, and Pennywise holding himself back, struggling not to run after her, tears streaming down his face.

Strangely enough, all of my own tears have stopped. All I feel is indescribable numbness. A cold has taken hold of me, chilling me to the bone, freezing everything that is me. I welcome the numbness, inviting it in. If I experience any more pain, I'm sure I'll shatter into tiny fragments.

With a deep, shuddering breath, I take Pen's hand.

"Let's go home. I can't stand being in this room a second longer."

Having signed my release papers an hour ago, I need to get out of here before I implode.

Pen's fingers wrap around mine, but even his warmth can't beat the cold I feel deep inside.

◊◊◊

Today is the day I've dreaded. We're laying Becca to rest at the Stormy Souls' cemetery. We asked for a quiet ceremony, just us and our families. The Restless Slayers wanted to come, but I asked that only Meghan attend as their representative.

The atmosphere between both clubs is strained, and Dad's patch over caused a wave of tension. It's not something I want to deal with today of all days. Instead of flowers, we asked for donations. The money will go toward buying a cuddle cot for the hospital, enabling parents to spend more time with their baby angels.

Everyone in attendance is wearing something pink and carrying pink roses as a means of saying goodbye. I can't abide the thought of earth falling onto Becca's coffin by our hand.

Ashley has barely looked me in the eye, and since coming back from the hospital, I've avoided her and Alex like the plague. Understandably, she's a beaming, joyful mother, but it hurts too much to see her with Alex in her arms. Especially today, when I am laying my daughter to rest. It's not personal; I mean, I envy her, sure, but… I can't even explain how I feel.

We've all gathered at the graveside. I'm here, but I'm not. My thoughts are racing without settling long enough for me to work out what I'm thinking. We opted for a non-religious ceremony, officiated by Ally and Dad.

I listen to their words without hearing them. When the time comes, Pen and I step up to Becca's beautiful tiny white-and-pink coffin and lay our roses on top.

My feet freeze, I can't move or do anything but stroke her coffin gently, not wanting to let her go.

Pennywise's arms come around me, steadying me as I sway, my knees so wobbly they almost give way. My tears splash onto the white lacquer, leaving tracks of my pain.

Our family members take turns passing on the other side of Becca, laying their roses down, until the white coffin top becomes covered in pink roses, giving the impression that Becca is resting in a rose garden.

We stay with Becca for a long while after, saying our own goodbyes.

Sleep tight, my baby girl. Mommy loves you to the moon and back. You will be forever in my heart.

29 — TANYA

THREE MONTHS LATER

Life has been hard, sometimes too hard to bear, and it's only Pen's and my shared grief that pulls us through the darkest nights.

Today is not a day I'm looking forward to. I have my final checkup appointment at the hospital.

I've showered and dressed, all on autopilot, and I'm now waiting for Pen to come home, ready to support me through this blasted appointment. After giving a lot of thought to our experience at the delivery suite, we reached out to the club's lawyer and submitted an official complaint against the hospital and the staff on duty that horrid day.

Those people should not work in patient care, and we will put up a fight, including taking legal action.

I'm pacing up and down the lounge when my cell rings. My display shows it's Dad.

"Hi, Dad, are you okay?"

"Yes, I'm fine, darlin', just wondering if I can pop over after work. Be nice to catch up."

"Sure, you're always welcome. You know that, right?"

What a silly question to ask. He's my hero. I can't imagine managing without his and Pen's mom's assistance. Dad patching over has been a huge blessing.

"Sure do, don't worry about feeding me, I'll bring pizza," he tells me.

"Great, see you later then, about six?" I'm glad I don't have to cook.

"Okay, sweetheart. See you then."

Well, that was short and sweet. Typical Dad.

At last, I hear Pen pull in with the SUV. We bought our own, so we don't have to borrow the club's whenever we need to go out. It's too cold to ride now. December in Duluth is harsh, so the bikes are in our double garage, stored for winter. I miss riding, more than I like to admit.

I grab my purse, keys, and jacket, set the alarm, and step out onto the porch.

"You ready, girl?" Pen asks as he folds me into his arms and kisses me soundly.

"As ready as I'll ever be." I grimace.

Pen helps me up into the seat, buckles my seat belt for me, walks around, and gets into the driver's side.

"Oh, before I forget, babe, Mom is coming over tonight. She wants to talk to us about something," he casually states.

"Dad called me a few minutes ago. He's coming over too and bringing pizza. It will be nice to have a catch up with the two of them,"

I twist the loose strands of my hair, which has grown much longer, trying to manage my nerves.

"Tan, darlin', it'll be okay. I'm with you all the way. We're in this together, sweetheart. No way will I give them the opportunity to hurt you again." Pen's hand drops onto my thigh, his warmth soaking into me, calming my frayed nerves.

My emotions are all over the place. One minute I'm sad, the next angry, then empty and burned out. And then there are the thousand times a day where I ask myself, what I did wrong? Was it my fault? Should I have noticed something wasn't right?

"Tan, honey, stop."

I didn't realize I said those words out loud.

"Baby, there is nothing you could have done differently. It wasn't your fault. You did everything right, did as the doctors told you. You have every right to be sad, to be angry. I am too. Some days I feel like I want the world to stop turning, because I want to get off.

"It kills me to see you so upset all the time, because I don't know how to help you, make it easier for you. It kills me that being close to our daughter means going to her grave. Some days, I'm so angry I want to cave someone's head in. Instead, I go to work every day and pretend everything's normal, when nothing is normal anymore." Pennywise heaves out of tortured breath.

"I love you, Pennywise. So damn much. You are my everything. Please, never forget that," I choke out.

His hand squeezes my thigh, hard. "We'll get through this together, one way or the other."

Watching the hospital get closer, the mere sight fills me with dread.

Pennywise parks, we register at reception and are led to the outpatient suite. Thank God, not the delivery suite or the OB/GYN department. Dr. Ritter, who I remember from my time in the emergency department, comes to greet us.

"Miss Frost, Mr. Nixom, please come in. I was asked to take over your care," he tells us as we walk into the spacious office and take a seat.

Another suited man stands with his back to us, staring out of the window.

"May I introduce you to Mr. Waters. He's the clinical director of the hospital. He'd like to speak with you. Is that okay?" Dr. Ritter asks, looking from me to Pen.

"I don't know what we have to talk about." Penny's icy tone could have double frozen Frosty.

Mr. Waters, a young-looking guy considering his position, sighs.

"Miss Frost, Mr. Nixom, please accept my and the hospital's sincerest apology for what you've been put through. The care, or should I say non-care, you received at the hands of our staff was unacceptable, and let me assure you, neither of the staff in question is still working for us. I realize that this is no comfort to you in this situation, but let me assure you, lessons have been learned, and all our teams are now receiving special training, to prevent an incident like yours ever happening again."

"And you think a lukewarm apology is enough for what you put Tanya through? For what all of us went through?"

Pen's fury is getting the better of him, and his voice has risen several octaves.

"Your apology changes nothing! My daughter is still dead. The events have decimated my fiancée and myself. I've seen a lot of things, but what happened here is by far the most traumatic experience any of us could have had!" he shouts, his face about three inches away from Mr. Waters'.

I almost feel sorry for him. Almost.

"We would like to offer both of you, and anyone out of your family who requires it, grief counseling, free of charge. We have a trained counselor on contract, who you can contact and access at your leisure. You might have heard of Darcy. She's a renowned counselor at Debs' Haven. We will cover all the costs involved, and there is no limit to how many sessions you are able to access. Furthermore, we'd like to ask you to settle out of court with us. I know money doesn't bring back your daughter, but we feel we owe you at least some kind of compensation. We would like to keep this matter out of court.

"I'm sure you'll want to discuss this with your legal counsel. If you agree, have your counsel get in touch with me directly. Here's my card."

As neither Pen nor I make any move to take it from him, he places it on the desk.

"I'll leave you to consider our offer. Miss Frost, Mr. Nixom." He nods at both of us, turns, and walks out of the office door.

"I'm so sorry," Dr. Ritter sighs. "For your information, I didn't suggest this discussion take place here during your appointment."

"It's okay," I croak. "Can we get on with it, please? I just want to get out of here."

Dr. Ritter nods.

"How are you physically? Any pain?"

I shake my head. He takes my blood pressure and asks me to lie down on the examination couch. He takes out an ultrasound wand, which has me tensing and gripping Pen's hand so hard he hisses. Afterwards, we sit back behind the desk.

"Physically everything seems okay. You can resume your intimate relations now. If you then wanted to, you could try getting pregnant again. If you decide to try again, I assure you we'd check you every week, at least once. You'd be classed as high risk, hence the regular check-ups. I know it's not something you're considering right now, but I'm duty bound to give you the information."

Dr. Ritter struggles to look us in the eye.

"I normally don't discuss this with my patients, but I've been where you are. I understand how you both must be feeling. So please don't take it personally when I list all of your options. You have my greatest empathy. From experience, I can tell you that counseling really helped my wife and I. Please think about it."

The sadness in his eyes when he looks at us makes me believe every word he says.

"Thank you, Dr. Ritter. And I'm sorry for your loss," I reply quietly.

"As am I for yours," he tells us, before getting up and showing us to the door.

I leave the examination room lost in thoughts, but feeling a little better than I went in.

30 — PENNYWISE

The drive home passes in silence, both of us pondering the outcome of Tan's appointment.

Exhaustion catches up with us as we get home, and we both slip under the covers, hold each other, and doze on and off.

Later, we get up, shower together, and get ready for Mom and Masher turning up.

I already understand what it's about, and man, was I surprised when Mom dragged me out of Ferret's office earlier.

◊◊◊

"How's Tanya?" Mom asks.

I struggle hard to look at her as I reply.

"She's so sad and depressed, still railing at the world, caught up in her grief. She's not even opened Becca's bedroom door, despite the nursery furniture and decorations being gone, and the room painted."

"Oh, Son, that will be the most difficult thing for her to do. She needs time, and maybe grief counseling," Mom suggests.

"I've tried again and suggested exactly that, but she doesn't want to know."

It's clear I haven't covered my despair as well as I thought I had.

"How are you coping? Anything I can do to help? You know, you just got to ask, Noah."

"I'm getting by. Mom," I sigh. "Visiting Becca twice a week helps. It reminds me she's still here with me, always will be." My eyes burn with unshed tears.

Thankfully, Mom refrains from hugging me, because if she does, I know I will lose it.

"So, what's up, Mom? What did you want to talk to me about?"

"Noah, there's no other way to tell you this, but straight up. I'm seeing someone. Have been for almost a year now, off and on, and we want to make it permanent. He loves me, I love him, and he makes me happy."

I can't stop smiling. Happy news at last!

"Mom, that's great! I know you loved Dad, but it's been a long time, and I want to see you happy. I'm stoked!" I jump off the table and wrap her in a bear hug.

"Don't you wanna know who it is?"

"I don't care, as long as you're happy, Mom. You can tell him from me though, if he hurts you, he's a dead man walking!"

I don't miss Mom's deep inhale.

"You can tell him yourself; Masher is in the garage working."

"What did you say? Did you just tell me you're with Masher?"

My eyes almost pop out of my head.

"Didn't think you're hard-of-hearing, Son. You need me to clean them for you?"

"Masher, seriously?"

"Yes, Masher. You got a problem with that?"

"No, not at all. He's a good man. I'm just surprised. You kept that quiet, didn't you? I don't like that you kept him from me."

"Noah, with all due respect, I am a grown woman. I know what I'm doing and don't need to justify myself to you. We took a break to be there for you and Tan. You needed us more. Now you are getting on with trying to live. We are doing the same. He asked me last night to be his Old Lady, and I accepted. I just wanted to give you a heads-up, since Caleb saw us drive in together this morning."

"Mom, I have no problem with you and Masher. I'm glad you found someone who makes you happy. The fact he asked you to be his Old Lady makes me breathe easier. Means he's serious about you. I'm grateful for all you two have done for us. I don't think we'd have survived

without both of your support. But, as you said, life moves on, even if we're not ready for it. And I'm stoked for both of you."

"How do you think Tanya is going to take it?"

She worries her lip hard asking me that question.

"I'm sure she'll be happy too." I smile at her.

We chat on for a while until I have to go take Tanya to the hospital.

I hope I'm not wrong and Tanya is gonna be happy to see the two together. And if he doesn't make my mother happy, there'll be hell to pay.

For now, though, I'll keep it to myself. She has enough on her plate for now.

◊◊◊

We sit in the kitchen, coffees in front of us, when she looks up at me.

"Hey, Pen, what do you think? About settling out of court?"

"I don't know, Tan. What's your gut feeling?

"I think we should consider it. Going to court means having to give testimony, and the last thing I want is to relive it all. The nightmares are bad enough. I don't think I can deal with any more."

That makes me sit up and take notice. In all of my anger, I've forgotten how testifying in court might affect her. *Man, I'm a damn oaf.*

"Tan, I'm happy with whatever you want to do. If you want to settle out of court, then that's what we'll do."

"I thought about it on the way back. I'd like to take any money they offer and buy more cuddle cots for parents whose babies are born sleeping. It gives them more time to spend with them in a safe environment. I'd like to donate them in Becca's name."

"Baby, do you have any idea how proud I am of you? You'd be giving our baby girl a lasting legacy. I love that. Let's make some inquiries, call the lawyer and find out the next steps, yeah?"

Tanya's tear-filled eyes find mine as she nods at me.

I walk across to her, pick her up, and sit on the couch with her in my lap. She leans her head on my shoulder and sighs. Love and fierce protectiveness suffuse me as I hold her tight. This woman is something special, and she's mine, all mine. I'll never let her go.

We're still snuggled up as Mom's car screeches into our drive. I love my mom, but I haven't been in a car with her since I turned seventeen and passed my driving test. She drives like a complete lunatic, and just the thought of her driving makes me shudder.

Tanya jumps up.

"I'll get it, Pen, you stay where you are." She smiles at me. God, I love to see her smile again. It's been a long time.

She opens the door and steps out onto the porch. I can hear Mom and Masher talking, and then, "Ewww, gross!"

Tanya slams the door shut and rushes into the room.

"Oh my God, I just saw my dad snogging your mom's face off!"

She wrinkles her nose and rubs her eyes.

"Oh my God, I need eye bleach. I'll never get that picture out of my head," she exclaims, making retching noises while at it.

Mom and Masher step inside and close the door behind them.

"So, you have a dirty little secret." Tanya frowns at them. "How long has this been going on?"

"Oh, about a year," Mom answers, grinning at Tanya, while I hang over the couch, head down, trying not to laugh.

"A year?"

My woman can screech with the best of them. Masher covers his ears, but Mom just grins at her.

"Sorry, darlin', we would have told you earlier, but, you know, it's not been the time with everything happening. We made it official last night, so we're telling you now," Masher tries to explain.

"What he said," Mom chimes in.

"Daddy, you are such an idiot," Tanya rails on her father, then walks to Mom and pulls her into a tight embrace.

"Congratulations, Helen, can I call you Mom now? Let me warn you, he's a blithering idiot half the time and needs a tight rein. Thank you for taking him off my hands." With that she kisses Mom's cheek, and a bright mischievous smile lights her face and even reaches her eyes.

Masher fights the tears, and looking at me, he catches me wiping my sleeve over my eyes, smiling big.

He looks relieved Tanya's taken things so well, but I can't help myself and pipe up, "Please, can I call you Daddy now?"

The big man groans, turns, and bangs his head repeatedly against the wall.

31 — TANYA

“You lot will put me in an early grave, I swear. No, you may not call me daddy, nor father or father-in-law. Not happening. Have you lost your goddamn mind?”

Laughter explodes from deep inside me, and God, it feels so good.

“Give me that pizza, you heathen,” I command, and rip the squished pizza boxes out of Dad’s hands.

Helen follows me into the kitchen, and in no time, we’ve set the dining table

Dad and Pen are murmuring in the lounge.

“Come and get dinner,” I call out to them.

“Hey, girl, how are you doing now?” Mom asks.

“Better, Mom, a little better. We went to the hospital today; physically, I am okay now. They even suggested we could try again. Medically, they are right, but I found it insensitive. They made it sound as though I could replace Becca, when that’s just not possible. She’ll always be my daughter. They also offered bereavement counseling, which I agreed to. It helps that their counselor on contract is Darcy. I can schedule sessions with her directly and go to Debs’ Haven for them.”

She pulls me into a tight hug.

"I'm so proud of you, girl. Hey, if you feel up to it, would you like to meet with me and Chloe tomorrow? She's helping me plan a unique Christmas celebration. You could join us. It'd be great to have you on board, but only if you feel up to it." She winks at me.

"Mom, you are the second most devious person in this house, right after me, so yeah, I'll join you. Time to socialize again. Just sitting in the house does me no good. When and where?"

Mom gives me the info just as Dad and Pennywise enter. Pen grabs beers out of the fridge, hands them out, and we eat in amicable silence. I feel almost normal, and it's a fantastic feeling.

I lean forward onto my elbows and glance at my dad and Mom.

"You know I said about the hospital appointment, Mom? Well, that wasn't all. The hospital director turned up and apologized to us officially. You remember we put a complaint in and threatened to take them to court? Well, they want to settle out of court with us. How much for, I don't know yet, but I've decided whatever money they pay will go towards buying cuddle cots for the hospital. It'll enable parents to stay with their angel babies longer. What do you think?"

"Oh, love, I think it's a brilliant idea. I'll say it again, I'm so proud of you, how you are handling the situation and yourself. I'm sure we can get the club to help as well, to stock up funds if need be. Maybe have a Secret Santa for Christmas presents, and the boys put an equal amount of what they spend in a big piggy bank. What do you think?"

"Fab idea, Mom," Pennywise interjects. "I was only planning on spending twenty dollars on a present for Tanya, means a cheap Christmas for me."

Whack!

"Ouch." Pennywise rubs the back of his head.

"Twenty measly dollars? On my daughter? You better come up with something better than that, or else!"

"Yeah, yeah," Pen grumbles "I know, she'll kick my ass."

"Too right, with my steel toecap boots!" I glare at him before giggles burst free.

"Right, time for us to go. Don't want to be late again," Masher states.

"Yeah, well, we wouldn't have been late had you let me sleep last night," Mom sasses back.

"Lalalalala, not hearing this…"

Mom laughs at Pennywise sticking his fingers in his ears and squishing his eyes shut tight.

"Come on, Old Man, I know when we're not wanted." Mom snickers, grabs Dad's hand, and pulls him up.

"See what I got to put up with?" he mocks

"Self-inflicted, now deal with it," I reply.

I'm still smiling when the door closes behind them, though I wince at the screeching tires as they fade into the distance.

"Glad I don't have to ride shotgun with her." I shudder.

"Yeah, you and me both, sweetheart," Pen agrees, smirking. "Now, come here."

He crooks his finger at me with a come-hither move, which I'm only too happy to follow.

"Have I told you today how gorgeous you look? That longer hair really suits you and gives me something to hold on to." He winks.

"Really, is that so? And no, you haven't but thank you." I smile at him. "Are you buttering me up? What have you done this time?"

"I've done nothing. Been a good boy! Can't I tell my woman she's gorgeous?"

The indignation in his tone makes me bark out a laugh.

“Hey, not funny.” He leans forward, grabs hold of my sides and starts tickling me until I beg for mercy.

“Stop,” I gasp. “Please, please, stop, I can’t breathe.”

His smiling face hovers above me, eyes bright and mischievous.

“You have no idea how good it is to see you smile and hear you giggle. My spitfire is making a return, and I love it. Love you more than life itself.”

He leans in and touches his lips to mine in the sweetest, mind-blowing kiss I’ve ever received.

It stirs something in me. The need to be closer to him, to feel his skin, and I won’t lie, to devour him whole.

We got the okay, so nothing’s stopping us now.

Pen’s eyes mirror my own desire. He stands and holds out his hand to me. When I wrap my fingers around his, he leads me upstairs to our bedroom, undresses me with sure, tender movements, kissing me slowly, setting my body and soul on fire and freeing a deep longing in me that I haven’t felt in months.

When he has divested me of my clothing, and I’m in front of him in just my cotton panties and bra, he worships my body with his hands and mouth, trailing a cascade of kisses from my mouth to my neck, and down the center of my breasts. He reaches behind me and unclips my bra. Self-consciousness rips through me. My body has changed. My breasts are larger but softer; there's nothing perky about them anymore. Not to mention the stretch marks and pooch left behind from where I carried Becca.

"Hey, look at me." Pen's soft voice cuts through my ruminations. "You are beautiful. I love your softer curves, baby, from where you carried our daughter. These are marks of beauty."

He kisses my rounder hips, my stomach, every stretch mark he can find, and his hands roam my body with gentle caresses. He's blowing my mind, and his actions make me lose my embarrassment instantly. When he stands and lets me help him remove his clothes, I return every touch, every kiss with fervor. Administering to him what he did to me.

We fall onto the bed, holding each other, exchanging featherlight strokes, and tracing each other's bodies, unhurried, reaching a new level of intimacy. Warmth and desire suffuse me, sparking my arousal and gently raising my need for him. This is not fucking; this is making love to each other, and it feels so right. We explore each other unhurriedly, regaining our knowledge of one another and a closeness I find hard to describe.

When Pennywise finally grabs a condom and rolls it over his hard, pulsing manhood, I groan just watching him, pressing my thighs together so as not to come on the spot.

I'm so ready for him when he enters me in a slow, deep stroke and settles inside me, his mouth never leaving mine. Our tongues dance together, our breaths in sync, as though our hearts beat together to the same rhythm.

His deliberate, gentle strokes drive me insane, taking me higher and higher on a wave of desire and close interconnection like I've never experienced before.

The surrounding silence is filled only with whispered words of love and our whimpers and moans. When my climax hits, it literally blows my mind, making me see stars. Pennywise's long groan as he empties himself into the condom extends the fluttering and contracting of my walls, even though I think I can't take any more.

He leans up to put his weight on his elbows, so not to crush me, but I pull him back down to me.

"Pen, that was amazing. Best thing I've ever experienced," I whisper in his ear. "Stay with me for a little longer. I want to feel you inside me, our connection."

When he looks down at me, pure adoration shines out of his eyes.

“I’d love nothing more.”

32 — PENNYWISE

THREE MONTHS LATER

The new year brought a crap ton of snow. In fact, we had a white Christmas.

A Christmas no one will forget in a hurry. I'm still chuckling at the memories and the video recording that keeps finding its way onto the big screen in the bar.

Masher isn't as amused as the rest of us, but he takes it like a man.

We're on high alert, and all the Old Ladies have a brother following them whenever they leave the compound. Things are heating up again for us. Looks like the Restless Slayers have taken umbrage with us declaring independence.

Spen, of all people, has set up the patch over of a nearly defunct club in Madison, Wisconsin, so we now are the Mother Chapter of the Stormy Souls.

The Wisconsin guys seem okay, and Spen is staying with them, monitoring, setting them up right. His time as a Nomad is over; he's now treasurer of the Madison Chapter. He didn't want to come back to all the memories of Debs but keeps in touch with Ellie and Debs' Haven.

The second chapter pissed the Restless Slayers off even more, so all eyes are on the swivel, and Ferret is nailed to his chair and computer banks, trying his hardest to keep Ghost, the Restless Slayers' IT man, out of our systems.

There have been several attempted hacks. Luckily, Ferret is better than them. At least up to now.

Tanya not only has gone back to work at Zippy's tattoo studio but also took over her role with the Wild Pixies again. We try not to talk too much about club business at home. There we're just us—a couple in love.

Today is different, though. Raven and Ally have scheduled a joint meeting.

The brothers and sisters need to be put into the picture. What we discussed in our officers' meetings fills me with deep unease. I can't help but shake the premonition that something is coming for us, and hard.

Which would be shitty timing, since we're fresh out of prospects. Chris got patched in first thing after New Year's Day. We need to recruit, but it's the wrong time of year for it.

I mean, we're not actively riding in this freezing weather. So, what are our other options? Put an advert in the local newspaper?

I can see it now.

'If you want to join a 1%er club, get in trouble, and do all the shit jobs for a year, please send a resume to the Stormy Souls MC recruitment office?'

If only it were that easy.

I'm sitting in my office, twiddling my thumbs when the door crashes open, and Ferret looms in the frame, his face like thunder.

"Raven and Slender are busy. I need you in my office. Now!"

"Keep your hair on, man, I'm coming. Whose ass is on fire?"

"Mine!"

Cryptic as always. I shake my head and follow him to his office.

In the chair in front of Ferret's desk sits a young guy, somewhere between twenty and thirty, I guess. He looks fairly green behind the ears but is in riding gear and looks frozen solid. Like he was stupid enough to ride out here.

I grab a chair and plonk myself down next to Ferret.

"What's going on?" I ask, my eyes moving between Ferret and the young guy. Back and forth, back and forth, yet neither of them answers me.

"Ferret, why the fuck did you order me in here?"

"Yes, Daddy dear, why did you?"

The sarcasm rolling of that unknown biker hits me like a ton of bricks.

Hold on, what did he just say?

He looks at my tapes, stretches his hand out towards me and says, "Hi, Pennywise, I'm Kevin Owens, since my father here doesn't deem it necessary to introduce me."

"Hi, Kevin, pleased to meet you," I reply.

"Can we dispense with the pleasantries?" Ferret hisses through his teeth. "This little shit turned up here thirty minutes ago, claiming to be my long-lost son, asking to prospect." He growls. I've never heard Ferret growl nor seen him in such a state of fury. It's obvious he doesn't believe a word this Kevin guy is saying.

"Did the Slayers send you? To infiltrate us?" Ferret hisses.

I pull Ferret back into his seat as he's standing and leaning over the desk towards Kevin now, who just looks at Ferret, calm as a cucumber. Maybe there's more to him than meets the eye. He certainly has gumption to walk in here the way he did. Chris is at the gates. He's a great judge of character, and if he persuaded Chris, then he must have proof.

"Where are you from?" I ask him, ignoring Ferret, who is acting like a complete dick.

"I was born in Germany but moved to the US almost a year ago when I lost touch with my mother, who fled to the US two years previous. I've been searching all over for her, but with no luck. Last I heard she was in Superior. I did my research and found your club. Imagine my surprise when I found out that your IT guy is Zack Owens, the guy named on my birth certificate."

He shoves a folder across to me containing his passport, visa, birth certificate, the lot.

I quickly scan through the documents. They all look legit. Ferret rips them out of my hand and goes through them one by one.

"What is it you want from us?" I ask him, looking him straight in the eye.

"I'd like to prospect for you. In Germany, I was part of the Devil's Insurgence MC as a fully patched member." He stands, turns, and shows me the back of his cut, where the outline of previous patches is clearly visible.

"Out bad?" I ask, since there is no way we would touch him if he was, no matter who his father is.

"Nope, I left in good standing to search for my mother," he tells me, reaching into his inside pocket, taking out a letter, and handing it to me. It's a letter from his last Prez, singing his praises. If only half of this is true, I'd rip his arm off to join.

"I have to check up on this and take your references."

"Wouldn't expect anything else." He nods at me. "I would have spoken to your Prez directly, but he was unavailable," he adds. Shows he knows and respects the common courtesies.

"Fuck!" Ferret groans. He's hammering the keyboard like a man possessed. I can see the page he has opened. The German registry of births and deaths.

Kevin must take after his mother because he bears little resemblance to Ferret. He's tall, six-foot something, if I had to guess, with light-blond short hair. Ferret stands at just under six feet, has dark hair streaked with gray, and is as thin as a beanpole, where his son is broad built. Not sure whether he's podgy or muscled, he's wrapped up against the cold and hasn't bothered to unwrap himself so far.

"Regardless of whether you accept me as a prospect, I'd like to ask for your help. I need to find my mother. It's not like her to just disappear from the face of the earth. She's always kept in touch with me and my sister. My sister is going out of her mind with worry.

She's threatening to leave the UK, where she's studying, and come over here herself."

Ferret sits up straighter. "Anya is missing?"

"She's not gone by that name for a long time. She's Amy Peters now."

Ferret nods as I watch the conversation unfold in front of me. Ferret looks as though he's just been hit by a bus. I stand to my full height, staring at Kevin as though he's ridden in on a unicorn.

"Okay, man, follow me down into the bar. We'll see you get something to eat, and you can chill for a bit. There's a meeting in an hour. I'll make Raven, our Prez, aware, and we'll talk to you after. Does that sound okay?"

Kevin nods, stands, and follows me out of the door, leaving Ferret to do his thing and recover from the surprise reunion.

I knew he had a son. He sometimes spoke about his time in Germany in the army, though not often.

Kevin is following me down the stairs into the bar, and as I turn, he taps my shoulder.

"Any chance of getting a shower to warm up? I've been on the road the last week and could do with getting changed before taking you up on that offer of a hot meal."

"Sure, man, follow me." I lead him into one of the crash rooms we have for visitors and single guys who partake in the services the club girls offer.

"When you're done, see Clarity behind the bar. She'll show you to the kitchen. My mom will be in there; she'll see you right. I'll grab you when we're out of our meeting."

I nod at him and throw him the key to the crash room.

"Bathroom is the second on the right, down the corridor," I add, pointing in the general direction of the corridor.

"Thanks, Pennywise, appreciate it."

With that, I turn and head back downstairs, where the brothers and sisters file into church. It is oddly packed and strange to have women amongst us, especially my woman.

Since I know Raven does nothing without good reason, I prepare myself for the worst as I take my seat to Slender's right, waiting for the meeting to start.

33 — TANYA

It's been six months, yet it seems like yesterday. I don't think giving birth to my sleeping angel is something I'll ever get over. Slowly though, with the help of Mom, Dad, Pen, therapy with Darcy, and everyone else around me, I'm beginning to feel a little more human again, experiencing emotions other than grief.

Going back to work at Zippy's helps me regain a sense of normalcy, and being back as an active member of the Wild Pixies WMC takes my mind of my sorrow, affording me time to breathe.

Squashed into the Stormy Souls' church, a profound sense of dread comes over me as I take my seat between Vicki, Hazel, and Jules, with Caroline, Gypsie, and Greta to our right. Ally is at the top of the table, next to Raven, drumming her fingers impatiently, glaring around the room, her anger visceral.

It takes a few minutes until the room settles. I watch Pennywise step up to Raven, whispering. Raven's eyes go wide, his eyebrows hitting his hairline.

He nods at Pennywise, who retreats, taking his seat.

"Let's get started." Raven raises his voice above the chatter, and the room falls silent.

"Rainbow asked for a joint meeting, so I'll let her open."

Ally grabs the gavel and slams it onto the table.

"Sorry to drag all your sorry asses in here. I am well aware you've got your own issues. The Wild Pixies have been taking flak lately. We're well used to it, but it's getting out of hand. We'd like to ask the Stormy Souls MC for their support in this.

"Since you are now independent, I'd like to propose that the Wild Pixies WMC change dominant club to the Stormy Souls MC. We know each other well, and it makes sense. At least to me."

When I look around the table, most heads are nodding. A few remain indifferent, but hell, that's to be expected.

"Before any decision making, I'm gonna put you in the picture of what's been going on behind our side of the fence.

"We've always gotten shit from the male clubs, not taking us seriously. Snarking, ridiculing, and trying to gaslight us are just a few of the experiences we've had. Especially on rallies and outings where the Stormy Souls aren't present.

“This has recently escalated. By the Restless Slayers and two of the national big three.”

Ally nods at me. I stand, walk out of the door, grab the packet I left outside, and carry it back inside. I drop it on the table with a thud. All eyes are glued to me as I open it and drag out a huge funeral wreath decorated with ribbons depicting the Wild Pixies’ colors and brass knuckles tied to both ends.

Hazel, our SAA, reaches underneath the table, pulling out a white lily funeral arrangement, plonking it next to the wreath, with Vicki, Gypsie, and Greta following suit.

The silence in the room is deafening. Pennywise is up and out of his seat, so are Sparks, Slender, and Dawg.

“What the ever-loving fuck?” Dawg roars, staring a hole into Caroline’s forehead.

“And you didn’t think to share this shit with me?” Sparks snaps at Ally, who looks ready to kill him on the spot.

“Calm your shit!” I interrupt the chaos erupting around the table. “You’re not our dominant club, and as far as I recall, we’re not bound to justify ourselves to you. We’re approaching you now, since our dominant clearly doesn’t give a shit.”

I shove a letter I unearth out of my pocket towards Raven, who catches it and starts reading, his brows drawn together, face like thunder. When he finishes, he hands it to Slender, who passes it to Pennywise after reading it.

Pennywise glares at me, and I'm sure, if looks could kill, I'd be dead and buried right now. I stare right back, meeting his eyes, shrugging my shoulders at him, which of course incenses him further, but right now, I don't care. In this situation, I am here as the Wild Pixies Enforcer, not his Old Lady.

No doubt, I'll get to hear his private opinion when we're home alone, but for now, I don't care. I am his equal here, and the sooner he grasps that, the better. Just to ensure he gets the message, I tap my name and rank tape while staring him straight in the eye. An imperceptible nod tells me he's got my message, loud and clear.

"Ladies, before we get involved any further or at all, we need to discuss your application for the Stormy Souls MC to become your dominant club," Raven declares.

Ally nods at him. We all understand that rules need to be obeyed.

Wordlessly, Ally stands and leaves church, with the rest of us following, heading straight for the bar.

"That could have gone worse," Caroline snickers. "Although I'm not looking forward to the ass chewing from Dawg tonight at home." She sighs.

"Yup, I think most of us will be in the same situation." I wink at Caroline. "Be strong, woman, roar."

"Oh, don't worry." Caroline smirks. "If all else fails, it's a dry spell for him. That'll sort him out."

I can't help but cackle. "You are an evil bitch sometimes."

"Yup, and really, he loves me just like that. If I was little Miss Martha Jones, he'd be bored out of his skull. Gotta keep him on his toes." She shrugs.

I love Caroline. She's wild.

Her 'Hello, my lovely lady' appearance is deceptive.

She may give off the vibe of a kind, sweet lady, and most of the time she is, but man, that woman is tough. She wouldn't bring a knife to a gunfight. Caroline would be the one with a bazooka over her shoulder.

"Hey, Clarity, could I have a whiskey and coke, please?"

"Make mine a double," Ally groans from next to me.

Clarity stares at us, nods, and gets onto our orders. She seems like one of the nicer club girls. I can't stand Tequila. Ebony is okay, but Clarity I like.

She puts the drinks in front of us, a slight smile playing around her lips, but wrinkles her nose as Gypsie steps up. I got to say; I get it. Why Ally took her on, I don't understand. She looks like a homeless person most of the time. The only one of us who wears a denim cut, which if she ever took it off, I'm sure would stand on its own. It's that filthy. You can hardly make out the red and gold colors of our patch. Her long dark wavy hair is greasy, and man, she smells dire. Sometimes it's difficult to tell whether it's body odor or weed.

"Beer!" Talk about being rude, one of Gypsie's character traits. Besides being nosey and closed off to others. Her secretive manners rub me up the wrong way, so I try to stay as far away from her as possible.

Clarity puts a bottle of beer in front of Gypsie, and gets a "Thanks, bitch" for her troubles.

That does it.

"Gypsie, while you are in my house you will be courteous. Clarity's done nothing to you. In fact, she's brought you your beer, which is more than I'd have done. So, say thank you nicely, before I take you outside and teach you some manners."

I advance on her, grabbing her stinky cut by the lapels and lifting her until only her toes touch the floor.

She's only a half pint, five-foot something. How her little legs reach the floor when she's on her Harley is beyond me.

Her stare cuts through me like a knife. Her thoughts play out like a movie on her face. She'd love to punch me, hates me for reasons unknown to me.

"Thank you, Clarity," she sneers.

"Remember it for next time," I warn her before putting her back onto her feet.

34 — PENNYWISE

"Nothing ever goes easy for us, does it?" Raven sighs after the women leave the room. "This could poke a hornet's nest with a big shitty stick," he continues, sending the letter Tanya gave him round the table.

We received your request for support, and it is herewith denied. A proper 1%er MC looks after its own issues. Aside from the fact that you cannot prove that any of the threats you mentioned are real. Anyone could take pictures of pretty flowers and claim one of the proper MCs sent them. We no longer believe you are a proper MC, so are withdrawing our dominant status from you, informing you that you either notify us within fourteen days of your new dominant club, or we'll collect your patches, rendering you defunct.
Knuckles, President

Not only do we suddenly have a Wisconsin Chapter and beef with the Restless Slayers, now we're considering picking up a WMC as our support club. Honestly?

If it wasn't for a lot of our Old Ladies being members and our knowledge of what they are capable of, it would be a flat-out no.

That letter, though, makes me see red.

"What are your thoughts?" Raven throws into the room.

I stand.

"They've been invaluable to us, especially helping deal with the traffickers, and have supported us at every turn. I can't see how we could refuse?"

"Ally is a strong Prez. Her girls are solid," Sparks adds.

Chris, who's newly patched in, shudders.

"Apart from that thing, walking around in her stinking denim cut. She looks more like cousin It from the *Adams Family*, just It was cleaner," he exclaims.

"I won't vote for supporting a female MC," Moggy sputters. "MCs are for men, not little girls."

"What the fuck are *you* doing here, then?" Dawg replies.

The discussion goes back and forth for another ten minutes.

"Right, enough, boys," Raven bellows. "Let's vote!"

He points at Vegas, who starts us off.

"Aye."

Everyone votes Aye, apart from Moggy.

"Majority rules. The Wild Pixies WMC are our support club as of today. Ferret, get a communication to Knuckles. Let him know to stay where he is, if he values his nose unbroken."

Ferret nods at Raven's request.

"Better get them back in here and put them out of their misery," Raven says, to which Chris jumps up and walks out the door, returning a moment later with the Wild Pixies in tow, who sit back in their original places.

"Okay," Raven starts, looking at Ally. "We've agreed to take you on. Get with Masher next week to work out your subs rate and see you don't fall behind. There will also be a joint meeting every other month. You happy with that?"

Ally nods.

"Yup, more than happy. Thanks, boys, we won't let you down."

Ally stands and leaves church, followed by the rest of the Pixies.

They won't let us down; we're more than aware of what they are capable of. They've shown it time and time again, supporting us with the breaking of the human traffickers last year.

"Ferret has approached me about a personal issue of his. Listen up and keep an open mind." Raven restarts the official part of the meeting. "Ferret, over to you."

Raven nods in Ferret's direction and the large screen behind Raven springs to life, showing a picture of a light-blond-haired guy in his twenties or thirties.

"This is Kevin, my biological son," Ferret starts to gasps from all corners of the room.

"And before you ask, yes, I knew I had a child, but I haven't seen him since he was about eighteen months old. It was his mother's and my joint decision to sever contact, to save him from the to-and-fro tango we were dancing at the time. He needed stability, and it wasn't something I could provide. I was too fucked up, and to be honest, so was she."

Ferret looks around the table.

"Essentially, he's as much a stranger to me as he is to you."

I grab the letter I kept safe, and shove it towards Raven, who unfolds it and reads.

"Devils' Insurgence MC, huh? I know of them. They're about the only German club that bothers to come to Sturgis. What does he want?"

"He's searching for his mother, who was last known to be in Superior," I explain. "He wants to apply to prospect for us."

"Ferret, have you checked his credentials and history? Full background check?"

"Yes, Raven, sure have. It's all legit. Also took the liberty to call his Prez. I know that's your job, but I had to know whether he really is who he says he is. His old Prez was singing his praises. He was a sound brother to them. A patched member for four years," Ferret answers, looking sheepish. Going over Raven's head is not a wise move.

"I've had Pennywise put him in one of the crash rooms, so you can meet him after the meeting," Ferret adds.

"Ferret, you put a complete stranger into our house?!"

Raven's voice could cut glass. He's pissed.

"You and I will have words later!" he growls, pointing his finger at Ferret in a creepy way.

Man, I wouldn't want to be Ferret right now.

"Let's move on to the other elephant in the room, if you are not too busy doing your own thing, Ferret?"

The blond guy disappears from the screen and is replaced by the faces of Fury, Ghoul, Ghost, and their new SAA Jinx, who's supposedly a true son of a bitch.

"Fuck," Masher spits, "Jinx? Seriously? He's the biggest dick around and loves getting into pissing contests. He's not happy unless he can prove he's got the biggest dick."

"At least we know who we're dealing with here," Dougal throws in.

"Quiet, assholes, let Ferret speak!" Raven thunders.

"So, here we have the new leadership of the Restless Slayers," Ferret begins. "As Masher rightly noted, their new SAA isn't their best choice, but who am I to judge? Ghost has tried several times to hack our systems, unsuccessfully, may I add, but if it wasn't for my contact's assistance, this could have gone entirely different."

That has all of us sitting up and paying attention. Ferret is one of the best in his field. If he had to request assistance, Ghost is much better than we thought.

"I propose we invite Specter to check out our systems, in case I missed anything."

Sparks whistles through his teeth.

"Man, that guy is a legend."

Ferret grins.

"Specter is legend. We met while stationed abroad, a fellow gamer. We've known each other for thirty-odd years. Specter is a first-rate hacker and consults for the government as a freelancer."

"I couldn't think of anything worse than having a government agent in here," Moggy pipes up.

"Why, Moggy, got something to hide?" Slender needles him.

"No, but we are a 1%er club. Who can guarantee that Specter won't just be here to infiltrate and sell us out?" Moggy argues.

"I'll vouch for Specter," Ferret quickly says.

"Are you sure this step is necessary?" Raven cuts to the chase.

"Afraid so, unless we want Ghost to play havoc with us in the long run."

"Here's what I suggest. Ferret, do you have our more… sensitive information on a separate hard drive?" Raven asks, glaring at Moggy, who's muttering under his breath.

"Of course," Ferret replies.

"Okay, disconnect and store them in the bunker while Specter is here, so there's no chance of him accidentally getting into them. Once that is done, ask him to come and check our system."

Ferret gets out his phone and shoots off a message. The reply is almost instant.

"Specter'll be here the day after tomorrow. Gives me time to move everything sensitive into the bunker." Ferret grins at Raven.

The incessant ringing of Raven's and Vegas' cells interrupts Raven, who's hovering the gavel over the table. He places it down, grabs his phone, and answers. Vegas follows suit.

As if on cue, they both jump up, cussing filling the air as they run towards the door, with the rest of us following them through the clubhouse, out into the parking lot, and toward the gates. Where a shaking Meghan, Fury's daughter, is holding up Ghoul, who looks as though he's been through a meat grinder, and begging us to let her in.

Raven nods at Ratchet, who's on guard duty, to open the gates. Vegas is on his cell, and less than a minute later, Chloe is jogging down towards us, carrying her medical bag, followed by Tanya, who stops dead by my side and gasps.

"What the fuck?" she whispers.

I leave her standing at the open gates and check over Meghan's car. Ferret joins me with a bug sweeper, just to make sure.

Ghoul is naked from the waist up, and as I drive Meghan's car into the compound, I catch a glimpse of his back. The bastards have burned his patch off!

They threw him out bad. *What the fuck?*

I watch as Tanya and Slender grab Ghoul under his arms and drag him through the clubhouse and into a crash room.

Chloe issues orders, which send Sparks and Moggy running. Meghan, sobbing, sinks to the floor, shaking like a leaf in a storm.

Raven walks up to her, pulls her up, and helps her into the clubhouse, which is now rammed with Pixies and brothers.

Raven deposits a distraught Meghan into a chair, and Mom appears, holding out a mug of coffee, smelling suspiciously of brandy.

"Here, love, drink this." She places the mug in front of Meghan, who lifts it and takes a mouthful, shuddering as the taste of brandy hits her, but sipping it anyway.

Raven takes a seat, with Mom sitting next to Meghan.

"Sweetheart, what's going on?" she gently questions Meghan, her hand rubbing up and down her back soothingly.

"Dad has gone mad." Meghan looks at Raven, tears filling her bright blue eyes, flowing over and rolling down her cheeks. It's eerie how she doesn't sob. Those silent tears catch me right in my heart, which goes out to Meghan. She's only nineteen, still a child really, and has seen and experienced more than any kid her age should.

"Ghoul wanted out. I overheard Dad telling Jinx to deal with him. The club is different now. They got into drugs, and most of the time, Dad is off his head high. So are most of the brothers. I had to leave when he caught me eavesdropping and beat me black and blue."

She pulls up her sleeves, exposing finger-shaped bruises all over her arms. But when she lifts her top a few inches, her ribs are covered in bandages, and what isn't covered is bruised so badly the sight makes me want to wring Fury's neck.

She takes in a shuddering breath.

"I followed Jinx and the prospects when they dragged Ghoul outside and beat the hell out of him. Then, Jinx brought out a blowtorch," she sobs, "and burned his tattoo straight off his back." Meghan retches at the memory.

Mom leans in and draws Meghan into her arms. That's all it takes for loud sobs to break free. Mom shoots Raven and me a look. We both nod at her, knowing that she wants us to remove Fury's ass from this world for what he's done to the person he swore to protect above all else. His daughter.

"They just left him in the dirt," Meghan sobs. "He was Dad's best friend, and he left him in the dirt!"

She takes a deep breath.

"I brought him round and helped him onto the backseat of my car. I didn't even bother to grab any of my stuff but drove straight out the gate without looking back. Praying Ghoul wouldn't die before getting to you. I didn't know where else to go."

She turns her tear-stained face to Raven, who nods and tells her, “You did the right thing, Meghan. There’ll always be a place for you here.”

35 — TANYA

I'm on my way to the house when I hear a car horn sound from outside the gates. Curiosity leads me back down towards the gate, where I see Meghan's car outside the gate, the brothers running out from the clubhouse, and Meghan struggling to hold onto someone. It's hard to tell who it is from this distance. All I can see is a male shape leaning heavily on Meghan, body stripped from the waist up, sagging forward. When he lifts his head, shock runs through me like an electric current.

"What the fuck?" I whisper to myself as I recognize Ghoul, the Restless Slayers' VP. A man I've known for more than half of my life.

Raven motions to open the gate, and before Pen can stop me, I step forward with Slender, grab Ghoul under the arms, and together we carry him into the clubhouse, straight into one of the crash rooms. His body is battered and bleeding from wounds I recognize as Jinx's signature method of torture. But I nearly vomit when I see the full extent of his flayed back.

Christ, they burned his tattoo off with a blowtorch!

We gently place him face down on the bed, and I race down the corridor, emptying the contents of my stomach into the nearest toilet I can find.

By the time I get back to Ghoul, Chloe's arrived and is spreading the contents of her medical bag onto the dresser in the room. First, she sets up an IV, which will help rehydrate him. He has lost a lot of blood and fluids through the weeping burn on his back. Without hesitation, she adds a pain killer and antibiotic to the IV.

"Ghoul, I'm going to administer a sedative so I can clean your wounds and treat them," she explains to Ghoul, who doesn't answer, but simply nods.

I watch as she draws up the injection and administers it.

Slowly, Ghoul's staccato breathing evens out. Chloe dons her sterile gloves and gets to work, removing the loose, scorched flaps of skin off Ghoul's back. I pass her what she needs on autopilot. She asks, and I reach. Once she's done with his back, she smothers it in antibiotic salve and dresses it.

A very pale looking Slender and I then turn Ghoul over onto his back. A groan escapes the still heavily sedated Ghoul. Now I understand why Chloe sedated him. No one could stand that kind of pain. Chloe makes short work of Ghoul's front, and the cloth she's cleaning him with has to be changed three times because of the amount of blood it soaks up.

There are at least ten deep lacerations on his front, which Chloe stitches up and dresses. Then she sets his nose. The crunching noise nearly has me vomiting again.

Together, we remove all the pillows from the bed, undress Ghoul's lower half, and replace his dirty, bloody clothes with a pair of Slender's boxers and joggers.

"He needs to stay on his front for the foreseeable future," Chloe says as she washes her hands in the handbasin in the room. "Someone needs to keep a real close eye on him. If infection sets in, he'll be up shit creek. I wouldn't want to explain his injuries in the ER department. I want to find out what took place. Ghoul is one of the nicest guys I've ever met. I consider him a friend. No one hurts my family or my friends. No one."

A shiver runs down my back hearing Chloe's diamond-hard voice. Her eyes promise retribution. Chloe isn't a member of the Wild Pixies. Her being Raven's Old Lady would create too much of a conflict of interests.

But the way she holds my gaze tells me that she's about to step out of her Old Lady bubble. Raven's gonna have a conniption first, then shit a brick. I've never seen Chloe like this. Ever!

"Let us handle this!" Slender picks up on the violent vibes rolling off Chloe like avenging waves.

"You better!" she growls at Slender, her eyes never leaving mine. "Find someone to stay with him. He'll wake up soon, and with luck, the pain killer I added to his IV should kick in. He'll be woozy for a while. Let me know when the infusion runs low, and I'll put up another one."

Chloe throws everything lying around back into her bag. She slams the door behind her so hard it has me and Slender wincing.

"Shit!" Slender punches the wall.

"Yup, shit indeed. Chloe's riled. It's not good."

"I stay with him for now. You find someone to take over from me," Slender orders, and I don't bother telling him he's not the boss of me but leave the room in search of Raven.

I find him in the bar, nursing a drink, with Meghan and Mom sitting beside him.

"Raven, we need someone to sit with Ghoul, twenty-four seven. He's in a bad way."

Raven whistles, and all heads shoot up.

"Volunteers for twenty-four-hour guard shifts for Ghoul," he hollers.

Chris nods at Raven, a determined glint in his eyes, and says, "I'll take first watch," before heading upstairs to the crash rooms.

"I'll take second," Christmas adds, the words hanging heavy in the air.

"I'm third," Moggy speaks up this time, and his offer has me raising my eyebrows. It takes less than two minutes for the rota to be filled.

Everyone chips in. Pixies, Souls, it makes no difference. We all take our turns.

I find a chair and pull it up, sitting between Mom and Meghan, whose silent tears seem to be unceasing.

"Hey, sweetheart, I'm here now. Come here."

I wrap my arms around her, rocking her like a small child. I can't imagine what's going on in her head. Not only the worry about Ghoul, but everything else she must have witnessed. Fury never protected his daughter from what happened in the club. But judging by her inconsolable, diminutive figure, she must have seen more than any person should. Certainly not the club princess.

"Come on, honey, you can stay with us," I tell her, the warmth of my hand a contrast to the chill in her skin as I carefully pull her to her feet.

She clings to me like a little monkey. I give Pen a pointed stare, and with tender care, he gently disengages her arms from my neck, scoops her into his arms, and carries her out the door, her small body limp against his. I stroke her head the entire way home.

Meghan is still crying as we place her on the bed in a guest bedroom. I nod at Pen, who silently leaves the room. A few minutes later, Chloe arrives. She gives Meghan a sedative, and slowly, her sobs become hiccups, then sniffles, before she closes her eyes and drifts off to sleep.

"Fucking assholes!" Chloe rants in the kitchen, where I've pulled out three glasses and filled them two fingers deep with whiskey. Straight. No ice, no nothing. We each take a glass and down it. Immediately, Chloe holds hers out for a refill.

"I'm gonna kick Raven's ass to the curb if he doesn't do something about them," she continues.

Both Pen and I know she doesn't mean it. She loves Raven to distraction, but that she threatens it, as empty as the threat is, speaks volumes.

When Chloe grabs her stuff and leaves, with the instruction to call her immediately if Meghan needs a top-up, Pen and I fall onto the couch. Long ago, we agreed not to take club business home with us, no matter which club it concerns. Sitting forward, with my elbows on my knees, I stare at him.

"Once, just once, I wish there was peace all around us," I huff out.

"Agreed. I'm getting sick of this shit. So much crap has landed on us the last few years, it's not even funny anymore," he replies, standing and refilling our whiskey glasses.

When he plonks himself down next to me, I draw my knees up and snuggle into his side, switching the stereo on with the remote, catching a live rendition of Little Big Town's "Life in a Northern Town."

We sit back in silence and just listen; the music calming both of our frayed nerves.

"Hey, Pen?"

"Yes, honey?"

"I think I might be ready."

He sits up and turns towards me, his eyes searching my face, for what, I'm not sure.

"Are you sure? There's a lot going on right now. Maybe it'd be better to wait?"

"If we wait and let the club business dictate our private life, we'll never be ready, Pen. I talked this through with Darcy. She said that there's never a right time for kids. There'll always be things cropping up: money issues, relationship issues, outside influences, and so on. And you know what? She's right.

"We don't have money or relationship issues. We've gone through the worst imaginable experience and survived it. Together. I don't want to wait anymore. I want Becca to have a brother or sister we can share her with." With my eyes glued to Pen's, I rush out the thoughts I've been mulling over for the last week.

"Baby, I can't think of anything I'd like more than to fill your belly with my babies. As long as you're sure?" Pen's smile reassures my own insecurities.

"I'm sure." A smile creeps on my face as I realize my statement is completely true.

I yelp, surprised, as he lifts me and pulls me on top of him, stretching out on the couch.

"Baby, I love you more than anything else in the world. You are mine, always and forever," he whispers against my lips, before drawing me into a deep, tender kiss, which makes my toes curl and my heart melt.

36 — PENNYWISE

Tanya's speech hits me like an arrow straight through the heart. I'd have happily waited another six months, or even six years, for her to be ready. Her telling me she's ready to try again makes all the club business shit fall right off my shoulders, and now, all I want is to be close to her, be inside her.

I want to make love to my woman until she forgets all the troubles that surround us.

"Baby, I love you more than anything else in the world. You are mine, always and forever," I whisper against her lips, kissing her with all the emotion I've bottled inside. My heart opens wide and expands to treble its size, or at least, that's what it feels like.

I roll us over, so I am on top of her, my lips never leaving hers, my tongue gliding against hers, slowly tasting every inch of her. She tastes of sunshine and heaven and all things her. I can't get enough.

Sitting up, I straddle her and pull her T-shirt over her head. My eyes feast on the round globes of her tits, nipples pebbled, begging for my attention. I lift my arms, helping her whip off my top, and the feeling of her hands on my bare chest drives me wild, as does the scent of her perfume.

My hands glide up her sides, finding their way to her luscious breasts of their own accord. Blindly, I lean forward, sucking one of her nipples into my mouth and groaning at the feel of her pebbled skin. The salty taste of her essence whips me into a frenzy. With my dick throbbing hopelessly behind the confines of my jeans, I stand, help Tan up from the couch, and pull her behind me in my rush to get to our bedroom.

I need to be inside her, but not on the couch. My child won't be conceived in a quickie.

I'll take my damn time to worship her.

Tan's giggles behind me spur me on. I drag her through the bedroom door, closing it behind us, and push her up against the cool wood. My hands rest above her head, caging her in, while my mouth descends on hers, relaying the burning inferno flowing from me to her in just one kiss.

Fire running through my veins has me groaning her name; her little whimpers fan the already out-of-control flames.

She pushes her hands to my chest and walks us backwards until my knees hit the edge of the bed. Her piercing hazel eyes are almost black with need. I drop to my knees, sniffing along her crotch. Her sweet essence tells me she's soaking for me, as does the dark patch on her jeans.

Reaching up, I pop the button and lower the zipper, dragging the skin-tight denim down her legs, taking her black boy shorts with them, and inhaling deeply.

"Pen, please."

"Please, what, my firecracker?"

"I need you." The hoarse whisper of her voice does nothing to calm my stone-hard cock, making him jump behind my fly.

"You take what I give you, baby." My own voice sounds like it's been sandpapered.

I undo her boots and strip away her clothes with them, throwing them behind me. Standing and turning us, so it's her against the bed now, I push against her hips, causing her to plop down onto the mattress. Falling back to my knees, I open hers, exposing her to my gaze.

"This is the prettiest pussy I've ever seen, and it's all mine," I growl, lean forward, and feast.

Lapping my tongue through her folds, her taste explodes in my mouth. My groan against her pussy draws more whimpers out of her.

Licking and sucking, I go wild, ravenous for my Old Lady. Lifting one leg over my shoulder, she opens further to me, and I proceed to torture her with small licks and soft kisses on her clit.

Looking up over the expanse of her sweat-slicked skin, I catch her eye as she props herself up to watch me between her legs.

"Do you want to come?"

"Don't ask stupid questions, Pen. Please make me come," she whines.

A deep chuckle rises from me before I lean down and suck her clit into my mouth hard, gently biting down.

That's all it takes. Shouting my name, she comes beautifully for me, coating my face with her juices. I love it when my woman gushes on me. I lap up her release, stand, and hurry to get my jeans off. My strangled dick finally springs free, hitting my stomach, and I breathe a sigh of relief.

Tan shuffles up the bed and opens her legs wide as I sink down onto her, bracketed by her knees and with her arms coming around me, holding on tight. Without guidance, my throbbing, leaking cock finds its home as I sink into her, her tight heat pulling a growl out of me. Kissing her deeply, I know she can taste herself on my lips, and the thought turns me on so much more.

Our kiss deepens, all urgency suddenly forgotten as I slowly work my way in and out of her tight pussy, which strangles my cock with its constant flutters. Her whispers against my lips hit me deep.

"Love you, Pen, always. You are mine, and I'm yours. I'll love you for the rest of my life. Truly, madly, deeply."

My chest expands to bursting point by her sweet words. Our motions slowing, we tenderly rock into each other. Minimal movements are enough to set us both on fire. The experience is so deep and so profound it blows my mind. With languid strokes of our bodies and our hands caressing one another, we slowly rise to the pinnacle, and when we come together, it is with blinding intensity. My head explodes, the shards scattering far and wide across the universe.

"Pen," Tan whispers as soon as she's caught her breath. "That was…"

"I know, baby. The earth tilted on its axis for a moment there," I whisper back, peppering her face with kisses. When my lips find hers again, I breathe her breath as she breathes mine.

"Love you so much, Tan, so much more than I could ever explain."

"Same, Pen. You are my everything."

I roll over and open my bedside drawer, grabbing the small box out of it I've had in there for over a year.

I open it and hold it out to her, muzzling her neck.

"Baby, will you make me the happiest man alive and marry me?"

Tanya's eyes grow wide as she takes in the diamond-encrusted onyx ring. Tears fill her eyes and begin rolling down her cheeks.

"Yes, Pen, a thousand times yes! I'll marry you!"

Before I can put the ring on her finger, she throws herself at me, rolling us over, straddling me. She kisses me over and over again.

"Keep still, woman," I grumble, trying to catch her hand so I can place the ring on her finger.

She sighs, staring at the onyx and diamonds.

"It is so beautiful and unusual. I love it, Pen."

A blinding happiness radiates from Tanya, and I can't look away. She's stunning.

I pull her down, kissing her deeply, my heart lighter than it's been in months.

37 — TANYA

I'm so happy, I'm bouncing along like Tigger. Not even the unrest at the clubhouse can dampen my spirits. I feel for Ghoul, he's a good man, but if I allow myself to take all the current issues on board, it'll eat away at me until there's nothing left. And if there's one thing I've learned through my experience with Becca, it's that life is too short, and fate can be a cruel mistress.

So, I've decided, for me, it's important to find a small slice of happiness in this life, since it's not a dress rehearsal. No one knows what'll happen tomorrow, so you gotta live for today.

Last night was by far the happiest of my life. Not only the amazing, mind blowing, intense sex we had, but for Pen to propose, fills me with happiness to the point I feel I may burst.

I grab my bike gear. Thankfully, it's getting warmer now. I wrap up against the cool air and ride down to Ally's diner, where Terrie, Chloe, Ellie. Ashley, and Sarah are already waiting for me.

Ellie's brought Tucker, that gigantic dog of hers, who almost reaches up to my hip. As soon as I sit down, he lays his massive head on my knee, staring at me with his soulful, chocolate brown eyes. I can't help but grin at him.

"Who's a good doggy? Who's a good boy? Yes, you are, I know, Tucker, good boy." I ruffle his fur and the baby language I spurt out at him makes him tilt his head, looking at me as if to say *"Have you lost your mind?"*

Ellie stares at me, lost for words. I normally stay well away from Tucker; I'm not really a dog person. So, my loving on him raises eyebrows.

"What's wrong with you?" Sarah stares at me as though I've grown two heads.

"Nothing, can't I love on my favorite boy?"

"I thought that was Pennywise." Ashley cackles.

We're interrupted by Caroline storming in, face like thunder as she dumps a bag on the table.

"Fucking stupid idea!" she complains.

"What set your hair on fire this morning?" Terrie asks, eyebrows hitting her hairline.

"I'll tell you, but you gotta promise not to laugh."

Oh? This'll be good. I rub my hands together, waiting for the big revelation, putting mine on hold.

"I've been trying to knit Dawg a jumper." No sooner does her statement hit, we all cackle.

"Shut up, you bitches. I've been at it for two and a half years, and it still ain't finished. The sleeves are killing me!" Caroline grouses.

"Do they sneak up on you at night, wrapping around your neck, pulling tight?" Ally asks, appearing at the table with a tray of coffee mugs.

"Ha, ha, hilarious. I'm just about ready to throw this shitty thing in the garbage and tell Dawg to fuck himself when he needles me about it," Caroline groans and swipes her bag off the table onto the floor.

"No, Tucker, leave it!" Ellie shouts, and as we all turn, we catch sight of Tucker, knitting bag in his mouth, disappearing under the table behind us, shaking the bag as though it was a rabbit on steroids!

Caroline jumps up and crawls under the table, where a tug of war ensues.

"Give it back, you monster dog!" she shouts at Tucker, who just pulls harder, dragging Caroline out of sight under the table.

"No, you nasty dog! Give it to me! Tucker, I swear, I'll take you to the groomers and have you shaved bare! Ouch!" A loud clonk lets us know that she's hit her head on the tabletop.

"Tucker, I'm warning you!"

"Woof, woof," Tucker barks at Caroline, in obvious disagreement, before he backs out from under the table, still pulling on the bag, dragging Caroline behind him, who is still clinging like the Devil to the other end of the bag.

We howl like hyenas, tears of laughter running down all our faces, and Ellie shouts, "No, Tucker, bad boy, let go!"

Tucker gives an almighty pull. Caroline losing her grip and falling on her ass, does nothing to calm us down.

Ellie finally wrangles the bag away from Tucker, which, by this time, has an enormous hole in it. When Ellie sticks her hand inside the bag, pulling out a heap of chewed up wool and jumper pieces, she shudders.

"Ew, Tucker, really?"

Dog saliva drips off the end of her fingers.

Welp, there's no saving that jumper now.

"I hate dogs!" Caroline growls, plonks herself down on a seat, turning her back to Tucker, who looks mightily pleased with himself.

"Why don't you buy Dawg a similar jumper and tell him you finished it? Just remember to cut the store labels out." Terrie shrugs.

"Crap, why didn't I think of that?" Caroline whines.

Ally grabs a large bone-shaped cookie from behind her counter and gives it to a tail wagging Tucker.

"It's dog safe," she reassures Ellie.

"What do you think about Ghoul?" Ashley asks, looking at me.

"Don't know, and for now, I don't care either. I've got other, more important things on my mind" I answer, grinning and laying my hand on the table, waiting for them to notice.

Chloe is first.

"Oh my God, Tanya, what's that rock on your hand? Jesus, I need sunglasses. The sparkle is blinding!" She laughs.

"Does that mean?" Sarah winks at me.

"Yes, Pen proposed last night, and I said yes!"

The intensity of the squeals, claps, and giggles, makes me want to stick my fingers in my ears, but that would be bad form, not to mention look ridiculous. The girls nearly hug me to death. I think we all needed good news.

"As we're discussing news, I've got some of my own," Sarah pipes up, looking sheepish. "I didn't want to say anything, but I won't be able to hide it much longer. Dougal knocked me up."

"You had to go there, didn't you?" Ashley sulks. "Stealing my thunder. I've got another bun in the oven too, I think," she adds, not looking too happy.

"That's great news." I smile at both of them. And for the first time in months, I mean it. I am truly happy for my friends.

"Alex is only six months old," Ashley complains. "I'm on birth control, too. Damn Vegas and his super swimmers!"

"Leo is going on fourteen. How do you think I feel? I thought I was done with stinky diapers. Now I gotta start all over again," Sarah clips back.

"Erm," Ellie says quietly, a blush coloring her cheeks, "I'm four months along."

We all gape at her, our chins nearly hitting the table.

"Say what?" Ashley blurts.

"I'm pregnant." Ellie smiles. "It's a boy."

They all suddenly stare at me.

"Sorry, Tanya, that was insensitive." They look so contrite. I can't help but smirk as I put them out of their misery.

"We're trying again, so don't worry. Wouldn't it be cool if all our kids could grow up together?"

Terrie jumps up, comes round the table and hugs me tight.

"I'm so happy for you, Tanya."

"Mom, you might wanna let go of her and let her breathe," Chloe teases.

"Err, ladies, while we're all exchanging news"—Ally sighs—"Sparks and I are going for a trial separation."

And just like that, our happy balloon pops.

"Ally, I'm so sorry. What happened?" I ask.

"Too many arguments. Sometimes, I feel I don't even know him anymore." Ally pulls up a chair and sits. "Part of it is because of Wild Pixies' club business. Part of it is, we've just grown apart over the years. We've been married for ten, straight out of high school."

Ashley nods. "I remember."

"But you seem so good together?" Sarah looks at Ally, whose sadness is written all over her expressive face. She swallows hard.

"Appearances can be deceptive. You only see what we want you to see. What goes on behind closed doors is a different matter. I wish I could say it's all his fault, but it's not. It takes two to tango, and our tango has gotten more and more out of step."

I stand and wrap Ally in a tight hug.

"You're my girl, my family," I whisper in her ear. "I'm here for you, no matter what time of day or night. You've been my rock, Ally, through the worst time of my life. Now, let me be yours."

She imperceptibly nods, and I step back to let the other girls support Ally, while I watch, immensely proud of my family. Blood and sisters from another mister.

Although I admit as pride swells in me, I also contemplate ways of making Sparks suffer.

Seems the old Tanya has just made her reappearance and is back in action.

38 — PENNYWISE

The sudden change in Tanya is almost unbelievable. If this is the results of Darcy's counseling, I'll be happy to pay her double what the hospital is paying her. For the first time in months, I feel as though an enormous boulder has lifted from my shoulders.

I can't get the way we made love last night out of my head. It was so different; it felt… special. As a guy, it feels weird to wax lyrical about my love life, but this was so far removed from anything else we ever did, I just can't help but feel deep in my soul that we created a life last night.

Not to mention how overwhelmed I felt having sex for the first time without a condom in months. Here I am in town, trying to withdraw some money from the ATM, to get Tan a little present from an artisan jewelry shop. The bracelet I saw in their window drew me like a bee to honey. I couldn't believe when I tried to pay for it, and they didn't accept card payment. Cash only.

I watch my card disappear into the slot, punch my numbers in, and wait for my balance display on the screen before I take out cash. I'm nothing if not studious. We are well-off, don't get me wrong. Between Tanya's wages from the tattoo shop and my monthly cut, we've built up quite the little nest egg. I'm talking six figures here.

The account balance pops up, and my eyes bulge out of my head. Shit, the bank must have made a mistake. Aborting the transaction and grabbing my card out of the slot, I walk inside the bank and ask for a customer service agent.

"Good morning, Mr. Nixom. How can I be of assistance?"

"Good morning"—I look for her name tag—"Grace. I've just tried to withdraw money from my account and my balance seems excessively high. Could you double check and tell me what's going on?"

"Certainly, Mr. Nixom. Follow me over to the desk, please, and we'll get you sorted." Her flirty smile is getting on my nerves already.

Stupid bitch. What is it about women and a man in leather with a cut on his back?

Disgruntled, I follow her to the desk she sashays to and take a seat.

"Could I have your card for a moment, please? It has all the details I need to check. Oh, and could I see some ID, please?"

I hand over my card and driver's license.

"Thank you, Mr. Nixom. This will just take a moment."

I nod at her, nausea setting in at her over sweet irritating voice.

"Could I have a printout of the most recent transactions, please?" Better I ask her now than having to prolong this encounter.

"Sure, not a problem."

God, her saccharine smile is getting on my last nerve.

"Everything seems in order, Mr. Nixom. The last transfer in was from the Duluth Hospital Trust."

I stare at the printout she hands me and nearly fall off my chair.

One point five million dollars.

"Thank you, Grace," I stutter out before standing out of my seat and shaking her stretched out hand. "You've been very helpful."

"You are welcome, Mr. Nixom, here is my number"—she scribbles something on a piece of paper—"in case you need any further help."

She winks at me again, pushing the paper into my hand. I can feel my eyebrows narrow in irritation on their own accord

“I don’t think that will be necessary. My fiancée will be happy to learn you’ve tried so hard though,” I growl at her, making sure she understands she definitely overstepped.

Walking outside, I push my card back into the machine, take a deep breath, and withdraw what I need without looking at the balance again.

Returning to the shop, I pay for the bracelet and ask for an angel charm to be added to it as well as a motorcycle one. Then, I wait for it to be wrapped and place it deep into my pocket on the way out.

I know Tanya is at Ally’s. I saw her bike outside when I rode in, so I ride over, park next to hers, and walk into the diner. All the ladies are congregated at a table in the back. Caroline spots me first.

“Hey, Pennywise. What brings you here? Thinking about changing clubs?” She smirks at me.

Caroline is an exceptional woman. I like all our old ladies, but I have a soft spot for Caroline.

“No, darlin’, just come to see my Old Lady before I head back to work.”

Ally stares at me with a weird expression on her face.

“What’s up?” I look at her, knowing instantly something is off. Very off.

"You seen Sparks today?"

"No, Ally, why? What's wrong?" Ally is the strongest woman I know, so to see her puffy eyes and realize she's obviously been crying, has me worried.

"Can you send someone over to come and collect his stuff? He's moving back into his cabin."

It feels as though I've been hit by a semi.

What the hell is going on?

"We're having a trial separation." Ally adds, her nails digging into her balled fists.

"Oh, Ally, I'm so sorry. Do you need me to whip the asshole into shape?"

"If you think it'll help, be my guest."

"I'll sort him out," I promise before turning to my Old Lady. "Tanya, sweetheart, can I grab you for a minute? I need to show you something."

"Sure, babe, what is it?" She stands from her seat, squeezing past Ellie. Her delectable ass bending over the table has me hard within seconds. *Down, boy!*

Dusting my leathers off, I lead Tanya to another table and sit down with her opposite me.

"Tan, I went to the bank earlier. You need to see this." I hand her the statement just as her cell rings.

"Hang on, babe, it's the lawyer."

She looks at me as she answers the call.

"Yes, this is Tanya Frost. Yes, that's right. We agreed to the settlement. Really? You have? How much?"

Watching Tanya closely, her face turning pale reveals she just heard the figure.

"Are you shitting me? Oh my God!" Her screech is so high pitched I fear she might shatter the windows.

"Yes, thank you so much. If you could email me your bill, I'll pay it as soon as I've received your invoice. Sure, thank you so much."

Tanya is panting as she ends the call, her mouth hanging open, eyes wide. I smile as I reach over, closing her mouth with my finger.

"You'll catch flies, honey."

"Shut the front door!"

"What?" I burst out laughing.

"Well, since I'm certain you impregnated me last night, I thought I'd try to curb my cussing." She grins at me.

"Wow! One point five million dollars, that is significantly more than I expected. Mind you, how much is a life worth to them?"

Her eyes cloud as her thoughts wander to Becca.

"Do you still want to give all of it to charity?" I know the answer but ask anyway.

"Yes, absolutely. Well, maybe not *all* of it. I've been thinking. Could we use part of it to have a little memorial garden landscaped in the backyard?"

"Of course, the yard is big enough, and anything you want to do I'm on board with." I grab her hand over the table.

"Think about how many cuddle cots we can donate," she gushes. "And memory boxes and maybe a photography service for the hospital, so parents can have a lasting memory of their angel babies!"

Tanya's enthusiasm warms my heart.

"Tell you what, why don't you and the ladies make plans, honey, and we'll discuss this further at home? I wish I could stay with you longer, but I need to get back to work and kick Sparks' ass."

I love this woman so much. Tough on the outside, fiercely loyal, but with a heart of gold.

"Okay, babe, you go. And please, give Sparks a kick in the nuts for me." There she is. My fierce little psycho.

We both scuttle out of the booth. I drag her tight into me and devour her mouth, her little whimpers making me even harder than I already am as our kiss deepens. It takes everything I have to pull away, smack her gorgeous ass, and head outside to my bike, but I do it. I need to get back to the clubhouse to interview Ferret's son and see if we want him as our new prospect.

39 — TANYA

One point five million dollars! I nearly pass out when I hear that number, even more so when I glance at the bank statement Pennywise shoves at me, realizing it's already in our account!

I walk back over to our table, squeeze past Ellie, and plonk back down onto my seat.

"Tanya?" Ellie asks, staring at me.

"The settlement from the hospital has come through and landed straight in our account. One point five million. Can you believe it?"

Silence reigns as everyone stares at me, shock and surprise written across their faces.

"Oh my God, that's huge!" Caroline breathes.

"I know, right? Ally, could you grab a pen and paper? We need to make plans." I grin at them.

Chloe gets her cell out and starts scrolling.

"One cuddle cot is around two thousand dollars. I understand you intended ten, but that'll hardly make a dent your budget."

"Show me." I grab her cell from her and scroll through the site, seeing beautiful memory boxes, photo books, personalized plush toys, and so much more. My mind goes into overdrive with the possibilities.

Ally returns, not just with paper and pen, but also her laptop, which she shoves in front of me, open and unlocked.

“Thanks Ally, you are a star!”

I bring up the site Chloe has open on her cell. Grabbing my card, I place an order for ten.

Next, I find memory boxes and order a hundred, plus the same number of cream-colored baby blankets, a mixture of small appropriate plushies, and I find the link for an experienced specialist photographer. Placing the call and explaining what I want; she’s delighted to work with me.

An invoice totally ten thousand dollars hits my inbox, which I pay right away, securing her services for two years, or until the memory boxes run out. The rest of the morning, the ladies and I spend planning.

◊◊◊

When Pennywise walks in, all I have to do is lay the table. For the first time in a long while, I’ve prepared a home cooked meal, rather than getting dinner at the clubhouse. I’m too worried I’ll kick Sparks in the nuts if I lay eyes on him.

Pennywise sniffs as he walks into the kitchen.

"What smells so good? My mouth is watering."

"Slow-cooked brisket, honey-roast carrots, herb-mashed potatoes, biscuits, and red wine gravy," I reply, smacking his fingers as he tries to pinch a carrot off the plate.

"Let me give you a hand." He grabs the plates and cutlery out of my hand and lays the table, then returns for the serving dishes.

We make our plates and dig in.

"So, have you made any decisions?" he asks between bites.

Covering my mouth with my hand, I nod at him. Nothing worse than talking with your mouth full.

"Yes, I've ordered cuddle cots, memory boxes, blankets, and plushies. Oh, and I've hired a photographer. But we had other ideas, too. I wanted to run them past you and get your opinion."

"Okay, Tan, let's hear it."

"I'm thinking about setting up a charity for parents of stillborn babies. Where they can get counseling and stuff. First, I thought about doing it with Debs' Haven, you know? Connect the two services, but when I gave it some more thought, I think it might blur the lines too much and take the focus away from Ellie and Darcie's work. I spent thousands of dollars today, and it hasn't even made a dent in the compensation. Do you have any ideas?"

Pennywise leans back in his seat, gaze turned inward, brows crinkled in deep thought.

"I think, first, we have to set up a separate account and transfer the rest of the compensation into it. If possible, a high interest one, so the money can work for you, or whatever organization you want to set up, with a smaller amount in a checking account that's accessible at any time."

Worried he's leaving me alone with this, I have to ask, "Don't you mean we?"

"Of course, baby. But you will be the figurehead of this, while I'm more of a silent partner."

He winks at me before shoveling more food into his mouth.

"And if you wanted to, you could connect with Debs' Haven without taking away from Ellie and Darcie's work. You could ask Darcy if she'd be willing to undertake counseling for bereaved parents, and contract her as such. She was so good with you, baby. We could offer the counseling free at the point of access and contract Darcy similarly to how you've contracted the photographer. It would then be up to Darcy to design a leaflet, which could be included in the memory boxes."

Wow, why didn't I think of that?

"Another thing, you could hold fundraising events. For Christmas, you could plan a *light a tree candle* event. Hold a short service, offer coffee and cake, and give each parent the chance to light a candle on a Christmas tree for their child. I went to one of those after Flakey died. Chloe contacted a hospice and organized it. We raised quite a lot of money for the hospice. There's no reason something similar couldn't work for us.

"Mostly, though, you need to think about what you want this charity to be. Work out a concept. Speak to Ellie about it. She set up everything for Debs' Haven. She can give you all the advice you need."

I shove my now empty plate away from me, walk over to Pen, and wrap my arms around him, hugging tight.

"What the hell would I do without you, Pen? You are my violent, saving grace."

"Oh, Tan." Pennywise chuckles "You are my firecracker; a psycho one, too."

He pulls me onto his lap, swallows the last of his food, and kisses me until my toes curl.

◊◊◊

EIGHT MONTHS LATER

Frustrated as hell, I waddle to my new Hyundai Palisade, an SUV far too large for what I need, but Pennywise insisted on as soon as we found out I was pregnant again. If I'm honest, his overprotectiveness drives me crazy, but he means well.

I click the button, open the door, climb in, get ready and press start.

My anxiety skyrockets as I drive towards the hospital for my last prenatal checkup. I'm sick of them, since I've had one every week to make sure the baby is okay. Though, so far all is well, but it was with Becca too.

Pennywise has been to all of them with me, and today he's meeting me there, since he's been dealing with club business.

We've gone private this time. There's no way I want a repeat of the treatment I received last time. I have a different doctor, a different private midwife, and have been able to view the delivery suite, which I had no chance to last time.

This time, I've opted for a caesarean section, just to ensure my baby is safe. I don't care about the longer recovery time; I just need to give my baby a chance at the best start.

We've decided not to find out what we're having, nor have I allowed another baby shower. We've kept everything quiet and low key, despite both clubs wanting to make a big occasion out of this. At the end of the day, it's our baby, our decision.

The nursery has been re-decorated and the furniture replaced; it reminded me too much of Becca in its previous state. It's unreal to think Becca's been gone for over a year now. She has a little memory garden at our house, full of pink flowers and roses, which I tend carefully.

Who would have thought I had green fingers, but tending her garden gives me peace and a place to talk with her. It also draws Ashley, Sarah, and Ellie with their new babies. It's an oasis of tranquility and happiness.

Parking outside the hospital, I spot Pen's bike already there and him walking over to me, smiling.

"Hey, baby," he greets, leaning in and kissing me deeply.

Rather than going in, I'd like to ravish him here and now in the car, not giving a flying fuck about who sees us. This pregnancy has made me unbelievably horny. I could climb him like a tree all day long.

"Hi," is all I can pant out. I'm so breathless from his kiss.

"You ready, sweetheart?"

"Pen, I'll never be ready." My anxiety ratchets up from level eight to level fifteen.

"Hey." He helps me out of the Palisade and draws me into him. "We've got this, Tanya. This baby has been spied on so much it wouldn't surprise me if it comes out striking a pose! Everything will be okay." His soothing voice calms me a little, but I reckon when they take my blood pressure, it'll be sky high.

We step into the elevator bank and press the button for OB/GYN and delivery; me clinging to Pen like a demented monkey, him rocking me gently in his arms.

He's my pillar of strength.

40 — PENNYWISE

As we exit the elevator, Tanya clinging to me for dear life, my heart aches for her, for me, for Becca, and for our unborn baby. Despite trying to keep busy—and there's plenty of club business to keep me just that—my thoughts frequently stray to our last time. Okay, it happened in a different hospital, but the situation is too familiar for comfort.

Anxiety has a tight grip on me, yet through everything, I try to be strong for Tanya. It's difficult, but my brothers have been there for me all the way. I can't count the days I've sat in Raven's office with a man-sized box of tissues and cried. Got to give credit to Raven, he just sat and listened to me going on and on about my worries.

I've taken to guarding my name tape closely, not to have it turned into *Sad Bastard*, the crying clown from a popular painting.

I lead Tanya to the doctor's office, register us and we take a seat, Tan clinging to my hand, squashing it so hard my knuckles are bending out of shape.

"Miss Frost, Mr. Nixom?" The friendly, always smiling doc calls us in, as though he's waited just for us.

We take a seat in front of his desk.

"Noah." He nods at me, holding out his hand to shake mine.

"Tanya." He shakes her hand, smiling warmly at her. "How has your week been? Any problems?"

"No. Getting sick of not being able to tie my own shoelaces though. Good job it's warm so I don't need socks," Tanya grumbles.

Dr. Philpott throws his head back and laughs.

"Not long now, and you'll have your baby in your arms. Shall we go through?"

"Yes, Dr. Philpott, let's get this over with," Tanya replies.

Unsurprisingly, her blood pressure is high, but Dr. Philpott pays it no heed. We check her blood pressure at home every day, and the readings are much better there, not so anxiety driven.

"Your urine test is fine, just as expected," Dr Philpott says. "Would you get comfortable on the bed, please? I just need your abdomen clear. No need to undress."

Tanya lays down as instructed, pulling her sweater up and trousers down a little at the front. Today is different, as we have requested a 3D ultrasound.

Tanya hisses a little as the cold gel squirts on her tummy.

"Okay, let's see what baby Nixom is up to today." Dr. Philpot concentrates on the wand as he runs it over Tanya's stomach.

The *swish, swish, swish, swish* sound that comes out of the speaker makes me so happy it brings tears to my eyes. I look at Tanya, who's smiling, eyes glassy.

"Now, that's what I call a strong heartbeat. Are you sure you don't want to know what it is? Boy or girl?"

"No," Tanya answers for both of us. "We want it to be a surprise."

"Okay, don't look while I take some measurements. When I'm done, I'll switch over to 3D so you can see your baby properly."

We wait while he takes notes. His sudden laughter makes us both jump in surprise.

"Well, whatever this baby is, it's certainly cheeky." He laughs, turning around the screen so we can see.

There it is. Our perfect baby, sticking its tongue out at us while giving us a thumbs up at the same time.

"Well, you've got to excuse that, Dr. Philpott. It obviously takes after its father," Tanya teases.

"Hey! That's you, not me," I protest, chuckling to myself.

It is one thing feeling your baby kick and watch it playing havoc with its mom by twisting and turning, but it's another thing entirely to watch it live on screen, in 3D.

My heart swells and the tears roll down my face automatically. There's nothing I can nor want to do to stop them. They are happy tears.

Tanya's eyes are glued to the screen.

"Look, isn't it beautiful? It's got your hair!"

As I stare at the screen, looking closely; she's right. He or she has a head full of dark hair.

"How would you like to welcome baby Nixom today?" Dr. Philpott smiles at us. "I've got theater time, and both the midwife Andrea and I could deliver your baby this afternoon. She's on shift and waiting to hear. Baby is in superb condition, and from the measurements, I'd estimate about eight and a half pounds."

"What?" We're thunderstruck.

"Eight and a half pounds?" Tanya echoes.

"Yup, eight and a half. If we wait two weeks, it could be nine to ten pounds."

"Oh, hell to the no! That's huge. No wonder I can't move." She looks at me and with her finger nearly poking my eye out, she spits, “What the hell have you done to me?”

That does it. I laugh, sputter, then laugh some more, until I can’t breathe.

“I take that as a yes, then?” Dr. Philpott chuckles.

“Yes please, can you do it now?” Tanya’s eagerness is amusing.

“Be back at three P.M. and we’ll get you prepared and deliver this baby.” He smiles at us.

I look at my cell. It’s one P.M. now; there’s just enough time to dash to Ally’s, update her, and get back to the club to pick up Tanya’s bag and the necessary baby things.

“Holy shit,” I whisper. “Is this for real?”

“Yes, it is. I know you’ll have lots of erm… family who’ll want to come. We’ll clear out a private waiting room for you.”

“Oh my God, thank you, Dr. Philpott, thank you so much.” Tanya drags her sweater down, tugs her trousers up, grabs my hand, and pulls herself up from the examination bed.

He nods at her, smiling, and ushers us out.

“Pen, is this for real? I didn’t misunderstand, did I? He’ll deliver our baby today?”

“Yes, baby, that’s what he said.”

"Ouch, you little hooligan!" Tanya admonishes her bump. "You've just got to wait two hours, then you'll be out of your prison, and I agree with you in there, it's not a moment too soon."

I don't even have to lay my hand on her extended belly. I can see our baby moving around under the tightly stretched top.

I leave my bike where it is and get into the Palisade with her, relegating her to the passenger seat.

We stop at Ally's, sit down, and order a quick lunch. When Ally brings it to the table, Tanya grabs her hand.

"Ally, the baby is going to be delivered today. Can you let the Pixies know?"

"What?" Ally is hopping from one foot to the other like Rumpelstiltskin. "Ok, don't worry about a thing. I'll set the phone chain off. Oh my God, I'm so excited for you. I take it everything went well today, then?"

It's hard not to laugh at Ally. She's almost more excited than we are.

"Yes, everything went great," I assure her.

Ally, cell in hand, is not paying us any more attention. "Caroline? Baby Enforcer is on the way! Yes, this afternoon. Hang on…" She glares at us. "What time?"

"Three P.M."

"Caroline? Three P.M. Yes, the private hospital in town, same one Ashley, Sarah, and Ellie used. Yes, meet you there." Ally winces as Caroline screeches in her ear so loud even we can hear her.

Ignoring Ally making more calls, we eat our lunch, leave money for the bill on the table, and get back into the SUV.

By the time we leave the club property, it's just after two P.M., and we are loaded up with everything we could possibly need, including a change of clothes for both of us. No way am I going home tonight.

It takes less than fifteen minutes to get to the hospital and another five for us to be back in Dr. Philpott's office.

"There you are," he greets us, already in scrubs. "Follow me, and I'll show you to your home for the next two days."

Two days? Surely Tanya will be in longer after a C-section?

We follow him down a labyrinth of corridors until he stops in front of a door and opens it.

"Wow." Tanya whistles as we enter the vast room with a large bed, a pullout couch, and a big screen TV. This resembles a hotel room, not a hospital room.

The door opens and Andrea, our midwife, walks in.

"Hey." She smiles as she shakes my hand and hugs Tanya.

"I'll get ready," Dr. Philpott tells us, nodding at Andrea.

"I'll be ten minutes," she replies and turns to us, smiling widely. "I'm so excited for you. Before we start, I have a few forms I need you to sign."

She goes through everything with us, explaining as she goes along. We both sign on the dotted lines.

"Right, I'll let you get changed into your gown, Tanya. Then I'll be your chauffeur to the operating theater. While the anesthetist sets you up with your epidural, I'll grab Noah, and we'll get him changed into theater clothes. He can then sit with you all the way through."

Tanya disappears into the bathroom, and when she comes out, I try hard not to laugh. Her gown has purple and yellow flowers all over it, and she's so not a flowery girl.

"Sorry, we were fresh out of Harley ones." Andrea smirks.

"I hate yellow," Tanya grumbles as she gets into the wheelchair.

My hands are shaking as I push Tanya, following Andrea.

I leave her in Andrea's care while I get changed, shocked when I find yellow scrubs are the only ones that will fit me.

I groan and mutter to myself, "She'll never let me live this down." Then, I realize it's not Tanya I ought to worry about, but the brothers.

I take a minute to man up and walk through the doors that say *Operating Room 3*, my hair covered by, wait for it… a yellow cap.

Tanya, who's sitting on the table, the anesthetist behind her, howls with laughter as soon as she sees me.

"You need to keep still, Miss Frost," he reminds her.

"Sorry," she chortles, trying not to move, her face turning red, trying to hold in her laughter.

"That's it, we're in and I'm starting the epidural now. You can lay back. Careful not to dislodge anything," he says.

Andrea and I help Tan recline slowly and push a pillow under her head. Then a drape goes up in front of us. The machines she's connected to bleep incessantly.

"Are we ready?" I hear Dr. Philpott, but don't see him. He and the rest of the staff are behind the drape, apart from the anesthetist, who’s behind Tanya’s head, monitoring the machines.

41 — TANYA

"Are we ready?" Dr. Philpott's question drives my anxiety levels to infinity. My eyes fill with tears, and I clench them shut.

"Hey, baby, open your eyes. Everything is fine. I'm here; I've got you." Pennywise's soothing voice encourages me to open my eyes. "That's it; look at me, sweetheart. Everything will be fine. Are you in any pain?"

He strokes my forehead since my hair is under one of those ugly caps.

"No," I whisper. "Just scared, Pen."

"Me too, baby, but we've got this."

There is tugging and pulling at my stomach, making me tense. Pen tries to glimpse around the drape.

"You can come and watch, Noah, if you want; no fainting though."

"No thank you," Noah replies, his face indicating he's just caught an eyeful of something unsavory.

"Suction."

"Clamps."

"Spreader please."

"Andrea, get ready to receive."

More tugging and pressure. It's the weirdest feeling, and I grip Pen's hand tight.

"There we go, congratulations, you two; it's a healthy baby girl!" Andrea declares.

The cries of a newborn baby sound all around us, and I cry a river.

Andrea steps beyond the drape, moves my gown out of the way, and lays a beautiful, dark-haired baby girl on my chest, who calms as soon as she makes contact with my skin.

Pen rests his head next to mine, wrapping one of his muscular arms over both of us, cocooning us in warmth and happiness. Tears run unchecked down his face.

"I'm sorry, but I'll have to steal this little lady. She needs to be weighed, measured and properly checked over. Once that's done, Tanya, we'll freshen you up. Dr. Philpot is almost done with you. Then we can take you and your new arrival to your room for some family time. Are you planning to breastfeed?"

Wow, Andrea is thorough.

"Yes, that's the plan," Tanya answers.

"Okay, once we're back in your room you can try to latch her on. I'll be there to help, if you need me." Her smile lights up her entire face.

"Thank you, Andrea, I can't thank you enough," I sob, deliriously happy.

"You're welcome. It's a pleasure."

"Pen, go get changed and tell the others; there's nothing more you can do for us here. We'll be back in our room soon anyway," I request.

"Okay, babe, if you're sure you don't need me anymore?"

"No, it's fine, babe. Could you dig out some clothes from my bag so I can get changed, please?"

"Sure, darlin', anything you need." He leans over and his tender kiss brings tears to my eyes again.

Wow, I've turned into a crybaby.

I watch him turn and walk out while the theater staff fix me up.

Andrea passes me my baby girl before she cleans me up and I'm transferred into a bed. She removes my cap and gown, covering me with a warm blanket, then pushing me down to my room, where Pen has laid out a nightshirt with *Mama Bear* printed on the front.

Andrea gets me changed out of my theater gown and our baby girl dressed. It feels strange not to have named her yet, but it's something we want to do together, after we've become familiar with our little lady first.

"Please, Andrea, could you show me how to breastfeed her?"

"Sure." She smiles at me, bringing my daughter to me and placing her in my arms. She laughs as she sees the alterations Ally's friend made to the nightshirt. Instead of a closed top it has flaps with buttons over my boobs.

I open one of them, shuffle my upper body around a little, and hold my daughter to my breast. Like a pro, her little mouth searches around.

"Like this." Andrea's gentle voice and hands support my daughter, and I get the hang of it, everything becoming clear as my little one latches on and starts suckling. Feeling sweet relief as the pressure in my breast reduces a little.

"There you go, little one," I coo. "That's it."

She loses the nipple and screams until my eardrums threaten to burst.

Andrea helps me to get her latched on again.

"I'll get you a nursing pillow. That will make things easier and more comfortable for you."

I nod as she walks to the door.

"Andrea, could you go to the waiting room and get Noah and our parents?"

"Sure." She smiles at me and closes the door quietly behind her.

When it opens next, it's Pennywise, my dad, and Mom entering the room.

Our little princess fell asleep on my breast a few moments ago.

"Oh my God, how cute!" Mom's beaming, happy tears tracking down her face. "She looks just like Noah when he was born. May I hold her?"

"Nope," Pen decrees. "My turn first. I've not held her myself yet. You'll have to join the back of the queue."

Dad snorts, quickly shutting up as Helen elbows him in the ribs. I wince. *That'll leave a mark.*

Pen wraps our daughter into a cream fleecy blanket with little rabbits printed on it, which he produces out of one of our bags like a magician.

He walks to the window, holding our princess tight, murmuring quietly to her.

"See, my little angel, I understand you're asleep, but I needed to show you off to your big sister in heaven."

My heart breaks as he points his hand toward the clear blue sky.

"Hey, Becca, meet your little sister. She's just as beautiful as you, and we love her just as much. Watch over her for us from up there. Guide her right. I'll bring you a picture when next I visit you. She's precious, just like you, my little angel."

When he turns back toward us, we're dissolved in tears but smiling big. We know her big sister will look after our princess and love her as much as we do already.

"What are you going to name her?" Dad asks.

Pen comes and sits on the side of my bed. We both look at our daughter's balled fists.

"A strong woman in the making deserves a powerful name," Mom chips in, looking over Pen's shoulder.

We discussed names before now.

I watch as something clicks into place in Pen's face.

"Aria."

"Aria Rebecca Helen Nixom," I add. Becca and my mother deserve to be remembered.

"Hello, Aria." Pen hands Ari back to me.

"Are you sure?" Dad and Mom both stare at us.

"Yes, we're sure." Happiness radiates from me. My heart feels so full it's threatening to overflow. With love for my daughter, my man, and my family.

We all draw together in a family hug.

I hand Aria to Mom, whose happy tears threaten to leave a puddle on the floor. Pen crawls up onto the bed with me and wraps me in his arms.

"Tanya, I'm so proud of you. You mean the world to me, and so does this little princess."

He nods towards Mom, who's holding Aria, cradling her as though she's the most precious thing in this world, and she is.

"We did it, Pen, together," I whisper against his lips as they close over mine with a gentleness that almost overwhelms me. "Now let the hordes know they can come in." I smirk at him before kissing him back with everything I have.

By the time six P.M. rolls around, I'm exhausted.

The brothers, sisters, and their Old Ladies and Old Men have all turned out in force.

The room is rammed full of balloons, flowers, plushies, books, and anything else you can think of.

Pen is shoving the last stragglers out of the room just as dinner arrives on trays for both of us.

Ravenous, we don't care what it is but wolf it down, followed by large mugs of coffee. Decaf for me, but I don't care. All I want now is peace.

Our princess is asleep in her bassinet next to me and Pen crawls into bed with me.

"I need to hold you, at least for a while," he whispers in my ear.

Just then, the little lady makes herself known, fussing in her sleep. I lift her, put her to my breast, and let her drink. This time goes a lot better, and after fifteen minutes she's asleep.

I hand her to Pen, who changes her diaper, and she's back in her bassinet.

Pen snuggles me against him, and sleep drags me under before I can take two long breaths.

42 — PENNYWISE

Tanya is asleep within seconds.

I extract myself as carefully as possible. Waking her is not an option.

Sneaking around, I bring Aria's bassinet around to my side, before scooting back onto the bed, where Tanya softly snores. Suppressing my giggle at her cute little noises, I lay on my side, just staring at the little miracle in front of me.

I can't believe we made this beautiful tiny human who is utterly dependent on us. Love radiates from me, filling me completely, unfreezing a part of my heart I hadn't realized was there.

"I'll love and protect you for all of my life, with everything I have," I tell my baby daughter. "Just don't think you'll be dating before you're thirty. No, sweetie, not a chance. And once you do, me and your uncles will sit on the porch, polishing our shotguns."

Just at that moment, Aria opens her bright baby blue eyes, staring up at me, as though she understands me, wrinkling her little snub nose. It looks as though she's glaring at me.

"You're going to be a handful, huh? Just like your momma." I smile down at her. "I wouldn't have it any other way, sweet baby girl. Your momma is strong, independent, loving, cares for everyone around her, and protects who she loves something fierce. She loves hard, and if you grow up just like her, I'll be the proudest daddy ever."

Our princess clenches her fist, stretching her arm out, and I can't help but fist bump my newborn daughter, like the idiot I am.

Grabbing her out of her bassinet, I wrap her in my arms, rocking her gently, patting her little diaper-clad butt. It seems to calm her. Our gazes locked; eyes wide. She's a little night-owl, just like her daddy. I know it's a silly thought, but who cares? I'm so happy I could burst.

Next thing I know, Aria is fussing, searching against my chest. I must have dozed off.

There's nothing for it but to wake Tanya. Our little girl needs sustenance. For a second, I feel a pang of jealousy, having to share Tanya's amazing tits, but then I roll my eyes at myself.

"Tan, honey, wake up." I gently shake her awake.

She groans and hisses in pain as she tries to sit up.

"Shh, let me help you."

I place Aria in Tanya's arms, walk around the bed to her side, put my arms under her, and carefully lift her up the bed, pressing the button on the remote to bring the backrest up.

"Thanks, babe." Her voice still sleep roughened, as she murmurs.

Fascinated, I watch as she positions Aria and lets her feed while stroking her tiny cheek.

Once Aria is finished, I pass Tan a diaper and everything needed, watching Tan change our baby girl as though she's done it a million times before.

Returning our miracle to her bassinet, I turn down the lights, climb back into bed, and fall asleep as soon as my head hits the pillow.

Morning eventually comes after a night of feeding every two hours. We're both exhausted when Mom sticks her head through the door at ten A.M.

She's holding a takeout bag from Ally's, and I could kiss her for it. The food here is good, but nothing beats Ally's coffee and breakfast trays. The smell emanating from the bag makes my mouth water.

"Gimme, gimme gimme," both Tanya and I say simultaneously.

In her other hand, Mom carries a bag from a well-known baby retailer.

"I brought full-fat coffee for both of you; figured you'll need it. But first, I brought you this."

She sets down Ally's bag and opens the other one, bringing out a weird-looking contraption.

"You are a star; I love you forever!" Tanya exclaims, as she spots what Mom is holding.

"Yup, I thought you might want to express some milk so Pen can help with the nighttime feeds." Mom smirks.

Tanya almost rips the contraption out of Mom's hand, unwraps it, throwing all the packaging off the bed, connects a bottle to the machine, and immediately puts it to her breast.

Mom plugs it in, and Tanya presses a button.

"Oh, sweet relief." She sighs as the machine springs to life, and milk squirts from her breast into the bottle.

Ah! A breast pump. Now I get it. Although watching Tanya milking herself in front of even Mom doesn't sit right with me. Her breasts are for my and Aria's viewing only.

I am amazed, though, at how much milk actually flows into the bottle. When the flow stops, Tanya switches sides. Filling almost two bottles, Mom decants them into small baby bottles and places them in the mini fridge we have in the room.

"Mom, please let me have coffee," Tan begs, making grabby hands.

She's not supposed to have anything but decaf, but since she expressed enough, one caffeinated Ally coffee won't hurt.

I'll never be able to describe the feeling of feeding Aria while watching my woman sleeping.

Sat in the comfy nursing chair in the room, bare-chested, my daughter snuggled against me, listening to Tanya's steady breathing, peering down at my daughter who's sating her hunger, I feel at peace.

I'm not a soft man; I'm jaded, harsh and can be your worst nightmare if you cross me. So, these gentle, tender, overwhelming feelings are new to me and very much at odds with Pennywise, the Enforcer.

Now I get Vegas' fascination with his son, who's now walking. Another year and Aria will be doing the same. It's only now that I realize children don't make us weak men, but stronger ones, as the bonds we already nurture increase in strength through the additions to our family, blood, and brotherhood alike. As a whole, we grow stronger through our weakest parts.

Now we just have work harder to keep the looming threats at bay, destroying anyone who tries to come for us and our families. Pride swells in my chest like never before, and at this moment, I vow on my daughter's life that nothing bad will touch her. Ever.

When Aria finishes, I wind and change her, not minding the spit up on my chest, it'll wipe away. Her happiness is all that matters. I lay her back into her bassinet as her eyes are closing and settle to take a little catnap of my own on the nursing chair, with my feet up on the footstool. We need one like this at the house.

So, before I close my own eyes, I shoot a message to Chloe. That amazing woman will take care of it, I'm certain, so leave it in her more than capable hands.

Aria's fussing wakes me. I pick her up and almost retch from the stink emanating from her little butt. I place her on the changing table and remove her romper. Now I can't hold back the retching. She's caked in her own mess from neck to thighs. I press the bell. This is too much for me to handle. Still retching, I hold on to Aria, who's screaming her head off. I can't help it and vomit into the diaper bucket by the side of the table. Laughter peals behind me as a nursing assistant enters the room, joined by Tanya's hearty laugh.

“Oh, what have we here?” the nursing assistant coos. “One stinky baby,” she giggles, “and daddy in over his head. Time for a bath, I think.”

She has the good grace to wrinkle her nose at the stench my daughter is fumigating the room with.

“And when we’re done, we’ll help Mommy to get a shower. What do you think? Good idea?”

She talks to Aria as though she’s her best friend, opens the cupboard underneath the changing table, pulls out a baby bath bucket, shoves it at me, and orders like a Drill Sergeant, “Dad, fill this halfway in the shower, hand warm, no more.”

I click my heels, grab the bucket, and disappear into the bathroom. *Damn bossy woman!*

By the time I return, Aria is naked but clean, and I squirt some of the baby bath the nursing assistant hands to me into the water and froth it up with my hand.

“Right, Dad, hold her like this.” She demonstrates, handing Aria to me, correcting my grip and instructing, “Now place her into the water. Here’s a washcloth.”

I’m scared to death.

What if I drop her?

What if she screams?

What if the water is too hot?

Gently, I lower Aria into the water, and to my surprise, all my worries were for nothing. Aria kicks her little legs and seems to enjoy her bath. I grab the washcloth and bathe my baby girl, loving every second.

In the meantime, the nursing assistant helps Tanya out of bed and into the bathroom. A few moments later, I hear the shower come on.

I lift Aria out of the bath, place her on the towel that's been laid out, and wrap my baby girl up, gently drying her. I spot the bottle of lotion and apply it all over her, which seems to have a calming effect. I suppose it's similar to a massage. Then I dress her in a clean romper.

"Now you smell like the sweet thing you are," I croon, rocking her in my arms, humming "*Row, row, row your boat*" for good measure.

I can't wait to have both my girls home.

43 — TANYA

Finally, three days later, we're allowed to go home. My wound is healing well. I can get in and out of bed myself, shower, get dressed, and look after Aria.

Every day I gain strength and a little slice of normality back. Not the same as before. My new normality, though. I love being Aria's mommy.

Pennywise stayed with us the whole time, only leaving once for church and to get clean clothes for all of us. I think I vastly underestimated how many clothes Aria goes through in any twenty-four-hour period, making me grateful for all the presents we received.

I understand I said I didn't want any, but hell, I needed them. Ashley saw to people buying the right sizes and brought an enormous bag of Alex and Craig's newborn clothes in for me. Yes, she had another boy.

Honestly? I could have kissed her. Same goes for Sarah and Dougal, who brought in bags of Amelia's newborn clothes. She's still not forgiven Dougal for having a girl.

"Now I've got to go through that hormonal teen stage twice," she complained with a twinkle in her eyes.

Ellie and Slender welcomed a bouncing baby boy, who they named Arthur. He has a set of pipes on him, which rival a fire truck's siren!

The new prospect, Kevin, came and picked up Pen's bike, so now Pen is wheeling us toward the exit in a wheelchair to the waiting SUV. He takes Aria and straps her into the car seat, then comes back for me, leading me to the rear passenger door so I can sit next to Aria. He helps me in and buckles me up. His overprotectiveness is sweet but grinds on my last nerve.

"I'm not an invalid," I grouse at him.

"No, but you are precious cargo." He grins at me, oblivious to my ire.

With a *harrumph,* I slam the door shut as hard as I can. He laughs, and Aria screams.

Shit, I must have startled her!

"Sorry, baby girl, your Daddy can be such an asshole," I coo at her, stroking her face.

"Me? Never, I'm as sweet as cherry pie." Pen laughs at me as he gets in and puts the SUV in drive, gently pulling out of the hospital grounds and filtering into traffic.

As we pull up to our house, the first thing I spot is a 'Welcome Home' banner, and people milling around everywhere. All I want is peace and quiet, but alas, it seems that's not gonna happen now.

Dad opens my door as soon as we come to a stop, helps me out of the cage, and hugs me tight.

"So glad you're home, sweetheart." He kisses my hair before leading me around to the other side, grabbing Aria's car seat and carrying it inside for me.

I didn't realize how much I missed him.

Inside, everyone is congregating in the kitchen, Aria's stroller system is already set up so her car seat can clip straight into it. Looks like the men have fired up our grill, and the smell of cooking steaks drifts through the house.

Grabbing Aria's stroller, I push it through the house to the back porch, which now sports a ramp on one side.

God, I love these guys. They've thought of everything.

Pen follows us, so does Dad and Mom, leaving the men to empty the car and stow everything away. I need to spend time with both my girls and take a breath.

When I get to the memorial garden, the flowers are in full bloom, and their sweet scent invades my nostrils, acting like a balm. Tears fill my eyes when I spot the bench in the center of it all, in front of the pink rosebush I planted for Becca.

"Hi, sweetheart, Mommy is back. Look, I brought your baby sister." I look up, taking in the sunshine and blue skies, and as I watch, a robin lands on the bird feeding station I placed in the center of the garden. It stares at me, cocking his head this way and that.

Mum whispers behind me, "When a robin appears, a loved one is near."

Taking Aria out of the car seat, I cradle her and walk towards the bird, which is sitting still on the feeder, staring at us.

"Look, Aria, your sister has come to see you. Both my beautiful girls in one place."

Suddenly the robin chirps like crazy, still looking at us, regaling us with its beautiful song, then it lifts and flies away.

Tears stream down my face, happy tears. I believe Becca is giving us a sign that she's with us.

When I turn, Mom is crying in Dad's arms, Pennywise is wiping his eyes, and the ladies, who followed us quietly, are all doing the same.

All of them pushing their own strollers, holding a pink rose, which they place, one by one, into the vase in front of the pink rosebush.

I love my family.

Placing Aria back into her stroller, I hug each person in turn, hard.

The last year has been the hardest, most difficult one of my life. I wouldn't have gotten through it all without the support of my crazy, loving, protective, blended family, and I thank God every day for them.

"Okay, let's see what's on the menu." I smile at them, and we walk back to the house, chatting and laughing, where the men have set up an enormous table on the back porch, bowing with food and drink.

Pen and I take Aria up to her room. As I open her door, I notice the new addition of the nursing chair. It looks fabulous, and I'm sure it cost a bomb. I feed Aria, change her into a princess romper, and put her to bed.

"Sleep tight, princess," I whisper as I lean over, kissing her forehead and inhaling her sweet baby scent deeply.

Pen watches me from the door, his smile huge.

"Finally, all my girls are back home with me."

"You won't say that when it's your turn getting up at night," I joke.

"For my girls, I'll spend a hundred sleepless nights in a row. I love you, Tanya, so much it hurts. And

I love both of our girls to distraction. There's nothing I wouldn't do for you."

My man! He still has the ability to render me speechless.

"Come on, let's go eat before I ravish you here on the spot." He winks at me, dragging me out of Aria's room so fast I only just manage to snatch the baby monitor.

The rest of the day passes in a blink of an eye. Great food, conversation, and laughter determine the vibe of the day. When everyone finally leaves, I drag myself upstairs to our bedroom.

Pennywise is seeing the last stragglers off. The moment he comes up and snuggles in bed, Aria requests her last feed.

Pen gets up, puts a bottle I expressed earlier in the warmer on the side, and opens the door connecting our bedroom to hers. I listen through the baby monitor.

"Hey, princess, it's okay, Daddy is here. Are you hungry? It's just you and me tonight. Mommy needs to rest. It was a busy day. How do you like all your uncles and aunties? They all love you just as much as Mommy and I do. Good grief, girl, you are a stink bomb tonight.

"Aww, baby girl, everything'll be alright. Let's clean your cute little butt and get you fed. Then you gotta sleep, dream of flowers, butterflies, and unicorns for at least three hours, so Daddy can have adult time with Mommy. Yes, I know she's listening. She's nosy like that, see?"

I can't help but giggle. What happened to Pennywise the enforcer? He suddenly turned into Pennywise, the love-struck daddy.

Pen comes in, carrying Aria, grabs the bottle and disappears back into Ari's room.

"There you go, princess. Have at it. Yes, I know it's not Mommy's milk bar, but I'm afraid you'll have to make do. You are my sunshine, my only sunshine…"

I listen to Pen's calming voice, singing to our precious daughter. Right now, at this moment, I love him so much more than I ever thought possible. And I realize we can overcome anything and everything life throws at us.

As I'm lost to my thoughts, Pen steps through the connecting door, closing it gently, and climbs back into bed, wrapping me into his arms. And just like that, fire ignites in my belly, and the need to show him just how much I love him blazes through me. I'm not allowed yet though—doctor's orders.

Pennywise, however, has no such restrictions, and shows me exactly how he feels. His gentle touches making me feel so revered, loved, protected, it's all-encompassing.

Tonight, I am the happiest woman on the planet.

I know, from here on in, we'll weather any storm. Together. Always.

THE END

Printed in Great Britain
by Amazon

59060136R00205